This book is a work of fiction. Names, characters, businesses, places, organizations, institutions, events, and incidents are either the product of the author's imagination or are used fictitiously. Any resemblances to actual persons, living or dead, or locales is entirely coincidental.

ISBN 978-0-9829470-1-2

Printed in the Unites States of America

CHAPTER 1

I arrived on Alabama's death row April 1, 1996, three months after being sentenced to death for the murder of Maureen O'Brien, a popular Montgomery television news reporter. The only problem in this tragic scenario: I did not commit this gruesome act of which I was wrongfully convicted. Call it bad lawyering, a horrific black-on-white crime, or a trial that was doomed from the very beginning.

If the person or persons responsible for her murder do not surface within the next year, I will grudgingly take a seat in Alabama's infamous "Yellow Mama" and feel the surge of 2,000 volts of searing electricity roar through my defenseless body. Although resigned to this fate, I desperately cling to some small measure of hope that I will escape this impending date with the chair.

Over the last ten years, I have missed Grandpa Tyler's funeral, my best friend's wedding, my chocolate Lab Hercules, Mom and Dad's new house, and ESPN. The latter is probably near the top of the list, as the state doesn't provide cable TV to their death row inmates. Imagine the public outrage if that were a perk for those condemned to meet the ultimate punishment for their crimes. We have to purchase our own TVs, radios, and CD players from our money account – money sent to you by a select few friends and family approved by the prison administration. And, knowing Alabama politics like I do, some schmuck up the food chain -- a middle man – is making a profit from your purchases.

My days and nights pass with equal boredom in a six-by-eight windowless cell on row two of death row. The first thing you reluctantly learn about prison confinement is the day-to-day routine. It almost never changes. Breakfast at five, lunch at eleven and dinner at five. We get one hour outside in the recreation yard each day, and an occasional hour or two in a cramped library in another part of the prison complex – but plenty of time to ponder what we could have changed in our lives to escape this hell-hole we call home. The world could come to an end, and we'd be the last to know.

There are twelve cell checks a day, as if someone could possibly turn up missing in a setting so regulated by the almighty clock. If you're the fortunate inmate with a radio, TV, a few pen pals, and regular visits from family and friends, segregation from the outside world isn't so cruel for you as the guy whose family has completely cast him out of their lives, dooming him to endless days of monotony in a cage smaller than momma's walk-in bedroom closet.

Johnny Edwards, four cells down from me, has not had a visitor, other than his attorney, in over twelve years. Maybe because he killed his mother and father and brutally sodomized his 14-year-old niece before slashing her throat with a box cutter. Or the guy we all hate the most on the row, John Skillings, a five-star scumbag who set fire to his home, killing his estranged wife and four helpless children, who had no chance of escaping the blazing inferno. Contrary to the beliefs of proponents of capital punishment, a good number of us still possess some moral fiber, wherein we can judge others – unlike the way we would judge ourselves.

Depression and hopelessness are there to greet you every morning, when the first of three suspect meals are shoved through an opening in your cell door. Your circle of friends consists of eighteen to twenty-four guys you hang out with in the exercise yard, playing basketball or volleyball, and enduring the fresh air of Alabama's blistering summers, when both the temperature and humidity are routinely in the high 90s. Add another ten degrees to that in your cell, and you eat and sleep in your own sweat from May through September. And the two weekly showers you're allowed are terribly overrated.

We find solace in the smallest ways: a guard stopping by your cell to ask how you're doing, an unexpected letter from a home-town friend, warm water in the shower, a quiet night on the Tier, a breakfast without burnt toast.

Unlike general population, where the majority of prisoners see some light at the end of the dark tunnel, we are wards of the state for whom rehabilitation has no purpose and life has no meaning. Time is the cruelest enemy of all as we are forced to live out our days conforming to rules and regulations that enforce the bitter reality of hard time. All this before they eventually kill you.

CHAPTER 2

I was born on a cool October evening in 1970, the one and only child of Ralph and Margaret Tyler of Greenville, Alabama. How a lasting relationship ever developed between those two is still a mystery to those who knew them best.

Daddy was the oldest of eight children from a financially challenged family in nearby Crenshaw County, and Mom was the lone child of a middle class family in Fort Deposit, fifteen minutes north of Greenville. Ralph Tyler did just the minimum to get through high school, while Margaret Cummings was earning perfect grades from the first day she entered elementary school.

Their high school yearbooks reflected the educational abyss between them. Ralph's senior class picture carried the caption, "If there's a party, Ralph is hearty," while Margaret's promised, "Life has no limitations for Margaret." The day after graduation, Daddy went to work for an area Budweiser beer distributor, putting tax stamps on cans and bottles, while Mom was off to Alabama State University in Montgomery to pursue a degree in education.

They met entirely by accident. Ralph's old and battered Pontiac Chieftain rear-ended the Cummings' family sedan, a brand-new Lincoln Continental, in the parking lot of the Greenville A&P. It was love at first sight – at least for Ralph. Ralph had no insurance, but he agreed to pay the Cummings twenty-five dollars a week until the thousand dollar repair bill was paid in full. Margaret's father was so impressed with Ralph's determination to honor his commitment that he let his daughter date him. Three years later they were married.

By the time I had entered grade school, Mom had earned a master's degree in educational administration and was the assistant principal of a rural middle school outside of Greenville, and Dad had been promoted to salesman on a Budweiser delivery truck. Mother stressed only two priorities for me growing up: church and school. Wednesday nights and most of Sunday mornings were spent in the third row of our Baptist church listening to Pastor Roberts preach for the redemption of our sins. It seemed like the same old sermon every week. Daddy unwillingly tagged along at Mom's insistence, but his mind was elsewhere, not the least concerned about his soul or the damnation it could suffer in some mythical place called hell.

Football was the only sport Ralph Tyler played in high school, if for no other reason than to take out the frustration of living with seven warring siblings in a three-bedroom house. By his senior year, he was a solid 200 pounds on a six-foot frame that earned him All-County honors as a two-way lineman. Several small black colleges in Alabama had offered him full scholarships, but "Biggie," as he was known to his friends, didn't like the contents of any book unless it had to do with sports.

Daddy had a hobby that earned him his "mad" money as he called it. He and a close friend from high school spent their spare time cutting lawns in the Greenville area, making enough cash to fuel a gambling habit to which they both were marginally attracted. Mother was the primary breadwinner in the family, and if Ralph wanted to wager money on football games, she didn't want to know about it. But she knew, because he would carelessly leave pieces of paper around the house with the betting lines on college and professional games.

Daddy and I started throwing a football around in the backyard when I was still at a young age, and by the time I was playing youth football as a nine-year-old, he was convinced I'd be playing football on Sundays in the NFL. As a freshman, I had matured quickly into a 190-pound running back, and three years later I was a sculptured 215 pounds with 4.5 speed in the forty – with pads on. I had attracted the attention of forty Division 1 schools after leading our high school team to the state championship as a junior, but ever since middle school I was secretly committed to Auburn. After my senior year, in which I rushed for over 2,500 yards and scored 33 touchdowns, I signed with Auburn. Nobody else was ever in the picture, although I did take seven visits to other prominent schools, including Notre Dame and Oklahoma. In track, I was the state champion in the 100 and 200-meter dashes and the long jump, leading our team to a second place finish in the state track and field championships.

While Mom recognized my athletic achievements, she was even prouder when I graduated second in a class of one hundred twenty-three. She was forever ticked off at a social studies teacher who gave me my only B in high school for missing two meaningless field trips to the state capital while I was on recruiting visits to Texas and Florida.

The Auburn coaching staff had promised me

they wouldn't red-shirt me in my freshman year, choosing to play me on special teams as a punt and kickoff returner. I had three long kickoff returns for touchdowns, but it was the last one in the season-ending game with Alabama on national TV that made ESPN's top ten plays. With less than a minute to play and Auburn trailing 26-20, I fielded an Alabama kickoff in the end zone and returned it 102 yards for the game-winning touchdown.

I went into spring training listed as number one on the tailback depth chart, and was receiving reviews comparing me to Bo Jackson, Auburn's 1985 Heisman Trophy winner. I didn't disappoint the pre-season hype. Through the first eight games, I had rushed for 1,256 yards and twelve touchdowns, but in the ninth game against LSU in Baton Rouge, my football career was over in the time it took two LSU players to make a sandwich of me on a kickoff return. The collision tore the anterior and posterior cruciate ligaments in my right knee, and the prognosis was dire. I needed reconstructive knee surgery, and I was told I'd be lucky if I didn't need the aid of a cane to walk by the time I was forty. Auburn honored my scholarship through my senior year, and I graduated in four years with a 3.89 grade point average in pre-law and a double major in media communications and computer science.

CHAPTER 3

I'll always remember a conversation I had with Mom on my fourteenth birthday. Some friends had been invited over for cake and ice cream, and later in the day we engaged in a spirited game of tag football in the backyard. Mom, who had never matched Dad's interest in my athletic ability, was watching as I eluded defenders in a make-believe game between Alabama and Auburn. Later that night, as we watched the sun fade below the horizon from the back porch, she asked me an intriguing question. "Michael, have you thought about your future plans for life after college and what profession you want to spend the rest of your life doing?"

"A profession?"

"Yes, son, something other than playing football on Sundays. I've done some research and read that the chances of your playing professional football are less than one per cent. It doesn't matter if you're from Mississippi or Montana, the odds are all the same. You might want to think of a backup plan."

Knowing Mom would have an answer to almost anything, I asked, "What are the odds of becoming a doctor or an attorney?"

"Michael, assuming that you continue making excellent grades through high school and college, the odds are much greater. An exact number, I can't predict. Your great-grandfather, Leo Cummings, was an accomplished attorney in Atlanta, then served on a Federal court for eleven years before retiring in the early 1950s. For a black man in the South to achieve that legal status before it was popular – and that might be a bad choice of words – was almost unprecedented.

"Your father, whom I love dearly, despite his minor indiscretions, is the perfect example. He grew up in an environment that neither appreciated the value of an education nor the means to achieve it. But the combination of his brawn and charm has served him well. He earns more money than most of my teachers, but, had he taken the opportunity to further his own education, who knows what he might have accomplished? Your brain will get you farther than your brawn."

That was settled. At the age of fourteen, I made an early career decision.

"I think I'll look into law."

Mother concurred. "Good, now you're using your brain, Michael."

In September of 1993, I enrolled in the Clarence Darrow Law Center in Montgomery. I was one of forty-two first-year students, who, through an accelerated curriculum, would earn a law degree in two years. Channel 10 in Montgomery offered me a part-time job as a computer specialist and camera close-up man, and it was there that I met the woman who would change my life forever.

CHAPTER 4

Maureen Ann O'Brien walked into my life in the fall of 1993, eight months after she had graduated *summa cum laude* from Northwestern University's School of Journalism and Communication. Had she lived long enough to enjoy them, Maureen had three things going for her: intelligence, drop-dead gorgeous looks, and money – lots of money.

Her looks came from her mother, Vivian, a former Miss Wisconsin in the early 1950s, and the intelligence and money were courtesy of her late father, Reese O'Brien, senior partner in the Midwest's largest tort law firm.

Maureen graduated in early January, but didn't need a job. She needed financial advisors to manage the immense wealth her father had left, when, a month later, the firm's corporate jet plunged into the icy waters of Lake Michigan after takeoff from Chicago's O'Hare Field, killing Reese O'Brien and two associates. When the final tally of her father's estate was determined, it reached nearly fifteen million dollars. Maureen would receive a stipend of five thousand dollars a month for as long as she lived, or, as the will read, "until the money runs out." That would never happen.

Maureen's mother, who was already suffering mood swings from dealing with an absentee husband who routinely spent sixty hours a week at the office, not to mention week-long trips all over the country defending clients and raking in millions for the firm, was only one small step from the loony bin. Lake Michigan finished her journey.

Vivian O'Brien was now the permanent resident of a plush Chicago area assisted-living center that spared no expense in making life ultra-comfortable for its guests. Maureen stopped visiting her mother when her condition deteriorated so badly that Vivian didn't know what day it was, nor did she care. Bedridden and sleeping a minimum of eighteen hours a day, Alzheimer's had robbed her will to live, and at the age of fifty-five, Vivian O'Brien succumbed to the mind-numbing disease that still has researchers and scientists searching for a cure.

Maureen had felt the pain, too. Although she had been an accomplished soccer player who earned Big Ten Conference honors in her junior and senior seasons, never once had her father been present for one of her games in high school or college. There were musical and theatrical productions as well, but the ultimate snub was his missing her college graduation day while he was off suing some pharmaceutical company in England for defective birth control pills that had caused ovarian cancer in teenaged girls.

Maureen now bore the weight of the entire estate, but it did nothing to change her lifestyle. She had resisted the country club scene as a teenager, and refused to participate in the cultural ritual that recognized the new debutantes of society, opting instead to run with friends from the public schools, rather than the privileged kids from the private schools she had attended since kindergarten. She was more comfortable running with kids of blue-collar parents and lounging around in cheap blue jeans and flip-flops. And she gave new meaning to the term form-fitting jeans.

It wasn't as if she weren't aware of her allure. She simply chose to ignore it. Which, of course, had the opposite effect on everyone who came in contact with her. Spectacularly beautiful, she was tall for a woman – five feet ten – which allowed her to stand her ground and hold her own at eye level with most men. At a somewhat sheltered twenty-two, she didn't yet have the life experience to overcome the slight aura of her naivete that hovered around the edges. But she had an adventurous spirit that opened her life to endless possibilities arising from audacity, and a sparkling intelligence that opened her valedictorian mind to everything else.

She had grown up rich, courtesy of her neglectful father – wealthy, even by the standards of the wealthy – but she'd never flaunted it or used it as a weapon. She'd always felt that, in the face of the desperate, soul-ravaging need in the world, it showed poor taste to brandish the money and possessions all her friends in the private schools had frantically acquired while growing up. So, instead of sporting designer clothes and a penthouse condo, she dressed off the rack and would live within the modest means afforded by her future reporter's salary.

Maureen had employment offers from all the major networks and their affiliates, the destinations where many graduates aspiring to anchor the nightly news at NBC never make it past Topeka or Toledo. She was the equivalent of the top pick in the NFL draft, and she explained her choice of Montgomery. "Our family stayed there one night on a trip to Florida for spring break, and it seemed like a nice place." That was Maureen, always living in the simplest terms.

Channel 10 in Montgomery, an NBC affiliate, thought they had won the lottery. Now the question was what they would do with this Irish goddess. It didn't take long to figure out. After she did spot news reports for awhile, management decided to make her the hostess of a Sunday morning thirty-minute show, "Sunday Mornings With Maureen."

Initially, the idea was to have Maureen present stories on non-controversial issues, but this wasn't her niche. The show was a drag, and she convinced her superiors that her thirty minutes would be better served reporting on pivotal issues in Montgomery, not on some ice cream social sponsored by a local service club to benefit underprivileged kids.

Michael feared that one of her first assignments would be her last. With heavy camera in hand, he accompanied Maureen on a short trip south on U.S. Highway 31, where restaurant owner Joe Snidley, a former Imperial Wizard in the Ku Klux Klan, was celebrating his 85th birthday on July 2, ironically the same day the historic Civil Rights Law of 1964 was passed. In the early sixties, Snidley had attracted the attention of the FBI and the Secret Service when he'd made some rather uncomplimentary remarks about President Lyndon Johnson who had lobbied hard for the bill after the assassination of John Kennedy.

Snidley had allowed black customers to drive around to the back of his establishment and order their food to go, but he did not allow them to eat in the main part of the restaurant. "If Johnson wants to come down and eat with those niggers, he'll have to do it in the back. Ain't nobody tellin' me how to run my place, including the President of the United States."

Snidley finally relented, but it took two years before blacks felt comfortable being served in the restaurant, while the older blacks still retreated to the back door to get their orders. Maureen and Michael were coming unannounced at the height of the noon rush hour to interview the crusty old man.

"No, Maureen. "Don't think this is a good idea," Michael warned. "I just hope to God I'm not the only black face in the place."

"Don't worry, Michael, I'll charm him."

And Maureen did just that, exhibiting just enough cleavage to pique the old man's interest. He explained how he was misunderstood in the fifties, and that "Neegroes" didn't mind eating out of the kitchen door. "They was always in a big hurry, ma'am, didn't want to sit at a table and everything. You know?"

Maureen didn't care to know, so long as Snidley was performing a dramatic version of *mea culpa* and Michael's blood pressure wasn't entering the danger zone. After thirty minutes of nonstop questions and puzzling answers, Maureen had turned the flag-waving rebel into Kris Kringle.

"Lunch is on the house, including your 'Neegro' friend, too," Snidley bragged.

"How in God's name, did you ever pull that off?" Michael asked as they drove back to the station to edit the film for Sunday's show.

"Sex appeal, Michael. Didn't you notice that he never took his eyes off my breasts?"

A little embarrassed, Michael replied, "Well, Maureen, they were there for everybody to see."

"Would you rather I not dress in a manner that might offend you?" Maureen asked.

"I wasn't offended Maureen, just a little uncomfortable, that's all. I felt a lot of eyes were focused on me, too, and probably for all the wrong reasons. Sorry I brought it up."

The Snidley interview was a ratings bonanza, fueling her passion for more controversial topics. And there were plenty to explore. Hiring practices by the Montgomery Board of Education, sexual harassment charges at a well-known law firm, a proposal to hand out free condoms to students at the city's public high schools, and a father's law suit to allow his daughter to play football at a private school were just a few of the stories Maureen brought to her viewers on Sunday at 10:00 a.m. After two months, an extra thirty minutes was added to the show.

CHAPTER 5

Michael had become more than just a cameraman for Maureen. He had chauffeured her around Montgomery, as he soon learned that she had trouble remembering the best route to the post office, the bank, or the hair dresser. They spent a week house-hunting before she settled on a $200,000 home in a development south of Montgomery, a short fifteen-minute commute to the capital city. She could have easily written a check for twice that amount in east Montgomery, but she wanted space and privacy, and Southbrook Estates provided that and more. Her 2,000 square-foot home was situated on a one-acre lot, and the homes on either side of hers were a good one hundred feet away. It was her Camelot.

Although Michael enjoyed Maureen's company, he was uneasy in public settings when she doted on him, ignoring the stares of both blacks and whites, who viewed this unusual behavior with caution and apprehension. This was still the Deep South, where the social mixing of races was in its embryonic stages.

Michael knew a relationship beyond their work environment was strictly a fantasy. This wasn't his first encounter with an attractive woman of the opposite color. On a few of his football recruiting trips, white coeds were assigned as escorts to show him and other recruits a "good" time on their weekend visits to the school's campuses.

Despite his athletic prowess, he was bashful to a fault; a shield his mother had provided her well-mannered son. He understood the recruiting game, but Auburn had always been his one and only choice, and he was passive and disinterested with the flirtatious escorts on his six trips outside the state of Alabama. And, Margaret Tyler wouldn't have approved.

Like her late father, Maureen was so engrossed in her work that she found little time for Montgomery's night life. She took an art class at Huntingdon College, joined a service club, and volunteered at a local animal shelter, where she adopted two pets, a toy poodle she named Josephine, and a muscular black and white tom-cat she dubbed Napoleon.

She learned to play bridge and often subbed in a group hosted once a month by Monsignor Patrick Reilly at St. Boniface Catholic church, where he had served as pastor for the last eighteen years. He was a delightful gentlemen, who spared little expense in making this Thursday night gathering for his twelve guests a special evening. On one of her earlier shows, she did a piece on the people who were fortunate to be included in this elite mix of politicians, professors, newspaper editors, clergy, businessmen, and lawyers. It was here that she met attorney Anthony Romano, the South's self-professed "King of Tort Law."

Her first year passed quickly, and Channel 10 knew the partnership was short-lived. Maureen was on the major networks' radar screens, and it was only a matter of time before she left Montgomery to rub shoulders with the icons of the nightly news shows. Maureen Ann O'Brien was a star in waiting.

CHAPTER 6

Justin Basch was a twenty-six-year old shiftless malcontent, who was resigned to living a life devoid of any goals or worldly possessions. He lived with his paranoid schizophrenic mother, Catherine, who had driven his father to empty a bottle of barbiturates into a quart of beer one Sunday afternoon while watching an NFL football game. In his suicide note, he asked Justin to watch over his mother, whose own demise was predicated on the dozen or so pills she consumed every day just to make it through another twenty-four hours.

Justin was a substitute rural mail carrier, on call to work for three routes that originated out of Montgomery's Southern Branch of the United States Postal Service. Considering his lackadaisical trip through high school, where he earned less-than-average grades and was a classic nonconformist in a class of six hundred students, he managed to pass the postal exam on his first attempt. A little nepotism helped land the job where his late father's brother, Paul, was the postmaster.

Uncle Paul considered his nephew an under-achiever, but out of respect for his brother, he took on the kid with a stern warning: "You're on a short leash here, kid. Screw up and you're history." Justin subbed two or three days a week, including every Saturday morning, when he was expected to be at his cubicle by seven o'clock, casing mail for 243 stops on Route Nine.

Justin hated Saturdays, because they always followed a night of bar-hopping at seedy beer joints that closed when the sun was coming up. His mother overlooked his listless lifestyle, because he was someone who would listen to her daily litany of rambling delusions, which included a wide range of subjects, most notably that her deceased husband was really living in the attic and came down to eat and watch TV when she had retired for the evening. Justin's only meaningful obligation was to escort her to countless doctors' appointments, where she stuck out her tongue, said "ah," and was sent home with a new prescription. "This is the one that will make me better, Justin. You just wait and see."

His mother's cooking was dubious at best, so Justin relied on fast food drive-throughs, doughnuts, and occasionally showing up for work with a bag of his Krispy Kreme favorites. His six-foot frame carried only 150 pounds, and, burdened with stooped shoulders since early childhood and a face that only a mother could love, bachelorhood was likely.

He arrived for work on September 3, 1994, completely unaware how one stop on his route would change his life and turn him into a couch potato watching soap operas with his mother. He was in a hurry to finish his route so that he could take in Auburn's opening game of the season against Northeastern Louisiana with a Starlight Lounge pick-up he had "fallen in love" with the night before. The tickets to the game were courtesy of uncle Paul who said, "Bring someone you're proud to be seen in public with."

Justin was about halfway through his route as

he turned left off Highway 31 to Southbrook Estates. After servicing the fifty-five boxes in the area's newest sub-division, he would head back to Montgomery, and by mid afternoon another uneventful Saturday was in the books.

There was only one stop he looked forward to on the route, hoping a sighting of Maureen O'Brien was in the cards. And it was. He had one special delivery letter that required her signature, and his testosterone level was increasing by the minute. Would she be sunbathing at the pool, like she was back in August, when another piece of mail needed her signature?

As he made the turn into her circular driveway, he noticed that something was amiss. Josephine, her toy poodle, was loose in the front yard, running in circles with an incessant bark that was totally out of control for the young puppy. The letter was her only piece of mail today, and he cautiously approached the front door to 14089 Meadowbrook Lane. After ringing the buzzer and knocking on the door with no response, he saw that the door was slightly ajar, maybe a few inches.

"What the hell," he thought, "she must be home if the door is open." He stepped inside the foyer that led to the living room and called out her name for the second time. Josephine was right behind, still barking and racing up and down the hallway that led to Maureen's bedroom. There was an oppressive odor permeating the house, and Justin's instincts were telling him that something was terribly wrong. He walked slowly down the carpeted hallway, continuing to call her name. He looked in the study where she liked to paint, and then in a second bedroom that was more of a storage room. Only one room off the hallway remained, the master bedroom. He tapped on the door lightly, then entered the darkened room. His morning breakfast of cinnamon rolls and chocolate milk spilled to the floor. He was the first to witness the beautiful Maureen O'Brien's corpse, or whatever was left of it.

CHAPTER 7

Kneeling in his own vomit and trying to regain his composure, Justin staggered to the kitchen and reached his uncle on a desk phone, incoherently trying to explain the horror of his discovery. "Stay put, I'll call the police. And don't touch anything, you understand?" his uncle ordered.

Minutes later, a stream of Montgomery city and county squad cars were racing down Highway 31 to Southbrook Estates. Captain Daniel Rabas of the Montgomery Detective Division was the first to reach Justin. "How we doing, son, are you okay?"

"I've felt better, sir."

While the other officers were trying to secure the area, Rabas asked Justin to retrace his entry into the O'Brien home. "Now, take your time, Justin. Walk me through it."

Together, they entered the house and Justin pointed Rabas in the direction of the bedroom. "You wait here in the living room, Justin. I'll take it from here."

Rabas unholstered his Colt Cobra .38 calibre special and tiptoed down the long hallway leading to Maureen's bedroom. The Captain had witnessed more homicides then he cared to recall, but what he saw lying spread-eagled on what were once white satin bed sheets was incomprehensible even for him. Out of respect for Maureen, he turned away, then placed a call to Dr. William Jacobsen, the county's medical examiner. Under normal circumstances, he would have checked for a pulse, but the enormous blood splatter on the rugs, bed, and walls had to be preserved, and only Dr. Jacobsen would be allowed in the room. No pulse check was necessary.

As more squad cars arrived, the scene became even more chaotic. It was as if the subdivision had been awakened from a long hibernation; people poured out of their homes to get a first-hand view of the police invasion. Rabas shouted at officers to tape off the area, but people were already peeking in whatever window was available. "Get these Goddamned people off the property," he yelled to any officer within earshot of his voice.

Dr. Jacobsen was in the middle of an autopsy when he received Rabas' call and he told the Captain "not to touch anything." Where had Rabas heard that before?

Accompanied by two forensic specialists, Dr. Jacobsen arrived on the scene twenty-three minutes after talking with Rabas. The captain dutifully noted the time, as he knew this investigation would be like no other in his thirty-one years on the force. And shortly afterward the mayor himself was waved through the police barriers.

"Aw, shit," was all Rabas could say when he saw the city's perceived police chief arrive. He was wishing Mayor Zachary Bunde was also headed to the Auburn game. But he sighed .... *Let the circus begin.*

Rabas did his best to ignore the Mayor, who had been denied access to the house. That pissed of His Honor, and he hollered to know who was in charge of the investigation. "Captain Rabas is," Sergeant Donnie

Myers informed the Mayor, "and he says nobody but authorized personnel is allowed in the house. Sorry, sir."

"Christ, I'm the Mayor," Bunde protested; a fact that Myers shrugged off.

Rabas finally stepped outside and informed the Mayor of the situation. "We have a homicide unlike any I've ever seen, and the fewer people who see it, the better off they'll sleep at night. For those doing their work in there, taking even the slightest nap will be a monumental challenge."

Bunde asked who the victim was, and when informed it was Maureen O'Brien, he shook his head as if to ask why her. "I'll leave y'all to your work, Captain Rabas. Keep me posted, please."

"Will do, sir."

Dr. Jacobsen and his forensics team finished their work in about an hour and bagged Maureen's remains for the unceremonious ride to the county morgue. Rabas then had the officers fan out and check out homes in the subdivision for any clues that would start them on the path to solving this unthinkable crime. It was the Labor Day weekend, and grills and backyard pools were alive with activity, but even the well-to-do in this exclusive neighborhood would have their privacy interrupted for a few questions.

CHAPTER 8

Four weeks into the investigation of Maureen O'Brien's murder, Captain Rabas had no substantial leads. Channel 10 had offered a $25,000 reward for information leading to the arrest and conviction of the person or persons responsible for her death, but this had only produced the usual quack calls that led nowhere.

Minutes before he was to meet with the Mayor on his weekly update, Rabas received the first of two calls that would give new life to the case.

"Call on line one," barked his secretary, Sandy Smith. "Some senior citizen looking for the reward money. Speak loudly, I think she's hard of hearing."

"Good morning. This is Captain Dan Rabas, how can I help you?"

"Well, you can tell that snippy secretary of yours she doesn't have to shout on the phone. I'm not that hard of hearing."

"Sorry about that ma'am. Now who do I have the pleasure of speaking with?

"Alice Carmichael, Meadowbrook Lane, the subdivision south of Montgomery off Highway 31."

"I'm familiar with it, Mrs. Carmichael. We had a terrible tragedy out there a few weeks ago," Rabas said.

"Oh, I'm aware of that Captain. I live across the street from the poor lady's house. Lots and lots of people coming and going from there all hours of the day, Captain."

"Why don't you tell me about it?" Rabas asked. "You have my undivided attention, Mrs. Carmichael."

"Well that night she was killed, there was that white Channel 10 TV van in her driveway most of the night. I saw it several times before I went to bed."

Interested, Rabas signaled for his secretary to pick up and record the conversation. This could be the first break the department was looking for in the case. Rabas continued, "Mrs. Carmichael, what time in the evening did you see the TV vehicle in the O'Brien driveway?" There was no answer on the other end. "Mrs. Carmichael, are you there?"

Mrs. Carmichael was back on the phone again. "Excuse me, Captain, my tea was boiling over. Now, what was the question again?"

Rabas repeated the question. "What time was it you saw the van in the O'Brien driveway?"

"Oh, yes, the TV van. Right after the ten o'clock news, Captain. I went outside to look at the moon again. It was full that night, or close to it. I forget. It's a beautiful sight; nothing even comes close to it."

"Yes ma'am," the Captain responded. Before Rabas could follow up with another question, Mrs. Carmichael was going off about how such a peaceful neighborhood was forever changed. "It'll never be the same again, Captain."

"Yes, it was terrible. Mrs. Carmichael, how long did you stay outside to look at the moon? You said it was right after the news, is that right?"

"Yes, Captain, right after the news. There was that big story about the gambling raid at the Air Force base. My husband is a retired colonel, but he was in bed already."

"Ma'am, could one of my detectives come out and speak with you tomorrow? You tell me what's a good time for you."

"Oh no, Captain, my husband isn't feeling well. Doesn't want any visitors. Says I should stay out of it, mind my own business. You know?"

"Is that why you waited so long to call us, Mrs. Carmichael?"

"I don't know, maybe," and the line went dead.

Sandy Smith was almost in tears from laughter in the outer office. "There's a lead for you, Captain. Get right on it."

Muttering to himself, Rabas headed across the street to a meeting with the Mayor he wasn't looking forward to.

CHAPTER 9

"He's waiting for you, Captain," was the greeting from Madeline Bowers, Zachary Bunde's long-time secretary. "Tread lightly. He's a little grumpy this morning. Bad cards at the club last night, I think."

Bunde, who was in his third term as the Mayor of Montgomery, rose to greet the captain with his vise-like handshake that scared some people away from locking hands with the former amateur boxer. "Good morning Captain. Trust we're making some progress on this case. The negative national media attention we're getting isn't something we need."

"If you think it's bad now, Mayor, wait until an arrest is made and the trial begins."

"Where do we stand, Captain?" Bunde asked.

Rabas didn't know if he should share the phone conversation he'd just had with Mrs. Carmichael, but the mayor wanted a weekly update on the investigation, and her call, however erratic, was all he had. "I got a call this morning from a lady who lives across the street from the O'Brien residence who said she saw a white Channel 10 van in the victim's driveway around ten-thirty the night of the murder."

"And may I ask who our good luck charm is today, Captain?"

"A Mrs. Alice Carmichael, sir."

The Mayor flashed his celebrated smile. "Alice Carmichael, Captain? The same Alice Carmichael who claims UFOs tried to land in her backyard about two years ago?"

"Didn't make the connection, Mayor."

Bunde, who had earlier raised the speculation that Michael Tyler was a prime suspect in the case, repeated his beliefs. "Captain, I'm convinced the boy is involved, and I'm not the only person who believes that. I have some of my people out there doing some investigative work that are convinced, too." *Why I am not surprised at that, Rabas thought to himself.*

Rabas was tired of his own staff referring to Michael as "the boy," and now the Mayor was doing it, too. He wouldn't let the remark pass. "Need I remind you, Mr. Mayor, that Michael Tyler graduated from Auburn University in the top one per cent of his class, and is a second-year law student on pace to graduate next year? His family is rock solid; mother has a master's degree in education, and his father has been employed by the same employer for thirty years. Oh, and I forgot; his great grandfather was the first black Federal judge in the South. Is that the type of pedigree your use of the term "boy" comes from? That being said, Mr. Mayor, I have work to do. And should your 'investigative' people solve this case, give them each a key to the fricking city and a complimentary trip to Six Flags."

Bunde was offering his apologies, but Rabas heard little of it as he strode out of the office. As he passed by Madeline Bowers' desk, he commented wryly, "You're right, Madeline, the boss is a little edgy today."

When Rabas returned to his office, there was a message that an insurance company from Illinois had called regarding a policy on Maureen O'Brien. Before he could return the call, they had called a second time.

"Captain Daniel Rabas, Montgomery Detective Division. Sorry I missed your earlier call."

The caller identified himself as Lawrence Karbowski, an agent with the Illinois Midwest Central Life Insurance Company. "Captain, we just received a call from a Chicago attorney representing the estate of Maureen O'Brien, a Montgomery resident, about a million-dollar term life policy that was written a year ago. The family attorney informed us of Miss O'Brien's unfortunate death a month ago, and I thought you'd be interested in knowing the beneficiary of the policy."

"Yes, sir, who is it?"

"A Michael Cummings Tyler, 214 South Jackson Street, Montgomery, Alabama."

Rabas was silent for a moment, then asked the agent if he would fax a copy of the policy to him ASAP.

"I'll have it to you as soon as we get off the phone, Captain. And, how do you say it down there? Y'all have a nice day?"

"Yeah, something like that."

It was time to have another chat with Michael.

CHAPTER 10

Michael was at home studying for an exam at the Law Center, when there was a loud knock on the door. He peeked through the shade of the front window and the black Chevy Impala with blackwall tires meant a visit from the local police. He opened the door to find Captain Rabas and two detectives with whom he'd had an unfriendly encounter a week before at the Atlanta Highway Walmart.

Opening the door, he greeted his three guests. "Captain Rabas. Nice to see you. Wish you'd called ahead. I'm studying for a test, and I'm a little behind, what with work and everything. I hope this won't take too long."

"Well, Tyler, we're in the middle of a murder investigation, and we need to ask you some questions now," snapped Bailey Moore, one of Rabas' two smart-mouthed detectives.

"Put a lid on it, Moore," Rabas ordered. "This is just a courtesy call, Michael. A few questions and we'll be on our way. They're just here to observe."

"Well, as a courtesy to me, you can tell Mr. Moore and his pit bull they can observe from the car while we speak. They leave, or we don't talk."

"Fair enough Michael. Detectives, if you'll wait out in the car, I'll be out shortly." Moore pointed an accusatory finger at Michael as he and Miles Austin departed, slamming the door behind them. Michael returned the one-finger salute.

Taking a seat in Michael's living room, Rabas asked, "What the hell was that all about, Michael?"

"Ask them," Michael replied. "Now, what can I do for you?"

Choosing his words carefully, the Captain said, "It might be better if I issue you your Miranda warning, Michael."

Michael reminded Rabas that his detectives had already done that a week after Maureen's murder in an interview at the station. "There's no need to do it again, Captain. I already gave them a statement, and nothing has changed since then. Anything I say today is off the record, or we don't talk. Now, how can I help you today?

"I'm sorry, Michael. I'm under a lot of pressure from the Mayor and the press to get this case resolved. Earlier today, I received a call from an insurance company in Illinois about a sizeable life insurance policy Maureen had taken out on her life last year."

"And why would I have any interest in that, Captain?"

"Because you, Michael, were the sole beneficiary of a million dollars, two mil if shc dicd accidently."

"And that makes me a suspect, Captain? I'm also the prime beneficiary on my mom and dad's insurance policies and their estate – not as much – and they're very much alive and well. I wish I could say the same about Maureen."

Captain Rabas tried to assure Michael he wasn't singling him out as a suspect. "In most situations, this would be a major motive. We're talking about a substantial amount of money here, Michael."

Michael stood, stretching his right knee which

was throbbing today. "Captain, this is all news to me. Maureen never said anything about naming me as a beneficiary, and had she done that, I would have declined the offer. If that's the 'smoking gun' you have, you've got nothing. Now, I have a lot of studying to get ready for that exam, so please excuse me. Maybe we can talk at a later time. Lunch some day?"

"Good, Michael, I'll give you a call. Sorry for the interruption, and good luck on that test."

"Thanks, Captain."

Michael then retreated to his favorite chair and opened the textbook to the section on felony murder. Interesting topic, he thought.

CHAPTER 11

Three weeks later, Michael had just returned home from his twice-a-week run through the streets of Old Cloverdale, an historic part of Montgomery that also encompassed Huntingdon College. The high school football season was winding down, and he would be covering four games tonight, including the long-standing city rivalry between Robert E. Lee and Sidney Lanier. The game had long lost its luster from the 1960s, when both teams fielded the best programs in the state, but 10,000 fans would attend the game in ancient Cramton Bowl, and with post-season playoff berths on the line, it warranted video coverage. He would shoot footage of the four games, return to the station, and edit the video for about three minutes of air time on the ten o'clock news.

He was watching *Jeopardy!*, trying to match wits with a Casino dealer from Green Bay who was seeking his tenth straight win. The final *Jeopardy!* question was pending when the phone rang, and Michael picked up on the third ring.

"Michael, this is Sarah from Greenville."

Michael paused, trying to place the name. "Am I supposed to know a Sarah from Greenville?"

"Michael, we went to school together. I was two grades behind you, played basketball and softball."

"Excuse me, Sarah. Now I remember you. How are things back home?"

Not wanting to rehash their old high school days, Sarah's voice seemed urgent. "Michael, they just left to execute a warrant to search your parents' property."

Michael interrupted. "Who are 'they', Sarah, and how do you know about some search warrant?

"The Greenville police, Michael. I'm the dispatcher at the station. Went to work here about two years ago. They received a reliable tip that the gun used in the murder investigation of the TV lady you worked with might be hidden at their house, and they're headed out there now."

Michael assumed his parents, at least his mother, would be home to allow the search, and asked Sarah what the normal procedure would be if any incriminating evidence were found.

"Since it's the weekend, it might be Monday before anything is sent up to Montgomery. But if they find a weapon, they might run it up there tonight," Sarah said. "Are your fingerprints in the FBI database system, Michael?"

"Don't believe so," he replied. "No reason for them to be there."

But Sarah wasn't so sure. "Michael, if the police took fingerprints at the lady's house, and you were a frequent visitor there, as the rumors suggest, then either full or partial prints of yours will be on file. You better hope your prints are not on any weapon they find and can match. We don't have the FBI database system down here, so you've got a little time on your side. I get off work in an hour, and they should be back by then. I'll call you when they get back."

Michael decided he wouldn't wait. He called home and his mother answered on the first ring.

"Mother, what the heck is going on? Just got a call from a high school friend who said the police are coming to the house looking for a weapon." Margaret had always been the calming influence in the family, and even the presence of police on her property didn't rattle the middle school principal. "They just left, son, with something in a plastic bag. I think it was a gun."

"Well, dad had hunting guns, but no pistols or revolvers that I can remember, mom."

"No, it was a small bag, Michael. Please tell me what's going on."

"If I knew, Mother, I would."

Shortly after he talked with his mother, Sarah was calling again. "Michael, they found a .38 calibre pistol in your dad's outside work shed or shop that police say was probably used in the murder. One of the officers is leaving in about an hour to take up it to Montgomery. Good luck. I gotta get off the phone."

Michael remembered a discussion he'd had with his father a week after Maureen's death. "Son, don't forget this name – Roscoe Jenkins, owner of Jenkins Auto and Salvage Repair. He owes me a big favor, and I mean big. Call him if the police are ever closing in. He's a fixer."

CHAPTER 12

Roscoe Jenkins was the ultimate survivor, the sixth and last child of Louis and Yolanda Jenkins, born on an oppressive summer day in 1950. Burdened by life in one of the city's low-income housing projects, Roscoe had managed to distance himself from the family nest by the time he entered high school in the fall of 1964. His parents had severed what little relationship once existed for a life of petty crime that spilled over to Roscoe's siblings. Yolanda was serving a five-year stretch for food stamp fraud, while Louis was in and out of alcohol rehab centers most of his adult life. Roscoe's three brothers were frequent guests in the city jail for misdemeanors that kept them unemployed and penniless. Two sisters had added five illegitimate children to the welfare rolls, and were routinely seen walking the streets looking for someone with whom to share a bottle, bed, or a needle.

Roscoe's uncle, Ellsworth, fearing the youngest child would follow in the footsteps of his kinfolk, was granted indefinite custody when young Roscoe turned fourteen. It was Ellsworth who had steered his young nephew away from the housing projects that were infested with the unemployed and unemployable.

Roscoe graduated in the top fifteen per cent of his class, and at the urging of his uncle, joined the Marines fresh out of high school. He spent four years with the Corps, then returned home to Montgomery to aid his elderly uncle who was battling rheumatoid arthritis. Ellsworth, who no longer wanted the day-to-day responsibilities of running the business, said if Roscoe would pay him $1,500 a month to stay away, the business was his. Over ribs and a fifth of Chivas Regal, the deal was signed.

Roscoe's stint in the Corps was spent working in one of the base's two auto body shops, but it was his sideline job that gave him the most satisfaction. An off-base bookie, with whom Roscoe had placed sports bets, needed an insider on the base to handle his gambling interests for basketball and football games. It was common knowledge that the shop was taking the illegal bets, but so many high-ranking officers were regular customers that it was permitted to thrive on government property. Roscoe was earning two per cent on every dollar booked, and in a good week he cleared over two hundred dollars of non-taxable income.

He brought the concept home to Montgomery, where wagering on sports, especially football, was generally overlooked. A raid or two on an established bookie brought nothing more than a slap on the wrist in the form of a low-grade misdemeanor and a hall pass to continue. A donation of a case or two of top-shelf whiskey for the city employees' Christmas party didn't hurt, either. Roscoe, though, wasn't satisfied with being just another small-time bookie. He wanted the biggest piece of the gambling pie, and he had a plan. He would donate all the booze and beer to the party and sponsor two of the police department's summer softball teams. He also provided the Boys and Girls Clubs with new bicycles, and funds to help install new scoreboards for the city's eight junior high school sports fields.

Roscoe's gambling enterprise reached into state government, where he had an inside man in the Motor Vehicle Division who would, for a reasonable fee, produce a "spot-on perfect" driver's license, with backup data, to the prove the bearer of the license existed – at least on paper. Where there was a need, Roscoe was the man to call. Michael Tyler never made it to any of the four football games he was assigned to cover that Friday.

CHAPTER 13

"Back door, Michael, and be quick about it," Roscoe said before hanging up the phone. "Jesus," he thought, *"what am I going to do with this kid?"*

Michael's Toyota was crossing Madison Street, when two Montgomery black-and-whites were going in the opposite direction with their flashing lights and screaming sirens headed to South Jackson Street.

Except for Roscoe's German Shepherd, Buddy, who was never more than breathing distance from his master, the shop was empty. After Michael parked his Toyota in the rear of the shop, Roscoe said, "Let's talk in my office."

Taking a seat across the desk from a man he was meeting for the first time, Michael peered over a mound of paper and styrofoam cups that once had contained coffee or scotch, but now served as ashtrays for the relentless chain smoker.

"I know what you're thinking, Michael, I'm an unorganized slob. Actually, I know why every piece of paper is on this desk. See this yellow piece of paper under this stack?"

Michael nodded, "yes."

"It's an old invoice I'm three weeks late paying," followed by a hearty laugh.

"No, no, Mr. Jenkins, to the contrary," Michael remarked, turning his attention to the four walls that were adorned with an array of photos. "I'm impressed with all the pictures, and you're in on every one of them. How did you manage to get one with President Clinton?"

"He was in town campaigning in1991, and he stopped by to say hello. All kidding aside, Michael, I know a lot of people, because I help a lot of people. Every picture has a story behind it, but unfortunately we don't have time for that now. The police scanner says they have an APB out for you, so it's time we find a good hiding place for you. We'll discuss it at my house, where you can hide out for a few days."

Two days later, over pizza, ribs, and Michelob, Roscoe Jenkins laid out Michael's new identity and itinerary that had him headed to Pine Bluff, Arkansas.

"Pine Bluff," Michael said with an obvious hint of sarcasm. "What the hell is in Pine Bluff that maybe Atlanta doesn't have?"

"Several things," Roscoe lectured. "Pine Bluff has has only twelve Auburn alumni from over there in the last thirty years, and seven are deceased. On the other hand, Atlanta has ...."

"I get it, Roscoe," Michael interrupted. "Atlanta has hundreds of Auburn alumni, including a lot of jocks who are living over there now. But Pine Bluff?"

"Heh, take a nice deep breath, brother," Roscoe cautioned. I want you as inconspicious as a dimple on a golf ball. You can walk by the police station, talk to anybody you want, and no one will have a clue you're the infamous killer on the run from Montgomery, Alabama. Excuse me, 'alleged' infamous killer.

"Secondly, I have an old acquaintance in Pine Bluff who owes me a little favor. I won't get into the specifics, and unless he wants to talk about it, it's something between the two of us. Like, personal, you know?"

"I get it, Roscoe – personal. So who is this old friend that's so indebted to you?"

"Jeremiah Jones, entrepreneur of sorts, but on a larger scale than me."

"Larger than you, Roscoe?"

"No, no, not what you're thinking, Michael. He's legitimate. He owns an antique car restoration body shop that does extremely well, but he also has a lawn maintenance shop that will be your perfect hideaway for a while. Your daddy said you could take apart the largest Sears riding lawn mower ever made and put it back together in one hour when he was cutting grass back in Greenville."

Smiling, Michael corrected Roscoe, "Maybe two hours."

"Is that how you lost that pinkie on your right hand?" Roscoe asked.

"Yeah, something like that."

"Look, it's a great setup, Michael. He has a small apartment over his business which he will lease out to you and ...."

"Lease out, like pay rent?"

"Yeah, like pay rent, buy groceries, subscribe to Cable TV and the local newspaper. A normal person doing some normal things, Michael. You'll earn three hundred bucks a week in cash with no deductions to the State of Arkansas or the U.S. government. Now meet the new Michael Tyler – Tim Jennings, a 26-year-old Birmingham native who died of an unexpected heart attack two months ago."

"He's dead, Roscoe?"

"Yeah, dead. Don't ever have to worry about him

walking into your shop with a lawnmower problem, do you? Your vital statistics are almost identical – hell he could be your twin brother. Here's a duplicate of Jennings' driver's license, which is good for another three years. People don't turn in their drivers' licenses just because they die. Even if you're stopped for some driving infraction, you're Tim Jennings, who has a clean driving record. By the time this expires, you'll have your own as a free man.

"For money, here's two thousand dollars in twenties. You'll deal in cash only, no credit cards, no checks. Today you traded in your Toyota Camry for a Chevy Caprice. Insurance, registration, and proof of ownership make it all legal. Well maybe not quite legal, but you know what I mean. Any questions?"

"When do I leave, and will my parents know where I am?"

"Tomorrow morning. You have a reservation at the Holiday Inn in Meridian and should get into Pine Bluff late Tuesday afternoon. I'll be in touch with your mom and dad, but no, they won't know where you are. We can't risk any trails with phone calls, or mail. Look, Michael, you have every right to be skeptical about this plan, but hiding out in Montgomery isn't a risk we can take. Get a good night's sleep, son. You're good to go tomorrow."

CHAPTER 14

With a bear hug that left him almost breathless, Michael was in the arms of Jeremiah Jones. Jones was also a bear of a man, 250 pounds, well distributed over his six-foot-three frame. He'd been a small college All-American at Grambling College in football and a high draft choice of the New York Jets in 1975. But a bad history of concussions that began in high school derailed his pro career before it even started, and he returned home to work in his grandfather's restoration shop.

"Any friend of Mr. Jenkins is a friend of mine, Michael. We go back a few years. Think it was 1990 in Montgomery for an old friend's wedding. A little misunderstanding with the police that he took care of. If he didn't tell you the details, I won't either. It's a ...."

"Personal, Jeremiah."

"Yeah, personal."

"Roscoe says the law wants you for a murder you didn't commit. If Roscoe says you're clean, that's good enough for me."

"Thanks, Jeremiah. I know you don't need to hear it, but I didn't kill that lady."

Gesturing for Michael to follow him, Jeremiah said, "Now let me show you around the place. This is a little more than your average body shop. Oh, we fix up the bangers teenagers and drunks bring us, but restoring vintage cars is where the real money is. There isn't another shop like ours within 250 miles of here, so our services are in high demand. Owners want them to look just like they did the day they rolled off the assembly line and that's what we provide – at a very good price.

"The 1957 Chevy Corvette is the most popular model; probably have restored fifty or more over the last fifteen years. I have five employees who do nothing but restoration work, and just a little word of advice, Michael, don't ever refer to them as grease monkeys. They're highly skilled technicians at their trade, each earning around sixty thou a year.

"Now, Roscoe claims you have two areas of expertise that might be beneficial to me: computers and lawn equipment. An ex-con, who happens to be a first cousin of mine, is in the finals stage of prostate cancer, and we closed the shop across the street a few months ago. There's a small apartment above it you're welcome to occupy for fifty bucks a week. I'll be paying you three hundred a week in cash, so you should be able to live a comfortable, but not extravagant life style here in Pine Bluff.

"As you can see, my shops are not in the affluent section of Pine Bluff. Lot of rundown bars, businesses that should be closed for lack of business, and a hooker trade that has seen better days. Seventh and Union used to be a thriving area back in the sixties, but downtown redevelopment never got this far.

"Those two pit bulls roaming around the shop, Rocky and Max, are my version of Dr. Jekyll and Mr. Hyde. I have some extremely expensive cars being restored here, and the dogs are my insurance policy against any unwelcome intruders. They're a little wary of you right now, but as long as me or the help is around, you won't have a problem. After they get to know and trust you, they'll adopt you like they have everybody else around here. Any questions?"

All Michael Tyler could think of was, "When do I start work?"

"Well, why not tomorrow? Grass cutting is pretty much over, but we do a lot of equipment overhauls during the winter months, especially for the city. Now, the shop is a mess, because my cousin hated the paper work that went with the business, and it'll take you some time to get it in working order. I bought him a computer a few years ago to help with inventory and billing, and hell he never hooked the damn thing up. Whatever you need, Michael, to get everything up and running, just say the word. And I guess I should be calling you Tim from here on."

Jeremiah wasn't kidding. The shop was worse than the picture he had painted. It looked like a tornado had made a prolonged visit to the shop. Paper and parts were strewn all over the place. The upstairs apartment would suffice for a fugitive; two small bedrooms, kitchen, living room, and a bathroom with a shower, all for fifty bucks a week.

Roscoe Jenkins was right. Michael had a better gig in Pine Bluff than most people in the Witness Protection Program. He was free to explore the area, socialize a little in some of the better clubs, attend a few basketball games at one of the two small colleges, and take in some concerts and theatrical productions at the new Civic Center. He was wary about opening a checking or savings account, because it might involve a background check and possible fingerprints, so, like an old hoarder, he stashed away the extra cash in an old shoe box under his apartment bed. Roscoe had insisted that Tim Jennings was *clean*, but just how *clean* was his main concern.

The missing tip of Michael's pinkie had drawn only marginal attention in the shop, since he wore gloves most of the time. And when out in public he was in the habit of keeping the hand in his pants pocket. He checked out the main post office to see if he had made the FBI's Ten Most Wanted list, but was relieved to see he hadn't. Jeremiah had a casual acquaintance with a local agent, who said the list was reserved for the real "bad asses" of society. Michael had been accused of an unforgivable crime, and the assumption was that he had fled the scene of the crime in Alabama, but the FBI had yet to get involved in the search. However, it would only be a matter of time before they did.

CHAPTER 15

Near the end of Michael's first year, Jeremiah treated him to ribs and beer at his favorite hangout. The "Ole House," as it was affectionately referred to, had prospered for nearly five decades in an old predominantly black neighborhood of Pine Bluff. Long before the Civil Rights act of 1964 had challenged the landscape of socialization in the old South, Marvin Johnson had welcomed whites to his restaurant, which featured the barest of amenities. If you could overlook sitting at scarred picnic tables, and eating with plastic utensils from paper plates, then you obviously came for the ribs, chicken, hot cornbread, and cold beer and wine that had served three former Presidents, as well as numerous sports and movie celebrities.

Jeremiah called it Michael's "job review," but he never needed an excuse to visit Marvin, who was his East High School classmate. "Michael, you've been a Godsend to me. We're finally turning a profit in the maintenance shop, you've got everyone computerized, and hell, Gus and Max have accepted you. But all that aside, I do sense that you're just a little bored with our fine city. Something bothering you?"

How could Michael disagree with Jeremiah? He had been a gracious host to Alabama's number one fugitive, but Michael couldn't see hiding out in Pine Bluff for – what? A lifetime? He could never have a serious relationship with a woman, and there were some fine specimens in one of the clubs he liked to frequent. The guys at the shop asked him to go bar-hopping with them on occasion, but there were too many questions about Tim Jennings that he didn't have answers to. Besides, there was the finger thing which ultimately would give him up. The holidays were approaching, and he would miss the energy and passion his mother always put into this special time of the year. He was twenty-five years old and, admittedly, homesick.

"You're like Roscoe in so many ways," he told Jeremiah. "You can read people's minds without them opening up to you. I can never repay you for all your kindness over the last year. But I'm concerned about you and the successful businesses you've built, which will be jeopardized if I'm discovered here. I don't think you need a second-year law student to run down the charges they'll heap on you. Obstruction of justice and aiding and abetting a fugitive will get you ten to fifteen years of real hard time, and no lounging around with corporate honchos working on their bridge and tennis games in a federal country club. Is it worth the risk, Jeremiah?"

Jeremiah was silent.

"Well I'll answer it for you. No! I don't know what Roscoe did for you a few years back, but nothing is worth spending the next decade or two locked up in some dirtbag of a prison because you wanted to help out an old friend. I'm seriously thinking of returning to Montgomery, turning myself in, and trying to clear my name."

Jeremiah was silent for a moment or two, then responded. "Michael, I appreciate your concern for my well-being. There isn't a day that goes by when I'm not thinking the law will waltz through my front door, haul you and me both away, and destroy everything I've achieved. Yes, Roscoe was placing a big burden on me when he asked me to help you out. And, while we've created a monastery of sorts here for you, sooner or later – and I fear sooner – the wall of invincibility will come crashing down. Michael, I ...."

"I know Jeremiah, you don't have to say it. Contact Roscoe and tell him I'll be leaving over the weekend. We'll hook up in Montgomery, and I'll do the sensible thing."

Jeremiah smiled and took Michael's hand. "I can't honestly say that any black man in the South turning himself in for allegedly killing a gorgeous white woman qualifies for any smart points, but I'll call him tomorrow morning."

With the same bear hug he'd welcomed Michael a year ago, Jeremiah Jones held him close. Michael could feel Jeremiah's tears on his neck as they bid adieu. For a man who said he seldom cried, Jones did his share tonight.

CHAPTER 16

Michael drove straight through to Montgomery, arriving at Roscoe's home early Sunday afternoon. "Make yourself at home, my good friend. Let's enjoy the evening over beer and pizza and watch the Packers-Bears game tonight. We can talk later about what you want to do."

"Sounds great, Roscoe."

"You want a little action on the game tonight? The Packers are getting six in Chicago. The pros are calling it the lock of the year. What say?"

"Geez, thought gambling was illegal in Alabama, Roscoe. You can go to jail for that."

"Yeah, and I'll bring a thousand or so other guys with me."

"Give me a hundred on the Packers."

Roscoe had no allegiances in sports. "Don't bet with your heart, use your damn head," he had always professed. And he'd become a master at laying off bets to other bookies when the action was heavy on one team. Today had been an exceptional day. He was up four grand by five o'clock, and the two night games would bring in another one or two. Life was good.

"We got a couple of hours before the night games begin, Michael, so let's talk."

"You first, Roscoe."

"Where do I start, Michael. Alright, let's begin with Pine Bluff. Any trail that would lead authorities there can be easily explained. Jeremiah can say you walked into his shop one day looking for a job. You spent a year there and then informed him you wanted to return to Alabama. Jeremiah knew nothing about your past. Let's wait a few days, maybe till Wednesday. We'll call Detective Rabas, and he can formally arrest you and take you into custody. But before we get Rabas involved, we need to get you an attorney, a *good* attorney. Once the news of your arrest is public, there'll be lawyers coming out of the woodwork to defend you. They'll view it as a career-maker, especially when they win. This ain't no case for a public defender or rookie lawyer."

"Roscoe, I don't have that kind of money for a defense that will run in the thousands, and I can't ask my parents to dip into their savings, either."

But Roscoe was adamant. "Michael, I can name a dozen outstanding legal minds here who will walk all over each other to do it free. I believe in the profession it's called *pro bono.*"

Michael studied Roscoe, then asked, "Who?"

Do you know Anthony Romano? His family owns two Italian restaurants. He's made his millions in tort law, but does some work on the side for Channel 10's license renewals and other legal matters. His sister Rosaline is married to the TV weather guy. What's his name?"

"George Crawford. Yeah, I've seen Mr. Romano around the station a few times. Played football at Duke I believe."

"Michael, the guy's a real ball-buster in court. I took in one of his cases last year in that big sexual harassment suit at the base. Uncle Sam had to fork out two mil to a gal who claims she was bypassed for a job promotion because she wouldn't do her boss. He tore into that Lieutenant Colonel like he was in a bathtub with flesh-eating piranhas."

"But, Roscoe, he sues municipalities, insurance companies, big corporations and hospitals. I doubt he's ever handled a murder case, much less one with definite death penalty implications. I need someone with criminal experience, not a tort lawyer."

But Roscoe wasn't finished selling Romano to Michael. "The guy's a big Italian whose mere presence intimidates the hell out of opposing counsel. Let me call him and see if he's interested. The final decision is yours, but I'm voting for Romano."

Green Bay smacked the Bears by twenty and Michael cost his host a hundred. He declined the winnings, but Roscoe insisted he take the money. It would keep him well supplied with his favorite Snickers and Mountain Dews while he was in lockup.

On Tuesday morning, Roscoe, Anthony Romano, and his new client talked for the better part of three hours. Romano, who was in Atlanta working on another tort case, drove home immediately when Roscoe called. Tony, as he preferred to be called, never sugar-coated his words. "You're in a heap of shit, Michael. You'll be arrested, arraigned, denied bail, and locked up for over a year before the Circuit Court considers the case. Winston Kennedy, the Attorney General, will want to prosecute you personally to further his political aspirations, which have no ceiling.

He will use this trial to satisfy the reactionaries out there who think capital punishment is the end-all to violence in our society. There is no grey area in Kennedy's mind over the use of the death penalty. Death begets death, pure and simple. The guy's got a huge ego, but the voters like him; he's in his second term, the youngest ever elected to the office.

"Your obvious concerns over a tort lawyer going to war with your life on the line are acknowledged. But I have the financial resources not only to defend you, but also to find the person or persons responsible for this heinous crime. Someday, when you write a book and become the second John Grisham, include me when you thank the people who helped you along the way. And, finally, my services will be *pro bono*."

What could a twenty-five-year-old unemployed black man in Alabama about to be charged with the brutal murder of a beautiful white woman, say, except, "Thank you, Mr. Romano. I accept."

Roscoe proposed a toast. "To Michael. To his freedom."

Later that night, Roscoe told Michael the circumstances of his friendship with Michael's father. "It's a short story with a happy ending, Michael. Your old man saved my life one day in a little store I own about fifty miles south of here. It serves as an outlet to place some bets where this low-life jerk had run up a pretty good tab making bad bets on college games. I knew he'd be there late Friday afternoon, so I made it a point to be there, too. Sure enough, old Junior shows up to put down some more bets, but Johnny, who runs the store for me, said he'd have to clear his tab before he could make any more, and he took exception to it. When he saw me, he started running his mouth, calling me an Uncle Tom and other shit. About that time, when Junior pulls a knife on me, your daddy comes through the back door with a delivery of Budweiser. Junior doesn't see him, not that it would have really mattered. Old Ralph slams him in the kidneys with that gorilla fist of his and down goes Junior. The rest – well, I'll let your daddy finish the story someday. We never saw Junior again. He disappeared that day, and your daddy and I became instant friends – forever."

"He just disappeared?

"Yeah, disappeared."

"You had him wasted over a freaking gambling debt?"

"I didn't say that."

Before Michael retired for the evening, he asked Roscoe why Anthony Romano was so eager to take on his case. "Am I missing something here, Roscoe? A tort lawyer – and a good one I'm told – wants to jump into what will be an extremely highly-publicized murder trial. For what, Roscoe?"

"He's like a gambler, Michael. He loves the damn action."

CHAPTER 17

At ten o'clock on Wednesday morning, Michael's brief flight from freedom ended when, accompanied by Anthony Romano, he walked into Captain Dan Rabas' office and surrendered to the authorities in the matter concerning Maureen Ann O'Brien. He was booked, fingerprinted, photographed, and read his rights for the second time; all the obligatory protocols that, for the time it takes, tests your resolve to the core. He was then escorted to a holding cell near the city courtroom to await a three o'clock arraignment, where he would plead not guilty to the charge of first-degree murder. If convicted, he would very likely face the death penalty. With Winston Kennedy prosecuting for the State of Alabama, there was no doubt the death penalty would be sought.

Michael's only words at the arraignment were "Not guilty, Your Honor," after the charges were read by an assistant city attorney. Romano bluffed as if he might request bail, but erred on the side of being ridiculed, because only under the rarest circumstances do capital murder cases qualify for bail.

Wanting to push the State into a quick trial, Romano suggested that a preliminary hearing be held within seventy-two hours, but Frederick Carter, representing the City of Montgomery, argued that the city detectives hadn't completed their investigation, and asked that the hearing be postponed for a month.

Romano took exception to Carter's request for a delay. "My client is innocent of these charges, and will be proven so in court. There is no need to have him languish in jail while the Attorney General grandstands for the press and promotes his own political agenda."

Carter angrily objected, calling it a "cheap shot against our fine Attorney General."

"Bite me, Carter," Romano snickered.

Judith Robertson, the municipal judge, ignored Carter's obvious support for Kennedy, and said the Fifth Circuit Court, which would hear the case, would take over the matter of the preliminary hearing. "Take it up with Judge Christian, and good luck there."

If there was a true rogue in the Alabama Circuit Court system, Harold Baines Christian wore the robe with distinction. The grandson of a poor black sharecropper from Tuskegee, Alabama, Christian was the first African-American elected to the Circuit bench, and having survived four elections, was the longest-serving circuit judge in the state.

Christian despised politics and its ties to the judicial system, but every six years he filed re-election papers as a Democrat and won convincingly against conservative white opponents who outspent him and claimed they extolled the philosophies of the party with more zeal than the laid-back Christian.

When asked about his success as a circuit judge, he joked, "Getting elected four times is a good place to start. Politics doesn't make for strange bedfellows, it makes for particularly corrupt ones," Christian once remarked when sentencing a state legislator to a somewhat lenient prison term for bribery. "I should have sent the sorry bastard to a maximum security prison where he'd experience the harsh reality of prison life the very first day."

Christian was a private man who lived modestly on his $100,000 yearly salary. As an only child, he had inherited a fifteen-acre farm which once had produced cotton, peanuts, and soybeans, but the judge had no love for Macon County's farm land, and headed off to Atlanta's Emory University. After only two years in pre-law, Christian was accepted to Emory's law school, graduated second in his class, and then returned to Tuskegee to begin a private practice.

But after three years of practicing in one of the state's poorest counties, Christian had come to the conclusion that work in his home town was a lost cause. Years later in an interview with the *New York Times,* Christian said his limited practice there was a humbling experience.

"Two things worked against me: per capita income was in the lower third of the state, and too many people sought out the dog track as an easy fix to their financial problems. In three years, I had billings of $75,000, collected only $10,000, and covered my losses out of a small trust my father had left me.

"And then I did what I thought was the dumbest career move I could ever consider – I ran for political office. After four years as a state senator, I then won the most improbable election ever in the state; Circuit Court Judge of Montgomery and Macon County. I beat out a prominent white guy with fifty-four per cent of the vote."

Christian, an avowed bachelor, was four years into his first term when an old, established private country club in Montgomery offered him a golfing-only membership. When he inquired abut the social perks of the club, he was informed they had a cap on new members at the time. Other than a discarded one iron he'd found on his property on one of his weekend walks, he'd never swung a golf club in his life. He could be seen from the highway walking and swinging at imaginary objects with Rusty, his trusted golden retriever, at his side. He declined the club membership with a curt, "Not interested."

Christian, however, did have a few vices to which only his clerks were privy. He had implicit trust in their silence when it came to his gambling, and the occasional hooker from Atlanta, who, for one thousand dollars, would spend a long weekend with the reclusive judge. Was it just a coincidence that his previous ten clerks had moved on to lucrative positions in the legal profession?

CHAPTER 18

One week after Michael's arraignment, Winston Kennedy and Tony Romano met with Harold Christian to set a date for the preliminary hearing. Christian was recovering from major back surgery after falling in his Tuskegee home, and it was unlikely the sixty-eight-year-old judge was in any hurry to begin a new trial. His painkiller of choice was a bottle of Southern Comfort, which shared equal presence in his dimly-lit chambers with old law reviews scattered about, several antique clocks with varying times, discarded robes hanging over chairs, and his prized possession, an English peruke, he'd brought home from a trip to London.

Judge Christian's courthouse drinking was well documented, and he considered it an insult if attorneys meeting to discuss motions and arguments didn't cmbracc his affinity for thc bottlc. Christian had barely poured the first of two drinks for the two litigators, when Kennedy launched into Romano about his remarks at the arraignment. Christian jumped in to halt Kennedy's verbal assault. "Gentlemen, please. Is this what I can expect to hear from you two every day if this case goes to trial?" Pointing a finger at Kennedy, Christian warned, "From this very moment, I am issuing a gag order for you to refrain from any public comments on the case. You've been trying this case in public for a year, and it stops now. Anything you don't understand about my request, Mr. Attorney General?" Before Kennedy could answer, Christian said, "I'll take that as a yes. Mr. Romano, are you in agreement with the gag order?"

"Yes, Your Honor. I don't have any friends in the press, nor do I have any aspirations for political office."

Kennedy wanted to take exception to Romano's cynical but truthful characterization of himself, but let the remark pass. There were other days to wage their battle, but not in Christian's chambers.

Christian had a difficult time getting comfortable in his vintage leather chair, which also predated most of the furniture in the courthouse. "Mr. Romano, is there a need for a preliminary hearing to get a sampling of the State's case, or do you wish to have a grand jury consider an indictment now so we can go straight to trial? The jury is in session for the next ten days hearing other cases."

"We have a good idea of their case, Your Honor. It's not a slam dunk, but I want a jury of twelve to render a decision based on a tainted crime scene and other inconsistences that don't add up to a conviction. The State has enough evidence to warrant a trial, but the greater issue is the perception of race in the case. If we don't go to trial, you would be vilified in the press, not to mention the legal community. I haven't had the pleasure of appearing before you in court, but your reputation as one who doesn't give a damn what others may think of your unorthodox methods is what impresses me the most, Your Honor."

"Thank you, sir, for your glowing critique of my judgeship, Mr. Romano. Hopefully, I can use it in my second lifetime. However, I don't believe that was the question."

"Yes, Your Honor, we'll waive the preliminary hearing. Mr. Kennedy, go get your indictment. And if it's true that Montgomery grand juries will indict a ham sandwich, change mine to pastrami."

Christian couldn't resist a little humor. "I'll take ham, Mr. Kennedy. And since there are no motions to have a change in venue or to sequester the jury – two motions I would deny – we'll be back on November 5 for jury selection. I still need another two weeks of rehab with my physical therapist, so we'll see you then."

While Michael was sitting in the city jail awaiting jury selection, Romano was off on another safari seeking millions from a power company in Arkansas. The FBI and Alabama Bureau of Investigation visited Michael one afternoon, wanting the details of his disappearance after the weapon had been found in his dad's work shed. Jeremy Hopkins of the FBI acted as if he came bearing gifts, indicating the government would consider leniency with anybody connected with harboring Michael's year-long absence. "We're here to help you, Michael," Hopkins offered.

Michael mocked the Feds. "Doesn't everybody just love the bullshit, we're from the government, and we're here to help you. And in what manner can you help me or anyone else?"

Peter Weston from the ABI scolded Michael for his rudeness, but Michael interrupted the lecture and said, "Your own incompetence and the government's, too, is the reason I was on the run for a year. Sorry your feelings are hurt. I could have stayed incognito forever, but it wasn't exactly the lifestyle I envisioned. And what do I get for snitching on others, a year's supply of Snickers?"

Weston pointed a finger at Michael, who flipped it aside with the back of his hand. "Once I'm acquitted of this crime there's nothing you can charge me with. What laws did I break staying off your radar screen? None that I know of. Now, you can take your fancy briefcases with you on the way out, as I have a massage at three, dinner at six, and a little TV before lights out at eleven. This interview, or whatever you want to call it, is officially over. Oh, and by the way, I'll be sure to inform my lawyer about this impromptu visit, since you're not allowed to speak with me unless he's present, too."

CHAPTER 19

A month before the start of the trial, the county had mailed out four hundred notices to potential jurors. They were asked to respond by phone or mail if for any reason they couldn't serve. Because of the high rate of mail that was deemed undeliverable, a seventy-five to eighty per cent callback was considered acceptable. The notice is a legal summons to appear, and while it is time-consuming to chase down the non-responders, the court would occasionally make an example of a few of them for not acknowledging the notice. When made public in the local paper, it served its purpose that the court was serious about jury duty.

Romano knew the jury configuration would be crucial to his client. The notion that one is judged by a jury of his or her peers is suspect in the American jurisprudence system. Jury duty was something the average citizen had little or no time for, and the inconvenience of spending eight or more hours in a courtroom for fifteen-dollar lunch money wasn't appealing, even to the unemployed.

With the county's African-American population reaching forty-five per cent, Romano pondered what percentage of that demographic he needed to give Michael the best shot for acquittal. The older blacks, especially the women, would have no sympathy for Michael. *He was out of place with that white woman. He should have stayed with his own.*

Younger people of both races were usually the first to opt out for various reasons, so the probability of a jury comprised of older black women and middle-aged Caucasians leering at Michael throughout the trial was a mine field that Romano would have to navigate. Meanwhile, the prosecutor loved that scenario. Whites and older black women were his perfect jury.

So, fourteen months to the day that Maureen O'Brien's life was taken, Michael Tyler would finally face the chorus of people who would decide his fate. It was a chilly November morning, as the blistering Alabama summer had finally relented, giving way to delightful autumn days in the seventies, with lower humidity and less dependence on air conditioning.

After spending ten weeks in the city jail since his first court appearance, Michael was ushered into the courtroom by two hefty bailiffs. In the navy blue suit he'd worn three years ago when he graduated from Auburn University, he could easily have been mistaken for a young executive. A crisp white button-down shirt was accentuated by a powder-blue tie, and an American flag pin adorned his left lapel. He was an extremely handsome black man, who seemed quite lost and out of place in court as a defendant accused of this hideous crime. For years, he had envisioned defending clients, not being one.

In a rare departure from protocol, Michael was free of the handcuffs and leg irons that capital murder cases usually required. Romano had written Judge Christian requesting that his client be given both the appearance and presumption of innocence throughout the trial. At the bail hearing, Romano had grand-standed a bit, suggesting that bail could have applied here. "He's not going anywhere, Your Honor,"Romano countered.

"He's already done that once," Winston Kennedy replied. Counsel for the defense forgets that this is a felony murder case, not a simple misdemeanor for a traffic violation."

"Please, cut the sarcasm," Christian shot back. "Mr. Romano isn't serious. A little indulgence on your part would be appreciated."

From his lack of exercise, Michael's surgically repaired right knee had been giving him problems ever since his arrest. Spending eighteen hours a day cooped up in a small cell wasn't the type of physical therapy his orthopaedic surgeon had recommended. He limped noticeably as he walked toward the defense table, acknowledging his parents and family friends who took up the first two rows in the courtroom. Romano greeted them enthusiastically and engaged in some small talk with Michael, encouraging him to look confident. "Don't avoid eye contact with the jurors. They'll have their eyes on you more than some of the witnesses on the stand. Every movement will be scrutinized. And I mean every movement."

A portly bailiff asked for quiet as Christian strode to the bench and called the courtroom to order. The attorneys for both sides were introduced: Anthony Romano for the defense and Winston Kennedy, Attorney General for the State of Alabama, as well as two assistants, Roger Mulkay and Harrison Weaver. They would do "go-for" work for Kennedy, who viewed this trial as his next huge step up the rungs of the political ladder.

"Let *voir dire* begin," ordered Christian.

CHAPTER 20

Thirty days after jury notices were sent out, eighty-five of four hundred citizen answered the call for "Alabama's trial of the century" as one newspaper likened it. They were each given a number, divided into groups of twelve in the jury box, and, when called, would address the judge and answer a series of questions that would determine their qualifications to serve: Will serving on this jury cause a hardship to you or anyone in your family? Have you read, heard, or seen news coverage of the impending trial? Have you already formed an opinion as to guilt or innocence? Do you personally know the defendant or attorneys that will be presenting the case? And, because this is a death penalty case, could you impose the sentence of death?

The majority of the potential jurors would never make it past the second question.

One by one, the panelists were excused for causes not related to the case, and two hours later when court was recessed for a short break, thirty-five prospective jurors were thanked for their civic service, however brief it might have been. One of those dismissed asked when he would get his fifteen dollars for coming to the courthouse.

A smiling Christian said, "Check's in the mail." Christian usually took the questioning a step or two further than required to select the jury pool, and his colleagues on the bench often needled him that *voir dire* was not a TV quiz show.

When a twenty-one-year-old black female begged off because she was seven months pregnant, Christian seized the opportunity to delve into her personal life.

"Would this be your first child," Christian inquired.

"No, Your Honor, it's actually my second. And what does that have to do with me serving on a jury?"

Christian lowered his glasses, obviously annoyed that he was being challenged by some high school dropout and snapped back, "I'll ask the questions, Miss Lewis. Do your children have a father or fathers who regularly pay child support and take some responsibility for the privilege of bearing children with you?"

Unhappy that her personal life had been pried open in front of over one hundred complete strangers, Rhonda Lewis said almost apologetically, "Not on a regular basis, Your Honor. They doesn't have no job."

"Thank you, Miss Lewis, you are excused."

It was a recurring theme in the first three hours. Unemployed, uneducated, or unfit to serve on a jury that would determine the continuance of a young man's life.

Christian hated trials that attracted outside media, and he was already being denounced in the press for his limitations on courtroom coverage during jury selection. The press corps in the courtroom was limited to three area newspapers and one TV station that would provide feed to an adjoining courtroom, where a pack of hounds, as Christian referred to them, watched day one of *voir dire*. He did allow one minute for pictures of Michael as he entered the courtroom.

But *voir dire* was a small fire drill compared to the start of the trial, when the national media would invade Montgomery.

In a conference room over a late lunch of hot dogs from a local vendor, Romano told Michael that the morning's developments were not unusual. "You have to weed out the undesirables, and we'll do that. In a perfect world, we'd have moderately educated people who understand the basic principles of law and find satisfaction in performing their civic duty. But not in Montgomery, or anywhere else."

Day two was not as complicated. Using their eight peremptory challenges, attorneys pared the field to twelve, and Michael's jury was in place. The panel included a retired plumber, two state employees, a construction foreman, a county employee, a dental assistant, an Alabama State University librarian, a lounge owner, an electrical contractor, an apartment manager, a life insurance secretary, and a cocktail waitress, the latter of whom would attract a lot more attention than any of the potential witnesses. Eight men and four women – four blacks in the pool – including two alternates. It was as good as Romano could have hoped for.

Satisfied, Judge Christian scheduled opening arguments for Friday, November 18, the day before the season-ending Alabama-Auburn football game.

Christian's suggestion brought Kennedy out of his seat, questioning the judge on his timing. "Your Honor, most of my staff will be taking a long weekend to attend the game. The bar association has a luncheon planned for Friday in Tuscaloosa, and we'd like to be part of it. Why can't we start the following Monday?"

Christian wasn't moved by Kennedy's plea to

delay the proceedings to accommodate a football game, especially the one he loathed the most.

"Really, Mr. Kennedy. The world is going to stop for a football game, where 70,000 adults wave their silly pom-poms and get wasted on Jack and Coke? And assuming Alabama wins – and they are double-digit favorites – you and your political cronies will act like universal hunger has been alleviated, the war in the Middle East is over, and the price of oil has been stabilized."

"Well, Your Honor, I'm not aware of any betting line on the game. That type of gambling is illegal in Alabama, you know."

Christian relished these courtroom dogfights with attorneys, especially when they set themselves up for ridicule. "Really, Counselor. A close friend of mine placed a bet with a Mr. Roscoe Jenkins just yesterday, the same Roscoe Jenkins your office has ignored prosecuting for the last how many years? Take your sermon somewhere else and be here at nine o'clock tomorrow morning for opening arguments. Agreed?"

Kennedy took his seat without acknowledging Christian, and this ignited the judge's wrath. "Sir, you will stand and address me as 'Your Honor' with an affirmative response to my ruling, or you will be cited for contempt of court! And there will be no radio or television in your cell on Saturday, the day of the game. Is that understood?"

"Yes, Your Honor."

"And for the record, Counselor, Alabama is a 13-point favorite."

CHAPTER 21

The day before the Auburn-Alabama game, the second-year law student went on trial for the murder of Maureen Ann O'Brien. The State had loudly and publically decreed in the press that it would seek the death penalty if a guilty verdict were returned, and Kennedy boasted that the jury would follow his wishes.

Because of overcrowding in the county jail, and for security reasons, Michael was housed in the city facility, where he would occupy a single cell and initially have only minimal contact with forty-eight other men. Some were awaiting trial, while others were serving minimum time for misdemeanors. Michael was the lone resident with a felony trial looming, but he had an ally in Captain Rabas, who had led the initial investigation and had originally dismissed Michael as a suspect.

Rabas had convinced his superiors that Michael posed no threat to the other inmates, and thus he was allowed to interact with them during the six hours they were allowed out of their cells each day to use the recreation yard to play volleyball or basketball, or to frequent a room that included a color TV, pool table, and board games for them to pass the time.

The media crunch was what Christian had feared. Press credentials had been issued to forty-two TV, radio and newspaper reporters. At the last hour, Christian reluctantly gave his approval for the national cable channel, *On Trial*, to cover the big trial. Their coverage would serve as the feed to twelve Southeast stations that were also featuring the trial. Outside of the local newspapers, other media outlets occupied a room adjacent to the live action.

The Tyler entourage, which included his Mom and Dad, relatives, and friends, took up the first two rows behind the defense table. There were no requests from the O'Brien family, because those left on the family tree consisted of a handful of second and third cousins who had little interest in the trial. They were too busy issuing challenges to Maureen's bizarre will, which had provided two million dollars or so to various charities, a local animal shelter, her hair stylist, the BMW mechanic who serviced her car, and other casual friends. There was no mention of Michael in the will, as he was the sole beneficiary of her life insurance policy, which was also being contested by the Illinois life insurance company. If convicted, Michael would never see a dime of the insurance, and Maureen's squabbling and distant cousins would probably inherit those proceeds, too.

Through a lottery system offered by Christian's clerk, the remaining hundred seats were filled with onlookers who thought they were going to be part of – or at least witness to – Alabama legal history. At nine o'clock, the jury took their seats and waited for Christian to make his appearance. A bailiff called the room to order, asking everyone to stand for the Honorable Harold Christian. Christian especially loved the "honorable" part.

After the attorneys had been introduced for the record, Christian asked if there were any motions to consider before the beginning of opening arguments.

Romano once again saught bail, and Christian stopped him before he could complete the request.

"I've ruled on it before, Counselor, and I haven't changed my mind," Christian said, giving an irritated look to Romano. There were no other motions, and Christian called on the State for its opening remarks.

Kennedy rambled on for thirty minutes, likening Michael to The Son of Sam and the Boston Strangler. Though it is highly unusual for attorneys to object to the opposition's opening statement, Romano finally had heard enough, and he objected loudly from his chair to the Attorney General's unfair characterization of his client.

"Your Honor!" Romano shouted. "The Attorney General makes it sound as if Mr. Tyler has already been tried, convicted, and sent off to death row. Tell him to back off."

Amused at the bickering, and it was only day one, Christian complied with Romano's request. "Back off, Counselor."

When Kennedy had finished his tirade, calling on the jury to find the defendant guilty and impose the harshest penalty allowed by law, it was Romano's turn to present a different set of circumstances that would refute the prosecutor's bitter commentary on his client.

"The defense wishes to defer our opening statement until after the State has rested. Thank you, Your Honor."

Before Kennedy could reply to Romano's legal strategy, Christian ordered Kennedy to call his first witness. Trying to make the best of a bad situation, Kennedy stammered, "Your Honor, we were thinking you might adjourn after opening statements and begin testimony on Monday. Our witnesses aren't available this morning."

"Well, Counselor, that's not my problem. We'll adjourn until one-thirty. Go find your witnesses. You're up first. You know the drill. See you after lunch."

Kennedy, who was already treading on thin ice with Christian, declined another confrontation, but mouthed a racial slur to his colleagues at the table as they went over their witness list, hoping to find someone within an hour of the courthouse. A quick phone call to Dr. William Jacobsen, the county's chief pathologist, landed the State its first witness.

Jacobsen's life was his job. A normal week for the forty-six-year-old workaholic bachelor was eight to ten hours a day, six days a week, and no football game, even the state's biggest, could take him away from his work. Kennedy hadn't planned to call on Dr. Jacobsen as his first witness. He preferred to bring him in last to testify, because he wanted the doctor to explain the chilling horror of Maureen's murder as only he could. Jacobson's penchant for detail made him the ideal witness to use up an hour on the stand, but Kennedy needed more.

Kennedy then rounded up Justin Basch, the mail carrier, who was first on the crime scene. He was good for at least an hour, and wasting time was everything to Kennedy. Two witnesses, hopefully two to three hours, and then an early adjournment, as the Judge was known to lose interest by mid-afternoon, call for a short break, and then never return to the courtroom.

However, Christian took a hike after lunch, and a fuming Kennedy was left sitting with two witnesses, knowing that his absence was intended for him.

CHAPTER 22

Harold Christian was a man of limited social graces. Instead of a "good morning" to Thomas Hagan, his trusted clerk of three years, Christian didn't stray far from his pattern on Monday. "Did you go to that stupid game Saturday? Remember, I said I might fire you if you did."

Hagan enjoyed the banter with the Judge, only because he allowed it. "I do remember you saying I shouldn't go, but nothing about being fired for it. You should be happy. Alabama covered the spread and you're a thousand dollars richer for taking my advice."

"How did you know which side I had?"

"I placed the bet for you. Is there anything else, Your Honor?"

"Yeah, Hagan, look outside the window below. It's fifty degrees out there, raining cats and dogs, and people are standing around like we're going to hand over Mr. Tyler so they can hang him from one of those oak trees that's older than me.

"Just our good old Southern justice," Christian grumbled. "If this were a black kid on trial for killing a black women, even a prominent one, you couldn't get twenty people to show up. The trial would take one day, the killer would get probation and community service, and justice would have been served. Maybe a stretch, but you know what I mean."

Hagan agreed, even when he didn't. "Yes, Your

Honor."

"Look at those fricking morons out there. People taking a week off from their jobs, assuming they have one, to recharge the batteries of their bigotry. And now we're part of it, Thomas; reluctant actors in this damn charade they call justice. I'm sick of it already, and we've just begun."

The courthouse and jail complex took up an entire city block and was cordoned off with barricades to keep the demonstrators at bay. Only courthouse personnel, the media, spectators, jurors, and attorneys in the trial were allowed access to the six-story parking garage. Traffic was a snarled mess, and both sheriff deputies and city officers had converged on the site providing security.

"By the way, Hagan, what's the line on the Bears and Steelers tonight?"

Hagan, who had been placing Christian's bets since he was hired right out of Vanderbilt Law School, gave his boss a puzzled look.

"Your Honor, they played last night."

"Well, who the hell is playing tonight?"

"The Vikings and Cowboys in Dallas, sir."

"If the Cowboys are anything under seven, put a dime on 'em."

"A dime?"

"Come on Hagan, that's a grand."

"Yes, Your Honor. Just kidding."

"Oh, and, Thomas, get me the witness list from my desk in the conference room. Want to see who that grand-standing prosecutor is planning on calling to testify. He'd call on Mother Teresa if he could, but I understand stand she doesn't like to fly."

Thomas returned with the list and was curious

about the relationship between the Judge and the Attorney General. "Why the antagonism toward Mr. Kennedy, Your Honor?"

"Thomas, I've had only case overturned in thirty years on the bench. It was a capital murder case about ten years ago. A fraternity brother of Kennedy's kills his wife, which resulted in a guilty verdict when I tossed some hearsay evidence. The appellate court gift-wraps a new trial for him, the hearsay is allowed, and the jury sends him home a free man. One of those legal technicalities that allow guilty people to skirt justice. Kennedy was the guy's attorney, and he's never let me forget it."

Grabbing his robe, Christian patted his young clerk on the back and said, "Okay, let's get to work, Thomas."

"Oh ...... Your Honor, the Cowboys are favored by five, and you have them for a dime."

"Good. Dallas will cover that and a lot more."

CHAPTER 23

Kennedy's first witness on Monday was Alice Carmichael, the frail eighty-three-year-old great grand-mother of eight who claimed to have seen the Channel 10 van in Maureen O'Brien's circular driveway around ten-thirty the night of the murder. After being sworn in, she turned toward Judge Christian and asked, "Why do you make us sit on those hard benches in the hallway before we come in to testify?" Before Christian could even respond, Mrs. Carmichael added, "And you could turn up the heat a little." Christian gave a pained look toward a grinning Kennedy who was waiting to question the feisty woman.

"Mrs. Carmichael, would you please state your full name and address for the record."

"You already know that, don't you? All right, sir. Mrs. Alice Carmichael, 14088 Meadowbrook Lane, Montgomery, Alabama. I'm surprised you didn't ask me how old I am."

Kennedy breathed deeply, wondering if the only witness that could place the Channel 10 van to the crime scene wouldn't self-destruct on the stand. "Thank you, Mrs. Carmichael. Now, how long have you lived at your present residence on Meadowbrook Lane?"

"Oh, I don't know exactly, Mr. Kennedy. I could ask my husband, he's in the courtroom, the man with the tan windbreaker in the third or fourth row."

Christian, a man of little patience on the bench, interrupted the questioning. "Mrs. Carmichael, you and you alone are to answer the questions posed by Mr. Kennedy. Most of the questions require only a simple yes or no response, and if you must comment, please make it as brief as possible. Mr. Kennedy, you may proceed."

"At approximately what time did you observe the Channel 10 television van in the deceased's driveway?"

"Nothing approximate about the time. It was right after the ten o'clock news."

Hoping to change the pace, Kennedy asked a question that Romano would probably ask on cross examination. "Ma'am, do you usually stay up that late at night?"

"What? Just because I'm eighty-three-years old doesn't mean I have to be in bed as soon as it turns dark outside. Wait until you get old, sonny boy. You'll want to get as much out of each day as you can and that includes staying up as long as you want. Got that?"

Anthony Romano hid his face in his hands trying to conceal his helpless grin. He almost felt compelled to object to the state's witness just to get Kennedy off the hook, but this was too good to be true. *Reign her in you dope, before she ruins your case and makes mine.*

But Kennedy forged on. "Okay, Mrs. Carmichael, I'm sorry to suggest what time you should go to bed. But what was the reason you went outside after the news was over?"

"There was a gorgeous full moon that night, Mr. Kennedy. It was a little on the cool side, but I had a sweater on, one my oldest grand-daughter had knitted for me."

"And how long did you stay outside – I believe you said it was the front door, ma'am?"

Romano stood, as if to break the pace of the questions, but said nothing.

"Is there an objection?" Christian asked.

"No, Your Honor."

"Well, then take your seat and let Mr. Kennedy continue."

"And how long did you remain outside, Mrs. Carmichael, to observe the moon?"

"Maybe five minutes."

"While you were outside, ma'am, did you see the Channel 10 van in Miss O'Brien's driveway?"

"Of course, that's what you got me here to say, isn't it?"

"Mrs. Carmichael, you're here to testify whether you saw the TV van, not because I or anybody in my office suggested you say that."

"Yes, that's what I saw, the white TV van in her driveway. Is that all now? I have a noon luncheon at the Officer's Club. Fried shrimp today."

"Yes, ma'am, no more questions. Mr. Romano, your witness."

"Chambers first," ordered Christian.

CHAPTER 24

Before anybody could even take a seat, Christian growled at Kennedy. "Please explain, if you can, why it took ten minutes of gibberish for your witness to say that she thinks she saw a white TV van parked in the O'Brien driveway?"

"Your Honor, I didn't know she'd go off like that."

"Did you think of prepping the witness, maybe explaining what you expected from her on the stand?"

"She wouldn't come down to the office for an interview, and she didn't want us to come out to her house because her husband was ill."

"Well, he looked fine to me sitting out there in the third or fourth row in the tan windbreaker. You seemed amused by all this, Mr. Romano. Can't wait to cross-examine this nut case? Well, make it short. She has a lunch date, remember?"

Mrs. Carmichael had returned to the stand, nervously checking her watch to be sure she didn't miss the fried shrimp at the Officers Club.

Christian was more composed as he took his seat, assuring Mrs. Carmichael that she would be in time for lunch.

"Thank you, Your Honor."

"Mr. Romano, you may question the witness."

Romano knew that beating up on a senior citizen was risky, and he initially decided to tread lightly with her. “I’ll try to make this as brief and painless as possible, Mrs. Carmichael. It’s been some time, a little over a year, since you said you stepped outside – the front door – I believe you said after the ten o’clock news?”

Christian knew what was coming, another litany of that evening’s events he’d already heard enough of. “Mr. Romano, the nightly news is not on trial. Please move on.”

But Mrs. Carmichael was quick to add that the news that night was still fresh in her mind. “That’s the night they broke the news about the gambling raid on the base.”

“And why would that be of interest to you, Mrs. Carmichael? ” Romano asked.

Christian was about to bring this testimony to a screeching halt, but the persistent great-grandmother wouldn’t permit it. “My husband is a retired Colonel, and we play bridge with a group of friends at the base. Me and my partner made two grand slams the other night. Took home thirty bucks of their money. Oops, maybe I shouldn’t have said that, Your Honor. I’m sorry.”

“If that’s the only gambling going on out there, Mrs. Carmichael, there wouldn’t be a big investigation.”

Observing the clock over the bench, Romano nodded to Christian that he would have just a few more questions.

“I read your mind,” Christian said sarcastically.

Romano decided now it was time to get tough with the old lady. “Now, Mrs. Carmichael, is your home directly across the street from the deceased, or maybe to the left or right of it?”

“Just across the street.”

"Your Honor, I submit a photograph marked exhibit one that shows the Carmichael residence is approximately two hundred feet to the west of the O'Brien residence, but across the street, as the witness testified."

"Your point?" Christian asked.

"I'm getting to that," Romano replied.

"Well hurry," Christian groaned.

"Mrs. Carmichael, did you get a new pair of prescription glasses in September of last year?"

"I don't remember the exact date. Glasses are glasses. What's that got to do with anything?"

"A lot, ma'am. One month *after* you reported that you saw the TV van across the street, you received a new pair of glasses. I believe it was to correct your increasing nearsightedness. Is that an accurate statement, Mrs. Carmichael?"

"I don't know the exact week."

"Well, you have a great memory for the news of that night, but you can't remember when you got your new glasses."

Kennedy had heard enough. His witness was in serious trouble and needed a lifeline. Looking for relief from Christian, the Attorney General asked almost apologetically, "Your Honor, Mr. Romano is badgering the witness."

"No, he isn't. I want to hear more about her eyesight – or lack of it. Objection overruled."

It was approaching 11:15 and the clock above Christian's bench had now caught Mrs. Carmichael's attention. Her mood took a dramatic turn from feisty to confrontational. "I have a luncheon date at noon and I don't intend to be late. We were late last week and had to wait for an hour to be seated. Now what do you want to know about my eyesight – or lack of it, as the judge suggests?"

Romano handed Christian and Kennedy two copies of eye exams marked Exhibit Two, which noted a significant loss of distance vision, perhaps fifteen to twenty per cent. A year before the most recent exam, she had unwillingly given up her driver's license.

Romano asked one final question. "Can you say for the record, Mrs. Carmichael, that you are one hundred per cent positive that you saw the Channel 10 van in the O'Brien driveway around ten-thirty on September 2, 1994?"

The silence was deafening. The only sound came from a clock above Christian's bench. It sounded like a sledgehammer ticking off the seconds. "I think so," Mrs. Carmichael answered.

"You think so, ma'am?"

"I don't know. Yes, it was the Channel 10 van."

Romano had succeeded in tarnishing the only witness to the van's presence. "I have no additional questions of Mrs. Carmichael."

Kennedy rose as if to redirect, but was stopped dead in his tracks by Christian. "You can redirect after a short break, Counselor."

"No, no, Your Honor, the state has no more questions of this witness."

"Okay, Mr. Kennedy. Mrs. Carmichael, you are excused. Enjoy the shrimp today."

But as Mrs. Carmichael was leaving the witness stand, she uttered loud enough for the jurors to hear, "That black guy was always around. Could have been there that night, too."

Both Kennedy and Romano heard the remark, too, and it was Romano who was momentarily too rattled to speak. When he regained his composure, he objected vigorously. "Your Honor, Mrs. Carmichael was excused. Her comment, if recorded by the court reporter, or heard by the jurors, must be stricken."

Christian agreed. "Any reference to Mr. Tyler's presence at the O'Brien home on the evening of the murder must be excluded. Jurors, please ignore the remark."

Kennedy huddled with this team over lunch in the coffee shop, not sure what to make of Mrs. Carmichael's rambling testimony. Grant Weaver, one of Kennedy's aides, suggested that they could always call her back to clarify her earlier statements.

"Clarify?" Kennedy laughed. "She's history and so is our only witness to the van." A call that said was "urgent" was passed through by his office to his pager. Kennedy left the table and went over to the coffee shop's public phone, where he dialed the number. When the young man answered, Kennedy said, "Kennedy here. How can I help you?"

The caller sounded intimidated talking to the Attorney General, but Kennedy assured the male on the line, probably a teenager, that everything was "cool." He'd heard that from his 16-year-old son a million times. "How can I help you? And do you have a name?" "Fred will do." "Fred" was a lie, but Kennedy would have his office trace the number and look for any public records with the owner.

"I've been watching the Tyler trial on that cable station, and that batty old lady really put the screws to you today, didn't she?"

"Not exactly, Fred."

"Well, my girlfriend lives two houses down the street from the Carmichaels, and we saw that TV van in that driveway the night that babe was killed."

"Miss O'Brien?"

"Yeah, whoever. She was one hot chick."

Kennedy was only a second away from disconnecting the call from this rude kid, but he said he would get back with him in a day or two.

"Is there any reward or something?" Fred asked.

"No , Fred, we already have the killer in custody. We'll be in touch."

"Who's the mystery caller?" Weaver asked.

"Some cocky teenager who claims to have seen the TV van in the O'Brien driveway the night she was killed. Was with his girlfriend who lives down the street from the Carmichaels, probably making out in the car. Why the hell did he wait over a year before calling us? Wouldn't put much stock in what he's got to say, but Milkey, go back to the office and see who lives where on that street. And for God's sake, don't get in touch with our Mrs. Carmichael. Grant and I will try to get through the afternoon without another train wreck. Hopefully, the mail carrier will save the day for us. And he's a big risk. The boy isn't exactly *Phi Betta Kappa* material. You know?"

Romano and Michael briefly discussed Mrs. Carmichael's comments and whether it was grounds for a mistrial. Knowing Harold Christian's disdain for mistrials, the two agreed that it could be argued on appeals if Michael should be convicted. "The jury heard the remark, but there's no credibility in anything she testified to," Romano remarked. "Hell, her entire testimony should be ignored."

CHAPTER 25

Justin Basch took the stand, trying to look his best in a brand-new navy blue sport coat and white turtleneck sweater his mother had purchased for him when he received the subpoena that he would be a witness for the prosecution. Clothes were never a priority for the substitute mail carrier, who was more comfortable in sneakers, worn blue jeans, and t-shirts that showed his array of tattoos. Kennedy had not been impressed with the twenty-six-year-old slacker in his pre-trial interview, but he was the first person at the crime scene, and had discovered Maureen's body.

After exchanging some pleasantries, Kennedy tossed him some softball questions about his part-time job with the Postal Service. Basch, though, seemed distracted as Kennedy tried to make eye contact with him, and when he turned toward the jury box, he saw why. Debbie Finkel, the Starlight Lounge waitress, was in the front row, flashing her well-shaped thighs for everyone to see. Kennedy surmised that the two may have crossed paths, as Basch was known to frequent bars that offered pool tables, gambling machines, loud juke boxes, and easy pickups.

"Please tell the court about your job, specifically on the day of Sept.3, 1994," Kennedy asked. "It was a Saturday, right?"

"Yes, Your Honor."

That brought big chuckle from Christian, who

interjected, "Maybe we should distinguish whose who in the courtroom, Mr. Basch. Mr. Kennedy is the Attorney General for the State of Alabama, the chief prosecutor in this trial, and is asking the questions. Mr. Romano, to your left, represents the defendant, and because I wear this black robe, that makes me the judge."

"Thank you, Your Honor. Just a little nervous, that's all."

Christian assured him that it was okay. "Not unusual, Mr. Basch."

Kennedy returned to his questioning. "Back to September 3, Mr. Basch. Meadowbrook Lane is part of Route 9 out of the Southern Branch of the U.S. Postal Service?"

"Yes, sir. It's about halfway through the route. I usually get there about noon on a normal day."

"Was September 3 a normal day?"

"Well, it was until I came to Miss O'Brien's residence."

"Tell us about it," Kennedy asked.

"I had a special delivery letter that she had to sign for, so I got out of the truck and went to her front door. I rang the doorbell, but I noticed the front door was slightly open. Her poodle had got out, and was running around the front of the house barking like something was wrong. Miss O'Brien had a fenced area in the back where she would let the dog and cat out to play and do their business."

"To do their business?" Kennedy asked.

"You know, to – ?"

Christian jumped in to rescue Basch. "To relieve themselves, Counselor."

"Thank you, Your Honor."

"Continue, Mr. Basch."

"I rang the doorbell again, and when there was no answer, I pushed the door open and walked into the foyer. "Miss O'Brien, I have a letter for you to sign." She didn't answer, so I walked down the hallway to the study, where she liked to paint and watch TV."

Romano, who was already relishing a lively cross examination with the witness, mildly objected from his seat. "Is there a question forthcoming?"

"Overruled, Counselor," Christian said. "I'm sure there's one on the way."

Kennedy offered his apologies for Romano's interruption. "Sorry, Mr. Basch. You said you walked toward the study to see if she was home."

"Yes, sir."

"Was Miss O'Brien in the study?"

"No, sir, she wasn't. But I detected a strange smell in the house. I thought maybe the puppy had messed up or something, but she was housed-trained, and, since the door was open, I figured it might be something else."

Basch turned toward Judge Christian. "Your Honor, could we take a short break?"

Checking his watch, Christian said, "I have another court matter that needs my attention, so we're adjourned until tomorrow morning. Jurors, don't take advantage of not being sequestered, and don't discuss the case with anyone. And, please, avoid the television and newspapers."

But Christian had no other court business that required his attention. He needed a drink or two and an afternoon nap.

CHAPTER 26

Day two of the trial brought bright sunshine and sunny skies to Montgomery, in stark contrast to Monday's dreary weather that had held down the spectacle outside the courthouse. An hour before the trial resumed, people were milling around, all hoping to look into a TV camera and offer their opinions on everything from football to politics. And there were plenty of them.

In chambers, Christian was in unusually fine spirts, as his clerk offered him a cup of cappuccino. "Thomas, my boy, any thoughts on the first day of the trial that's being touted as the "Trial of the Century in Alabama?"

"As to your friendly disposition, Your Honor, I assume you're thrilled the Cowboys thrashed the Vikings by twenty-one points, or because I added just a touch of Southern Comfort to the cappuccino? As far as the trial, it's boring as hell. Trial of the century? You got to be kidding?"

"Thank you, son, for your astute observation," Christian noted. "Trust me, Thomas, it's going to be very interesting when Romano gets to cross the Basch kid. I think he's ready for a meltdown. Not a whole lot between the ears."

Justin Basch was back on the stand, dressed in the same attire he had testified in on Monday. After watching the television coverage of the trial on the cable channel, his mother told him not to “slouch” so much on the witness stand. Christian reminded him he was still under oath, and then nodded to Kennedy to resume his questioning.

Kennedy slowly approached Basch, asking him if he was more comfortable than his first day on the stand.

“Yes, sir, everything is fine with me.”

“Alright, let’s pick up where we left off yesterday. You said that after there was no response from Miss O’Brien, you walked down the hallway to the study, thinking she might be in there. Is that right?

“Yes, sir. It was a room with a wooden deck to the outside facing the back yard, where she liked to read and paint in nice weather. She was a very good painter, had entered a few pieces in art shows.”

Romano rose as if to make an objection, but Christian waved him off. “I know, Counselor, her painting and reading habits are not an issue here. Continue, Mr. Kennedy.”

“Thank you, Your Honor. If the defense would stop with these unnecessary objections, it might be possible to continue a fluent line of questioning with my witness.”

Irritated with the constant bickering, Christian signaled for the two attorneys to approach the bench. Removing his glasses, he stared at them for what seemed an interminable amount of time. “Okay, boys, here’s the question: Why do you think there are so many dead lawyers’ jokes?”

A puzzled look was all the two attorneys had to offer.

“Because of the way you act in here. You sound like two kids arguing who has the toughest dad in the neighborhood. Now, get back to work and act like adults. Mr. Kennedy, you have the floor."

"Your Honor, would you please have the court reporter read back the question?

"I'll do it for her,"Christian barked. "Before Mr. Romano could object to your question, I said, 'her painting and reading habits were not an issue here.' "

"Thank you, Your Honor." Turning towards the mail carrier, the Attorney General asked, "When you observed that Miss O'Brien was not in her study, what did you do next?"

Basch paused briefly to collect his thoughts, then replied, "I knocked on her bedroom door, which is across the hallway from her study."

Kennedy asked, "Was it open?"

"I wasn't sure, so I knocked on the door again and called out her name, but there was no answer. I realized then that it was open a little, so I pushed it forward and went into the room. That's when I saw her on the bed. God, it was awful! Blood was everywhere! I got sick to my stomach."

"Are you feeling okay, Mr. Basch?" Kennedy inquired. "Do you need a minute or two to compose yourself?"

"No, sir, I'll be all right."

"Okay. Did you check her pulse, or anything else, to see if she was alive?"

"Are you kidding, Mr. Kennedy? There was a hole in her stomach the size of a – it was huge. And most of her face was missing, probably from a gunshot.

"Objection!" Romano shouted. "Witness is not qualified to offer this opinion."

"Sustained."

Kennedy continued. “What did you do next, Mr. Basch?”

“I called my uncle, who’s the postmaster at the branch I work at. He was on his way to Auburn for the game against some team from Louisiana. Forgot the name.”

“What phone did you use?”

“”I used phone in the kitchen.”

“What did your uncle tell you to do?”

“He told me to wait in the mail truck and that he would call the police.”

“How long before the police arrived?”

“Maybe five to ten minutes. A bunch of police cars showed up. There were people all over the place, you would have thought ....”

“I get the picture, Mr. Basch. Thank you. No more questions. Your witness, Mr. Romano.”

CHAPTER 27

Anthony Romano bided his time, a ploy that always unnerved a witness who was about to face an aggressive cross-examination from the opposing attorney. He approached Basch, stopped and turned to face the jurors, then scanned the courtroom, as if looking for divine guidance. He would play the waiting game until Christian tired of the delay.

"Mr. Romano," Christian asked. "Do you have any questions for this witness, or is he free to step down? Maybe a short break?"

"No break necessary, Your Honor, and yes I do have few questions for the witness. Mr. Basch, other than breaking every rule in the post office manual regarding entering a residence, you seem to know a lot about Miss O'Brien's house, especially the layout. Not to mention the pets' bathroom habits, as well as the fact that she liked to read and paint on the deck. Maybe even the men in her life?"

That brought an angry objection from Kennedy. "What makes you think Mr. Basch knew anything about her personal life or who was involved in it?"

But Christian wasn't buying the argument. "Overruled, Counselor. I believe that's precisely what we're trying to determine here today. It obviously had something to do with her death."

All of a sudden, Justin Basch couldn't find a friendly face in the courtroom. He knew what was coming: embarrassing questions about his possible relationship with the deceased, and his mother, who blindly defended her son's indiscreet lifestyle, at home watching the trial on television with friends. And now that juror Debbie Finkel, who never gave him the time of day at the Starlight Lounge, was messing with him again, giving him racy looks and taunting him with her tongue.

Romano, sensing Basch's sudden nervousness and vulnerability, plowed ahead. "Other than delivering mail to Miss O'Brien, were there any other times you may have been a guest in her home?"

"No, yes, maybe a couple of times, I don't know for sure," Basch whispered, completely out of range of hearing for the jurors.

Romano wouldn't let up. "I barely heard you, Mr. Basch, and I'm only a foot away. Do I have to repeat the question for you?"

Basch sprang out of his chair as if it were spring-loaded. "No, dammit, I heard you the first time! I suppose you want to know if I had sex with her! Right? Y'all want to get off on that, don't you? Well, I did, and it was the best damn sex I ever had! She was screwing a lot of guys, and I thought, why not me? I bet my buddies a hundred bucks I'd make it to bed with her, and I did! I even got pictures to prove it! Now, you happy?"

Michael buried his head in his outstretched hands, not wanting to believe these accusations against his beloved Maureen.

"Did you kill her, Justin?" Romano shouted at the top of his voice."You did it, didn't you? She would never have sex with a loser like you, so you killed her out of rage. You're one despicable human being, Justin

Basch, sitting here and lying on national television. You took an oath to tell the truth. Or did you forget the words you said when you placed your hand on the bible? "So help me God." Christian jumped into the fray."That's enough, Mr. Romano. Chambers now! Both of you!"

Christian went right to the bottle of Southern Comfort, filling a four-ounce tumbler to the rim. "I'd offer you a drink, gentlemen, and I think you both need one, but I'm looking at an empty bottle. Sorry for my lack of hospitality.

"Now, Counselors, I don't intend to turn this trial into material for a porn flick. We have a national audience looking in, and, while some sadists out there are salivating over Mr. Basch's braggadocio, we're going to adjourn for the morning and reconvene at two. And, Mr. Kennedy, I strongly suggest you reign in your blowhard. That's all."

CHAPTER 28

Sitting dazedly in the courthouse holding cell, Michael took a pass on the inmates' lunch for the day.

"How's it going?" asked a guy who was serving six months for drug possession.

"Not worth a damn right now," Michael replied. "We just got hit with a haymaker in there. If you don't mind, I'm going to try and take a nap. Got a few hours to kill before the afternoon session starts."

"Okay, brother, good luck in there."

Michael's thoughts drifted back, and, he remembered almost every day he'd ever spent with Maureen on their weekly assignments for her Sunday morning show. There had never been a harsh word between them, even when she toyed with him over interracial relationships and the racial biases of the turbulent 1960s. She would always press her index finger to his lips, saying, "It's okay to hurt, but we live in different times. The shackles are off, Michael. You're free. Future generations of black people will never have to suffer these indignities again. Do I have to recite verbatim, which I can, Michael, Martin Luther King's historic speech? 'Free at last, free at last'..."

And then she would bring up the Joe Snidley interview, and they would laugh, no matter how many times she'd bring it up.

James Riley, a young deputy Michael knew from a rival high school, stopped by to escort him back to the courtroom. "The food ain't that good here, no good desserts, so I'll bring you a piece of my momma's apple pie tomorrow."

"Thanks, James, really appreciate it."

"And don't believe all that jive talk that dude said about your lady friend in there. He disrespected her. He needs his honkie ass kicked by some of the brothers."

Extending his hand to his friend, Michael, said, "I feel better already."

Two days after Justin Basch's fantasy testimony, two friends of James Riley waited outside the Starlight Lounge that Basch frequented. He exited the lounge around midnight, highly intoxicated, and struggled to his car behind the bar, where he had the misfortune of encountering a pair of weightlifting freaks, who, as they like to say in the South, "Beat him with an inch of his life."

In the hospital, where he was being treated for broken ribs, a disfigured nose, numerous lacerations and bruises, Basch told Captain Rabas the testimony of his sexual fantasy was one huge fabrication to impress his drinking buddies. That portion of his testimony was stricken from the record, and he was eventually charged with perjury. Taking into consideration the savagery of the beating Basch took for his fifteen minutes of fame, he got off lightly with five years' probation, two hundred hours of community service, and a fine of one thousand dollars. He also lost his job at the post office.

CHAPTER 29

After the lunch break, Romano declined to call Basch back to the stand, knowing he had done major damage to the young man's credibility.

Kennedy's first witness of the afternoon was Captain Dan Rabas, head of the detective division for the Montgomery Police Department. After a brief resume of his thirty-one year career with the department, Kennedy asked Rabas if he had been the first officer on the scene at 14089 Meadowbrook Lane.

"There were six patrol cars that were called to the residence in question, and I happened to be in the lead car with two other detectives. Yes, I was the first to enter the house."

Kennedy asked, "Is the O'Brien residence in the Montgomery city limits?"

"No, it's actually in Montgomery County, but we received the call. The subdivision borders the city, maybe a thousand feet or so from the city limits, but we patrol the area for the county. It is also adjacent to Lowndes County to the south."

"Were their officers called to the scene?"

"No, but one squad car was already there when we arrived. They must have picked up the call on their scanner. It probably was in the neighborhood."

Kennedy wanted to know if the Lowndes County officers had a role in initial the investigation.

"No, but some officer who claimed to be a deputy

detective for the county wanted to know what was up. I told him we were investigating a possible homicide, and that between our city and county departments, we were very capable of handling the investigation. They're good folks and all, but we didn't need their help."

Kennedy checked his notes and then posed a long series of questions for the captain. "Was the mail carrier who discovered the body still on the premises?"

"If you mean Mr. Basch, yes, he was sitting in his mail van."

"Did Mr. Basch's uncle make the initial call to you requesting your assistance?"

"Yes, a Paul Basch, who identified himself as the postmaster at the Southern Branch."

Kennedy wanted to know about the procedures when police arrive on a crime scene.

Rabas explained in detail that, "After looking at the body, it was obvious a crime had taken place, but our coroner and his forensic team would survey the scene and estimate a time of death."

"When did the coroner arrive?"

"Around one-thirty. Doctor William Jacobsen, the county's coroner and chief medical examiner."

"And how long did he stay, Captain Rabas?"

"He was there an hour at the most."

"Did Dr. Jacobsen determine the exact cause of death?"

"No, he said he would perform an autopsy later that day, and that we'd have the results in hand by Sunday afternoon at the latest."

"Captain, it was pretty clear that Miss O'Brien had been shot to death?"

"Yes, there were two indentations in the head-board of the bed frame that appeared to have been caused by the bullets. The killer or killers removed them, then disfigured the holes making it almost impossible to determine the gun used or calibre to make a match if any gun were found. She was shot at extremely close range."

Christian interrupted the questioning, calling for a fifteen-minute break, but it would probably last much longer. At two-thirty, Christian's clerk informed the court that they were adjourned until nine o'clock Wednesday morning. He then headed off to a state liquor store for a quart of Southern Comfort, and then to Christian's estate to take care of Rusty's needs. The judge would be sleeping in tonight.

CHAPTER 30

Thomas Hagan greeted the Judge Wednesday morning with his favorite morning treat: bagels, cream cheese, and cappuccino. He noticed the seal of the new bottle of Southern Comfort hadn't been broken, which meant the trial might get a full day of testimony.

"Did you have a good night's rest, Your Honor? You seem to have an extra bounce in your step today."

"Thomas, I've never felt better. I missed Rusty sleeping next to me, and I trust he was glad to see you last night. Thanks for looking after him. Now, what's the lineup of the State's remaining witnesses? I'm hoping they can rest by the end of Friday."

Thomas retrieved the witness list and handed it to the judge.

"No, son, you read it, please. Print is too damn small."

Thomas scanned the list to see who was left. "After Captain Rabas, who should be finished this morning, including cross, there's a state ballistics expert, the county medical examiner, an insurance executive, and a sportswriter from western Georgia."

Christian frowned and asked, "A sportswriter? What the hell will he testify about?"

"His bio says he played football with Tyler at Auburn in his freshman year. Wanna bet he says Tyler was chasing white women?"

Christian inquired, "How many witnesses does

the defense plan on calling?"

"Five, Your Honor." Hagan seemed perplexed. "Wouldn't you expect more in a death penalty case?"

Meanwhile, Harold Christian was enjoying a good laugh.

"And may I ask why you find so funny about the defense's witness list?" Hagan asked.

"Thomas, let me tell you a quick story. About five years ago, we're trying some punk black kid who had a rap sheet as long as my arm. He's about to do some serious time as an accessory to murder, and his court-appointed attorney is adding new witnesses every day. He's up to twenty, and the State is questioning the validity of the list, which has a lot of Willie Joneses and Jimmy Smiths on it. I suppress the state's motion to cull the list, because names likes Jones and Smith shouldn't be too hard to run down and verify, right? So the moral of the story is this: our state statute on witness lists is a little vague, and thus open to interpretation, which is why we have judges like me to settle these little courtroom battles. Consider this, son. Winston Kennedy loathes Anthony Romano, first, because of his family's status, and second because a tort lawyer, and one of the best around, is challenging him in court – on a *pro bono* basis, at that. Don't be surprised if the witness list grows a little each day. Now, who do we have as of today on Romano's list?

"Two former coaches, a professor at the Law Center, a Baptist preacher from Greenville, and the station manager at Channel 10."

Christian grimaced, asking Thomas if he saw a suspicious pattern here. "Are you thinking what I'm thinking, Thomas? Five character witnesses, all of whom will speak glowingly about the kid, but probably nobody who can give the defense what it needs the most – an airtight alibi for Tyler on the night Maureen O'Brien was murdered."

The ever-inquisitive Hagan was in step with his boss. "Do you think Romano might rest without calling any witnesses and head right to closing arguments? That's a pretty risky move considering it's a death penalty case."

Christian agreed."Damn right, Thomas, that's exactly what he's going to do. That's why he skipped his opening remarks. Wish I could put money down on it."

"I can call Roscoe, Your Honor."

Captain Rabas returned to the stand, answering questions from Kennedy about the early hours of the investigation. "Detective Rabas, during the course of the initial investigation Saturday, did you encounter the defendant at the crime scene?"

"Yes, Mr. Kennedy. Mr. Tyler arrived about an hour after the call came through of a possible homicide at the O'Brien residence."

"Why would he be there?"

"Mr. Tyler has a police scanner at his home, and he must have heard the call."

"Captain, were you aware of any special relationship between the defendant and Miss O'Brien?"

Romano was on his feet, objecting to the term "relationship."

Christian was quick to overrule. "I think we should hear about the 'relationship,' whatever the context might be."

Rabas, who still believed the State had the wrong man on trial, glared at Kennedy. "I wasn't aware of any special relationship between the two, Counselor." Kennedy wasn't deterred by Rabas' apparent defense of Michael, asking the captain what, if any, discussion the two might have had.

"Michael was visibly upset, assuming that something was terribly wrong in the O'Brien home. I didn't let him enter the residence, so we talked outside by the pool."

"Did you eventually tell the defendant that Miss O'Brien's body had been discovered in the residence?"

Romano objected. "Your Honor, the state insists on referring to my client as the defendant. He does have a name. Mr. Kennedy, meet Michael Tyler. A little respect would be appreciated."

Kennedy shot back, "He should have showed Miss O'Brien some respect on the night of September 2."

Christian, by now, was long past the point of digesting any more dialogue between the two attorneys, banged his gavel and called for a brief recess. "You both need to step outside and enjoy a whiff of our beautiful November morning. And before you return, leave the attitude outside. I've had enough of this nonsense."

Melissa Williams, the reporter for *On Trial,* was on the courthouse steps interviewing a local attorney, who, like many, was taking in the trial on closed circuit TV. "Is this normal, the animosity between the principal attorneys in the case?"

Walter Craven, who had practiced law in Montgomery for twenty-five years said, "This is only the beginning. There's a little history between the two, and, while Judge Christian seems annoyed over the rancor, he's actually enjoying it. A couple of years ago, he tossed two combative attorneys a pair of boxing gloves and said, 'Five minutes. May the best man win.' Enjoy the show."

CHAPTER 31

After the short break, Captain Rabas was back in the witness box with an obvious chip on his shoulder as Kennedy peppered him with questions that had been asked and answered in his earlier testimony, and Romano was quick to point that out to Christian.

"Move it along, Counselor," Christian warned. "Your penchant for backtracking is unnecessary and time-consuming."

Kennedy pored over his mates, offering a weak, "Sorry, Your Honor," before resuming the questioning. "When you spoke with the defendant, excuse me, Mr. Tyler, did you consider him a suspect?"

"No, not initially. We spoke only briefly, maybe ten minutes. I told him it was probably best that he leave the premises, and that I would talk to him later in the day. He was obviously distraught over his friend's death, so I personally escorted him back to his vehicle to see that he left the property."

Kennedy seemed intrigued over the Captain's apparent concern for Michael, but he trod lightly on the subject, because he knew an objection from Romano was forthcoming. "Do the two of you have a past, maybe a friendship the court isn't aware of, Captain?"

The Captain was about to do a Mrs. Carmichael imitation, but then thought better of it and answered the question. "If you knew your history, Mr. Kennedy, you would know that Michael Tyler and I are both graduates of Auburn University, although we're three decades apart. We both aspired to play football, but our careers were cut short by similar knee injuries. We had one other thing in common: we both played on a state championship football team in high school; Mr. Tyler at Greenville and yours truly here at Robert E. Lee. That's the extent of our 'relationship', or 'friendship', as you so phrased it, Counselor."

Christian appeared amused, leaning in the direction of the witness, cautioning Captain Rabas. "While the counselor might have a slight memory lapse in anything connected with Auburn, please allow him some latitude in his line of questioning. Fair enough, Captain?"

"Yes, Your Honor. Excuse me for my sarcasm."

"No problem. It's contagious today, Captain Rabas. Mr. Kennedy, please continue."

"Captain, after Mr. Tyler had left the property, what was your next course of action?"

"We left forensics complete their work, then I had eight officers spread out in the neighborhood knocking on doors and asking for any information that would help us in our investigation. Considering the hour of the crime, we didn't come up with anything helpful from any of the residents."

"With the exception of .... Mrs. Carmichael?" Christian butted in.

"Well, she actually called me a few weeks later. She apparently wasn't home when we canvassed the neighborhood, but we have her testimony."

"Almost in concert, Kennedy and Christian said, "that we have." Muffled laughter rippled through the courtroom.

Kennedy's thoughts were elsewhere, perhaps on the juror Debbie Finkel who again was torturing anyone privileged to see the hem of her short skirt edge upwards over her thighs. He looked to his co-counsel and they mouthed a lunch break. "Your Honor, could we break a little early for lunch?"

"No problem, Counselor. Resume testimony at two-thirty."

Michael returned to his cell, and there was a slice of apple pie his friend James Riley had promised. A note read, "One other thing. Some of my bros had a little run in with Mr. Basch. He won't be disrespecting women anymore." Your friend, James.

In chambers, Christian nervously eyed the new bottle of Southern Comfort Hagan had retrieved for him yesterday. Christian had gone almost a full day without a drink, so he cracked the seal on his favorite libation and enjoyed a liquid lunch. Hagan awoke him at two o'clock.

CHAPTER 32

When court resumed at two, Captain Rabas was relieved when Kennedy said, "We have no additional questions of Mr. Rabas. Your witness, Mr. Romano."

Anthony Romano had made his millions in civil suits cross examining corporate CEOs and public officials, most notably police officers and detectives who might have erred in their investigation procedures. He strode to the edge of the witness box like a matador ready to apply the *coup de grâce* to an already wounded bull.

"Captain, would you say that the preliminary investigation of Miss O'Brien's homicide was done according to the book?"

"The book, Counselor?"

"Yes, Captain, the book. Or your department's own version. It calls for the crime scene to be secured to eliminate any possibility of evidence contamination. Crime scene tape should encircle the property to keep onlookers and the media at bay. Road blocks should be set up at least 200 feet from the property, east and west in this case. And traffic should be rerouted, so that only police and emergency vehicles are allowed near the property."

"Yes, I would assume so," Rabas replied.

"Really? Your Honor, I submit five pictures, marked Exhibits five through ten of the crime scene, taken by a young amateur photographer who resides in the subdivision. These six photos show the activity on the O'Brien property. They are time-stamped to show the chaos on the property thirty minutes after the first fleet of city and county squad cars arrived at 14089 Meadowbrook Lane. I count no less than twenty-five unauthorized people outside the home, trampling over possible evidence that could help lead us to the *real* murderer, not to my client, Michael Tyler."

Handing the photos to Rabas, Romano asked, "Does this look like the investigation is going by the book, Captain? Don't answer that, I'll do it for you. To me it looks like a summer block party, Captain. All that's missing is a keg of beer, women in bikinis by the pool, and dogs chasing frisbees."

"Your Honor," Kennedy begged.

"Is there an objection, Mr. Kennedy? Going once, twice, three times."

Before Romano could ask his next question, Rabas tried to defuse the fire Romano had lit. "Your Honor, let me explain."

But Christian offered little help. "Captain Rabas, Mr. Romano will ask the questions he wants specific answers for, and if you allow him, he will probably want a good explanation for these pictures. I certainly do. Mr. Romano, please continue."

Romano then turned his questioning to the inside of the O'Brien home. "Captain, how many people would you say were in the residence at the height of the investigation?"

"Well, that's hard to say, Mr. Romano. I wasn't counting, if that's what you mean."

But Romano pressed on. "Ten, maybe fifteen police and forensic personnel milling around a three-bedroom house. Close quarters, wouldn't you agree,

Captain?"

That brought an objection from Kennedy. "The Counselor is testifying for the witness, Your Honor."

"Sustained," growled Christian.

That produced a sly grin from Romano, who was in full offensive mode. "Maybe I can help you with that, Captain. I have five more exhibits, numbers eleven through fifteen which are pictures taken in various parts of the house by the forensics team. You can do the head count if you'd like Captain."

Dan Rabas casually looked at the five photos, showing little interest in any number Romano was seeking. There was a long pause before he admitted he couldn't give an accurate count. "I don't know how many people were in the house."

"Well, maybe I can help you some." Romano offered. "In the five photos, there are eighteen different people doing what we hoped the department book said they were supposed to be doing. Heck, I'm surprised Mrs. Carmichael isn't in the kitchen baking cookies."

A beleaguered Kennedy rose to object, but Christian waved him off. "We could all use a good cookie now."

Romano pressed on. "Captain, a man's life is at stake here, and this crime scene is bogged down with the usual overkill of officers and investigators from both the city and county who have no business being there. And look, the sleuth from Lowndes County you told to hit the road is back, smoking a cigarette by the pool. What part of *adios* didn't he understand?"

Christian intervened again. "Are you asking a question or offering an opinion, Mr. Romano?"

"Probably both, Your Honor."

Romano then switched gears. "Captain, I assume

forensics did a complete sweep of the residence for fingerprints, right?"

"Yes, prints were lifted from every room in the home, even the courtyard. We were told she hosted a cookout a month before her death for maybe twenty or thirty people, which would account for all the different prints."

"And most of those were partials or smudged prints Captain Rabas?"

"Yes, but no prints that could help us."

"I would be interested in the victim's bedroom, Captain Rabas. Anything that might indicate one or more people might have been in the bedroom the night she was murdered."

"We recovered two different sets, including the victim's, from the back of the headboard on the bed."

"Were there any database matches from any of the prints lifted from the residence?"

"No, sir, none at all."

Romano made light of the results. "I guess it means lots of law-abiding citizens must have attended the cookout. Your Honor, were you invited?"

Harold Christian wasn't flattered at Romano's suggestion. "No, I wasn't Mr. Romano. Do you have any other questions of this witness? If not, let's move on. The state has other witnesses to call."

"Yes, Your Honor. Just a few more questions of the good Captain. Mr. Rabas, you did obtain a search warrant to search Michael's home on South Jackson Street? Is that right?

"Yes, we did."

"How long after the Saturday in question did you do that"

"I believe it was shortly after Mrs. Carmichael

called."

"Well, what in particular, were you looking for, Captain?"

"Well, the obvious items were a gun, clothes, and shoes that might have blood residue. There was a tremendous amount of blood in the bedroom, and, considering how close the shooter was to the victim, he couldn't have avoided getting the victim's blood all over his clothes."

"Did you find anything that would indicate Mr. Tyler was involved in this shooting?"

"No, sir. He, of course, could have disposed of them elsewhere, like the gun that was found on his parents' property."

"Your Honor, I object to his comments on the gun. That wasn't the question I posed."

"Sustained."

"Captain, did you check his company van or personal car for blood splatter?

"Yes, we did."

"And, did you find any?"

"No sir."

"Just one more question, Captain, Were Michael Tyler's fingerprints found in the bedroom or any other room in the O'Brien home?

"No, sir. We didn't have his prints on file at the time."

"Well, when you finally obtained his prints, were they a match to the prints on the victim's headboard or other areas of the house?"

"No sir."

"Amazing, isn't it? You can't find any evidence to link Michael Tyler to the crime scene, yet here he sits, wrongfully accused of first-degree murder."

Romano decided to close the cross. "Captain, you've had a long day here, and I'm going to cut you a little slack. I think we all get the picture of how this investigation went. I'm through with this witness."

Kennedy shook his head in dismay. How did his first three witnesses turn into fodder for the defense? He needed the two forensic experts to save his case.

CHAPTER 33

Winston Kennedy's final witness for the day was Lawrence Karbowski, the insurance agent for Illinois Midwest Central Life Insurance, who had sold Maureen the million-dollar life insurance policy.

"The State thanks you for making the trip south, Mr. Karbowski, considering the little time you will be on the stand."

"That's okay, Mr. Kennedy, my wife and I are making a mini vacation out of the trip."

"Mr. Karbowski, you are the agent who sold Miss O'Brien the life insurance policy?"

"Yes, sir, I believe it was less than a year before her untimely death."

"I'm curious as to why Miss O'Brien bought the policy from your company. Was there any sort of history between Illinois Central and the deceased?"

"Yes, we had sold some policies for members of her father's law firm. Our vice president of sales was a personal friend of Mr. O'Brien."

"Mr. Karbowski, why would an individual who had just inherited an estate in the vicinity of ten million dollars purchase a term life policy on her own life?"

"That's a good question. There would be some tax liability in the event of her death, but the estate could handle that amount. She had a will that was well designed to divide the estate to different people, churches, schools, and charities, just to mention a few of them. Miss O'Brien insisted she wanted to purchase the policy, and named Michael Cummings Tyler as the sole beneficiary."

"What was the annual premium on the policy, Mr. Karbowski?"

"Oh, about four hundred dollars and change, Mr. Kennedy."

"When the insured buys a policy, regardless of its amount, are there any specific guidelines in naming a beneficiary?"

"Not really, Mr. Kennedy, but all policies ask what relationship the insured has with the beneficiary, such as spouse, relative, business associate, or just a close friend. Miss O'Brien indicated Mr. Tyler was a friend."

"What is the status of the policy now?"

"It's in limbo. Because the defendant is charged with this crime, he cannot receive the assets of the policy until his guilt or innocence is determined. The policy also featured a double indemnity clause for accidental death, which made it worth two million dollars."

"The state thanks you, Mr. Karbowski. I Have no further questions at this time, Your Honor. Mr. Romano, you may question the witness."

Anthony Romano had only two questions for the agent. "Mr. Karbowski, are the beneficiaries usually aware that they are to receive the proceeds of these policies?"

"Well, in the case of business policies or those between spouses, yes. But those between friends, who knows? We had a policy three years ago, where an individual was the recipient of a hundred thousand dollar policy, and didn't know he was the beneficiary."

"One last question, Mr. Karbowski. Is it possible that Michael Tyler had no knowledge that Miss O'Brien had named him the beneficiary of her policy?"

"Yes, it's highly possible. Unless, of course, their relationship was something other than ...."

"Withdrawn, no further questions, Your Honor."

Kennedy was on his feet, shouting, "Redirect, Your Honor."

Both Christian and Romano know what was coming.

"Unless what, Mr. Karbowski? Please finish what you were about to say before you were so rudely cut off by Mr. Romano."

"Objection, Your Honor," Romano hollered.

"Sustained."

But Kennedy wouldn't let up, wanting to know more about the relationship. "You stated, 'unless' – unless what?

Romano was on his feet again. "Asked and answered, Your Honor."

An agitated Christian slammed his gavel hard on the wooden block. "Sustained, excuse me, overruled. May we have a sidebar, gentlemen. And I use that term loosely."

The two attorneys stood shoulder-to-shoulder waiting for Judge "Almighty" to unleash his wrath on the two adversaries. Instead he, he simply glared at them, for as long as the courtroom clock took to tick off sixty seconds. And then, "Each of you can leave me a check for five hundred dollars before the end of business hours today." They both looked bewildered, extending palms upward as if to question Christian's displeasure.

"Gentlemen, I can make it a whole lot more if

you'd like. Mr. Karbowski's testimony is completed. He is free to continue his short vacation in our fine city, with the Court's thanks. Mr. Karbowski, you may step down. Court is adjourned until nine o'clock tomorrow morning."

CHAPTER 34

Winston Kennedy was hesitant to call Francis Herring, the sports editor of *The Cartersville Times* in southwestern Georgia, but after speaking with Herring on the phone, Kennedy decided he couldn't hurt the case. Herring promised he had some interesting things to say about that "hotshot" football player, as he referred to Michael.

When he took the stand on Friday morning, Francis Herring looked nothing like a college football player, past or present. His second chin was only the beginning of a body that had been stuffed into clothes two sizes too small. Kennedy slowly approached the witness and thanked him for making the trip over from Georgia.

"Glad to help out, Mr. Kennedy. Got lots to say about your boy Tyler."

Before Romano could even raise an objection, Christian did it for him. "Young man, let me explain a few things about courtroom procedure."

"All right, judge, you're running the show."

Christian folded his arms for a moment then poked an index finger that came within inches of coming in contact with the smug sportswriter's nose. "For openers, you are in contempt of court, which will cost you five hundred dollars. You will answer direct questions from the two attorneys, and you will offer your opinion only when you are asked for it. If you're trying to impress some folks back home in Georgia with your haughty attitude and disrespect for our courts here in Alabama, you have failed miserably. Do I have to repeat that, Mr. Herring?"

"No, sir. I mean no, Your Honor."

"Thank you. Mr. Kennedy, you have the floor."

Kennedy nervously checked his watch, debating with himself if Herring would be a reputable witness. *Five minutes with this Georgia cracker, that's all,* he thought. "Francis, are you familiar with the defendant, Mr. Tyler?"

"Yes, Mr. Kennedy, we played football together at Auburn."

"What year or years would that have been?"

Herring thought for a moment. "That would be the fall of 1989."

Continuing on the theme of football, Kennedy wanted to know if he and Michael had any social connection outside of football. "Were you in the company of Mr. Tyler socially, like the college hang-outs, bars, and restaurants?"

"We were only eighteen, Mr. Kennedy. Weren't supposed to be in bars and clubs, especially if you were concerned about staying in shape. And we didn't want to break the law."

Considering Herring's girth, Kennedy wished he'd said nothing about staying in shape. "Mr. Herring, back to my question about seeing the defendant in a social setting."

"Oh yeah, saw him around a few times, always had his eyes out for the white women."

Anthony Romano jumped to his feet, almost knocking over the defense table. "Objection, I don't believe that was the question, Your Honor."

"Well, he probably answered what would have been the next question, Counselor," Christian offered. "I'll allow it."

"A mind reader in our midst, Your Honor?"

"Careful, Mr. Romano."

Kennedy was rattled at the exchange between Christian and Romano, and fumbled through his notes trying to collect his thoughts. "Sir, is it your sworn testimony, that Michael Tyler, enjoyed the company of white women at Auburn?"

"Yes, sir, that's my testimony."

That was the message Kennedy wanted the jury to hear, but Francis Herring was unmistakably the wrong messenger.

"I have no more questions of Mr. Herring, Your Honor."

Michael was tugging at Romano's suit coat, asking him to call for a short break. "Your Honor, may we have a ten-minute break?"

Christian agreed. Time for a drink.

In a conference room off the courtroom, Michael was frantically telling Romano, "This guy's a damn liar. I don't know who the hell he is. And that crap abut running after white women. No way, Mr. Romano."

Romano assured Michael he would crucify him on cross examination. "Michael, I've done my homework on this dope. After I get through with him, the State will wish they never had taken his phone call to come and testify. Trust me."

CHAPTER 35

Francis Herring took the stand again, but the smugness was gone, perhaps in anticipation of a harsh cross-examination. Romano didn't waste any time bearing down on his prey. Offering a slight smile, he asked, "Mr. Herring, or are you more comfortable with Francis?"

"It doesn't matter."

"Good, we'll go with Francis. And remember, sir, you're still under oath. You stated in your earlier testimony that you were a teammate of Michael's at Auburn in 1989. Is that an accurate statement?"

"Yeah, that's what I said."

"Your Honor, I have a copy of the Auburn football program for the 1989 season opener against Northeast Louisiana, which I offer as Exhibit twenty-one. On page six, which lists the team roster, nowhere do I find a Francis Herring of Shell Lake, Georgia. And the team photo on the opposite page is also missing the same Francis Herring. If that's just a coincidence, please explain it to the court, Francis."

Herring was flustered, searching for the right explanation. He loosened his tie, much to the relief of his eighteen-inch neck, which looked as if it had ligature marks from his constrictive accessory.

"I was a walk-on during my freshman year. We don't get scholarships right away, have to earn them the hard way. Hopefully by the time you're a junior or senior, so we weren't included on the team picture."

"Or maybe you missed picture day, Francis? What was it?"

"I don't know. Don't know."

Romano said he understood the walk-on program. "I walked on at Duke and didn't earn a full ride until I was a sophomore. You took a lot of crap from the other players and coaches? You know, not good enough to get a scholarship right out of high school, like Michael. You had to earn it the hard way, right?"

"It wasn't too bad."

"What position did you play? Running back? Lineman?

"I was a linebacker on the scout team. That's where all the walk-ons played."

Romano pressed on. "Did you ever come in contact with Michael in drills or scrimmages?"

Eager to impress the court, or mostly himself, Herring bragged, "Yeah, I popped him a few times on a goal line drill. He fumbled the ball, just like he did against Ole Miss game that cost us the game."

"Well, Francis, I'm sure Michael doesn't need to be reminded of that one play. He had a pretty decent year for a freshman, wouldn't you agree? I believe he was named the Southeastern Conference freshman of the year, right?"

"I guess so."

Without leaving his seat, the Attorney General asked, "Where is Mr. Romano going with all this football talk, which has no bearing in this case?"

Christian agreed. "Move it along, Counselor."

"Yes, Your Honor."

"Francis, did you finish out the season?

"You mean the team or the school?"

"The team, Francis. Were you invited to the season-ending team banquet, and did you receive an invitation to come back the following spring and give it the good old college try again?"

"Not quite, sir."

"How do you mean, not quite? Did you quit, get cut? What?"

"I sprained an ankle and it never healed properly to let me play again."

"And how far into the season did this happen?" Romano asked.

"After the second or third game."

Romano was setting the trap, and Herring was about to walk into it. "Francis, I have an affidavit from your scout team coach. It's dated October 3, 1989, and it says, and I quote: 'Francis Herring was dismissed from the scout team for a myriad of reasons.' I won't embarrass you by reading them in court, but here's a copy for you and the Attorney General. Please, go over the letter and read it closely. Take your time. Are the reasons listed by the coach accurate, Francis?"

Herring's eyes were glued to the floor, searching for an answer that would explain his failings as a college football player. He slowly raised his head, briefly looking at the letter before meeting Romano's steely stare and said, "Most of them are true."

"Well, which ones aren't, Francis?"

Kennedy rose to object, but said nothing and sat down.

"Just a few more questions," Romano promised, "and then you can be back on your way to Georgia. You didn't complete your freshman year at Auburn, did you?"

"Not exactly, sir."

"Francis, we deal in specifics here. Did you or did you not complete your freshman year at Auburn University?"

"No, sir, I left about midway through the year."

Romano wanted specifics, not estimates, from the witness. "I have another affidavit from your former landlord at 25 Cottage Drive that says you moved out on December 15 with no prior warning, owing the landlord two months' back rent. How we doing for specifics, Francis?"

"That's about right. But there was a misunderstanding about the back rent."

Romano dismissed Herring's attempts to give his version of the dispute. "The court isn't concerned about your beef with your landlord. I own rental property here in Montgomery, and the excuses by tenants failing to stay current with their rent are all original – at least in the eyes of those about to evicted. What I really want to know about is your claim that Michael Tyler, in your own words, had 'eyes' for white women."

"Yeah, that's what I said."

"Could you be more specific, Francis? Times, places, dates that would establish some type of pattern you seem to suggest here? My client's reputation, specifically his life, is on the line. Times, places, dates, Francis. Now, dammit."

Christian leaned over the bench. "Watch your language, Mr. Romano."

Kennedy, knowing his witness was going down for the ten-count, tried to stop the slaughter with a pleading, "Your Honor, Mr. Romano is badgering the witness.

Christian countered, "Counselor, if Mr. Herring

had been more forthcoming about details, Mr. Romano would certainly be in a better mood. Overruled. You may continue, Mr. Romano."

Romano waited, arms folded, anticipating an answer. "Francis, maybe I should repeat the question for you?"

"No, that's it. Nothing more to say about it."

"Well, you haven't said anything about it, so what's the truth here, Francis? Did you ever have the occasion to see Michael in the company of white coeds that would lead you to believe he was hitting on them? I believe that's the phrase young people like to use these days."

"No, sir."

Romano was now nose-to-nose with Herring. "Let me sort this out, Francis. Your drove 150 miles to Montgomery to weave some cock-and-bull story about my client hitting on white women. Is that your story? Can you, for once, tell the truth before you're cited for perjury?"

"I lied sir. I'm sorry."

"You're right on both counts. You're a liar and sorry, too."

Kennedy was on his feet again. "Objection, Your Honor. The Counselor's remarks should be stricken from the record."

"Withdrawn, Your Honor. And, speaking of the records, I do ask that Mr. Herring's entire testimony be struck. Asking the jury to make sense of this liar would be an onerous burden, Your Honor."

Christian agreed. "Are there any more questions of Mr. Herring?"

There was silence for a moment, then Romano turned to Christian and said. "I have no additional questions of this witness." But he then did a quick one-eighty and stepped toward the sportswriter. "I ask the court's permission for one more question."

"You still have the floor," Christian gestured.

"Francis, who owns the paper you work for in Georgia?"

Not sure what Romano was soliciting, Herring said sheepishly, "My daddy."

"Praise the Lord. Thank God for our daddies," Romano sneered as he returned to the defense table. "*Now*, I am through with this witness."

Christian adjourned the trial until Thursday with the usual instructions to the jury "not to discuss the case with anyone and don't let media reports, or family and friends hinder your good judgement. And, Mr. Herring, I'll see you in my chambers."

CHAPTER 36

Winston Kennedy decided to save his two most compelling witnesses for last. They were James Hanley from the state ballistics lab and Dr. William Jacobsen, the county medical examiner. Kennedy declined to call "Fred," the teenager, who claimed to have seen the Channel 10 van in the O'Brien driveway the night of the murder. An interview with the high school dropout had left Kennedy with the distinct feeling that he would turn into another Justin Basch or Francis Herring.

Anthony Romano's witness list didn't include anybody that would offer a different spin on the forensic evidence, since the ghastly details of Dr. Jacobsen's findings couldn't be disputed. Romano also questioned the wisdom of whether it would be beneficial to cross-examine the doctor, who had a reputation for being overly dramatic on the stand.

The Attorney General would go with Hanley first, and it would be a short question-and-answer session, since the gun found in Tyler's Greenville residence was a likely match to the crime scene.

"Good morning, Mr. Hanley. Thank you for coming."

"Good morning to you, Counselor."

"Mr. Hanley, were you called to the crime scene on the Saturday in question?"

"No sir, I was in Birmingham at a high school class reunion."

"Did you eventually visit the crime scene at 14089 Meadowbrook Lane?"

"Yes, when I returned home Sunday, and I met Captain Rabas of the Montgomery Police Department at the residence."

"Did he brief you on their findings?"

"Yes, forensics had searched the residence for spent bullets and casings and found none."

Kennedy thought about his next question, but went ahead anyway. "Was it possible to tell what type of gun was used?"

"No, not initially. But then a .38 calibre pistol was found on the Tyler property in Greenville, and because the defendant's fingerprints and the victim's blood were on the barrel and handle of the gun, the assumption was made that it was the weapon used to kill Miss O"Brien."

Anthony Romano rose to object, but Christian waved him off. "You will have the opportunity on cross, Counselor."

Romano just shook his head in disbelief at Christian's dismissal. It was Harold Christian at his worst.

Kennedy then asked, "Did the indentations in the headboard give you any idea what type of bullets were used?"

"No, Mr. Kennedy. It appeared that a knife or something had been used to alter the impressions after removing the bullets. We made a mold of the holes, but they weren't very helpful."

"Then what is your theory on the type of bullet used?"

"We were led to believe that hollow-point bullets were used, because they leave a greater impression than a standard .38 bullet."

"Two more questions, Mr. Hanley. Who was the gun registered to?"

"The defendant, Michael Tyler."

"Was it possible, Mr. Hanley, to determine when the gun had last been discharged?"

"Yes, maybe within the last month or so."

"Thank you, sir, I have no more questions for this witness."

Romano had several. "Mr. Hanley, you said you assumed a .38 calibre weapon was the gun of choice. Can you offer a probability – say maybe fifty per cent that it was a .38.

Hanley thought, then responded, "I'd say ninety-five per cent."

Romano scowled at Hanley, obviously not in agreement with his estimate. "Really? Two holes that were severely altered to disguise the calibre of bullets, and you come up with ninety-five per cent? How about fifty per cent again, maybe even lower?"

Hanley wasn't the least ruffled at Romano's suggestion. "Mr. Romano, ballistics isn't an exact science, but if it will make you any happier, I'll go with ninety per cent. The defendant's prints and victim's blood were all over the gun."

"One final question, Mr. Hanley. If you were trying to hide a weapon used in the commission of a crime, would you hide it on your own property, or in this case, your parent's property?"

"I can't speculate on that, Mr. Romano."

"I didn't think so. No more questions."

Christian entertained a short recess by the State, because Dr. Jacobsen was late getting to the courthouse.

Twenty minutes later, the County's top medical examiner was sworn in, and Winston Kennedy, who was armed with photos and reports that would depict a grisly murder scene, began his interrogation.

"Good morning, Dr. Jacobsen."

"Thank you, Mr. Kennedy."

"In all your years as a medical examiner, have you ever witnessed a crime scene like that at the O'Brien residence?"

Romano thought to object, but he knew the pictures were forthcoming to illustrate the doctor's observations.

Dr. Jacobsen paused as if he didn't want to be reminded of the horror he'd observed and said, "I've been doing this for twenty years, Mr. Kennedy, and no, I have never seen anything like I witnessed in that house. The destruction those two bullets caused is indescribable. What kind of monster could do that to another human being?"

Romano passionately objected. "Your Honor, I don't believe that was the question. If the good doctor is accusing Mr. Tyler of being a monster, I request it be stricken from the record."

"So noted, Counselor. Just stick to the facts, Dr. Jacobsen."

Kennedy resumed his line of questioning. "What did the autopsy provide?"

"By law, we have to perform one, but there was nothing substantial to be gained in this case."

"How so? " Kennedy asked.

"The bullets, which we ascertained were hollow-point, caused so much damage to the victim's chest and head that there was little left to examine. I did find a large trace of Rohyponol in her blood which led me to believe she had probably been drugged before she was killed."

Kennedy then approached the jurors' box with twelve identical photos of the deceased, asking that they be marked Exhibit A. He turned to the jury box, at which point Romano posed an objection. "Your Honor, Dr. Jacobsen's testimony should suffice. There is no need to prejudice our case with these inflammatory pictures."

Christian was quick to overrule. "I understand the graphic nature of the photos, but the jury needs to see them."

Kennedy took his time, handing one to each member of the jury. "I think these pictures speak volumes of the atrocity of this slaughter. We treat animals we hunt in the wild with more respect than the killer did Maureen O'Brien."

The jurors must have thought they were holding live hand grenades, as each one took a quick glance and turned the photo over and placed it in their laps. The Alabama State librarian asked to be excused, and Morgan Franklin, the macho construction foreman, was right behind her, as if he were about to lose his breakfast.

"I believe we can all use a short recess," Harold Christian ordered. "Let's reconvene in about thirty minutes." He wouldn't need thirty minutes to knock down two healthy shots of Southern Comfort.

Anthony Romano looked uncomfortable as he viewed the photo, and quickly buried it under a pile of papers in front of him. He reached for his twenty-dollar silk handkerchief to wipe his brow, which was soaked with perspiration, then hurried out of the courtroom. Michael retrieved the photo from under the stack of papers on the desk and looked at it without any expression.

Twenty minutes later, Christian's clerk said the court would resume testimony at two o'clock.

CHAPTER 37

Dr. Jacobsen was back on the stand, hoping his appearance would be brief. Kennedy approached the witness slowly, as if he didn't want to ask his next question."Sir, were you able to determine where the shots originated from?"

"Yes. The abdominal shot originated from within the victim's body. Death was instantaneous. The head shot was made at point-blank range, after the victim was already dead."

Kennedy hesitated, then asked, "From what part of the deceased's abdominal area did the first shot originate?"

"The gun appeared to have been inserted in the area of the pelvic. With such a short distance to travel through the body, the result was – devastating. And maybe that word doesn't do justice to this slaughter. One bullet was sufficient, but two ....?"

Kennedy wanted to expand on the effects of a hollow-point bullet. "Dr. Jacobsen, Mr. Hanley indicated the prevailing opinion was that hollow-point bullets were used. Would you please describe for the court the effects of such a bullet on a human body."

"When a hollow-point bullet strikes a soft target, like a human body, it causes extreme expansion or fragmentation on direct impact. This process is called mushrooming, resulting in extensive tissue and organ damage to the victim."

Winston Kennedy paused before asking his final question, one that he struggled to pose. "Doctor, was there any evidence of sexual assault on Miss O'Brien?"

Dr. Jacobsen didn't hesitate. "No, Mr. Kennedy. As I said before, the autopsy was inconclusive. There was massive organ damage from the mushrooming effect of the two bullets. I had absolutely nothing left to work with."

One more question, Dr. Jacobsen. "Were you able to determine a time of death?"

"Not a specific time, Mr. Kennedy. I placed the time of death around midnight."

"Thank you, Dr. Jacobsen, I have no additional questions."

Anthony Romano squirmed in his chair and shook his head in the direction of Christian that he had no questions for Dr. Jacobsen. He did, however, offer one last comment. "I still object to the photos being introduced as evidence."

"You made your objection earlier, Mr. Romano, and I haven't changed my mind on the matter."

"Exception, Your Honor."

"So noted. If there are no other matters before the court, we are adjourned until Monday. I have a personal matter to attend to in Atlanta, so y'all have a nice long weekend. And, jurors, please remember the guidelines imposed on you regarding any discussion of this case among each other, family, and friends."

The Attorney General was frantically waving his hands to get Christian's attention as he prepared to leave the bench.

"Your Honor."

"Yes, Counselor."

"The State rests."

CHAPTER 38

The Honorable Harold Baines Christian was dead of a massive heart attack the moment he hit the ground on his estate outside of Tuskegee. Rusty stayed beside his master for twenty-four hours before his body was discovered early Sunday morning by Thomas Hagan, who routinely visited the judge for brunch and an educational session: "Christian's Law," the judge called it.

Christian's death reverberated throughout the courthouse Monday morning, and anyone who'd even had minimum contact with the judge over the last thirty years had a favorite story to tell anyone else who was willing to listen.

Stories aside, Michael's trial now faced an unpredictable future. Montgomery's other Circuit Court Judge, Robert Morrison, was on sick leave, battling lung cancer, and his return was in doubt. The Alabama Supreme Court stepped in immediately and assigned Birmingham Circuit Judge Brian Brendle to finish the trial.

But Anthony Romano had other thoughts on the Supreme Court's selection, and he unwisely took them to the press. He questioned the decision, arguing that it would take too long for a new judge to review all the testimony, and that a mistrial should be declared. He should have stopped there. But he didn't.

Romano cited Brendle's record in death penalty

cases, suggesting the second-term judge had presided over twelve such cases, all resulting in guilty verdicts. But the difference was that the five white defendants had received sentences of life without parole, while the seven black defendants were sent to death row. The most disturbing issue, though, was the alarming racial bias in the sentencing of the seven blacks; all from Jefferson County. Each jury had recommended life without parole, but as Alabama law provides, Brendle overrode their sentences and handed down the death penalty.

Romano mocked Brendle's sentencing record, saying "We're aboard the Titanic with no life jackets."

Brendle took exception to Romano's remarks and slapped him with a one thousand dollar fine for contempt of court. Romano made light of the fine, saying he wasn't aware that contempt of court charges could be applied when comments were made outside the courtroom. He was wrong, and he knew it, so he showed his sense of humor, sending the judge the fine in one dollar bills.

After a one-week lull in the trial, Brendle arrived in Montgomery to oversee what remained of it. The State had rested, and now it was Romano's turn to deal with a judge whose history in dealing with black defendants was troubling.

Brendle's first order of business was an *ex parte* meeting with Romano in Harold Christian's chambers. Romano knew better than to start another confrontation with Brendle and he offered an apology for his earlier remarks that sounded sincere, but both knew it wasn't.

Brendle, not known for his wit, tossed Romano an actual life jacket and said sarcastically, "Put it on,

Counselor, you'll need it in there." He then offered Romano what he called some free legal advice. "If you make a spectacle in court, I'll throw you off the case, then go after your bar license. For a tort lawyer used to pocketing a few million a year, that could be a real career-changer. I'd hate to think you might end up waiting on tables at your uncle's restaurants. Is there anything you don't understand about my order?"

Romano didn't immediately respond to the Judge's warning, so he asked him if he had heard him correctly.

A somber Anthony Romano nodded, "Yes, Your Honor."

"Excellent. Now go out there and give your client the best defense he deserves. Just one other thing, Counselor: there's been a change in the dress code. Your client will wear the more traditional orange jump suit for the rest of the trial, and he will be shackled, as all death penalty cases usually require. Understood?"

But Romano couldn't resist testing Brendle's ruling on this issue. "Do I understand what you said, or what the rules of courtroom decorum are in Alabama, Your Honor? There is no specific rule regarding the defendant's clothing, only an opinion that appropriate dress apparel can be substituted for the guilty-looking jumpsuits. Shackles are also an option, depending on the defendant's conduct in and out of the courtroom. You seem to have a problem with that."

"Excuse me counselor," Brendle interrupted. "You don't talk to a judge like that. Understood?"

But Romano wouldn't be deterred."Since Mr. Tyler is innocent of these bogus charges, he can show up in a white tuxedo with a red carnation in his lapel, if he so chooses. Judge Christian approved my client's choice of wardrobe in the preliminary hearing, and also ruled that handcuffs and leg irons were not required. I believe it's called judge's discretion, sir."

"Yes, counselor. And it is my discretion that Mr. Tyler will wear the jumpsuit and be shackled as I just ordered. But to humor you a little, the tuxedo would add a nice touch. Anything else?"

"No Your Honor."

Michael had spent the short break in the trial making entries in the journal he had started when he began his flight from Montgomery to Pine Bluff. The most important ones would come over the next two weeks during which time a tort lawyer, and a very good one, would argue for his life. His parents had visited him twice in the city lockup, and relayed to him what most people watching the trial were professing: their son was innocent.

Romano was in Nashville, seeking damages against a hospital in the death of a middle-aged man who had died on the operating table during a routine hernia procedure. It took only three days for the hospital to admit negligence, and the jury awarded the family five million in damages. Romano came home with a check for one-and-a-half million dollars.

CHAPTER 39

Anthony Romano had given the State his final list of witnesses, and, as predicted by Judge Christian, had added a few more to send Winston Kennedy's minions scouring the Southeast for the Jimmy Smiths and Willie Joneses of the world. The list included a James Smith in Memphis. The Memphis phone book listed forty-eight James Smiths.

Kennedy's motion to delay the trial for two days because of a death in the family was granted, and it gave Romano time to discuss with Michael his defense strategy. They were sitting in the jail's conference room, Michael sipping on a Mountain Dew and Romano with his customary bottle of water.

"You want to do what?" Michael asked. "You want to rest without calling any witnesses? That's suicidal, and you know it. The only worse scenario would be yours truly defending myself."

But Romano was insistent on resting the case and presenting it in his closing remarks. "Michael, the only evidence linking you to that murder is the gun, which was obviously planted by the killer to frame you. The motive that you were after her life insurance policy is pure speculation, at best. Hell, you weren't even aware she had purchased the policy. And the Channel 10 van in the driveway. Didn't you give Maureen a ride home Friday evening because her BMW was being serviced? I don't think anyone can believe Mrs.

Carmichael's inconsistent testimony about what she saw or didn't see when she stepped outside to take a peek at the moon. Michael, not asking you to testify is by no means precedent-breaking legal strategy."

Michael thought for a minute and then asked the question that everyone would be asking:"Isn't it a sign of guilt if I don't take the stand? What are the odds?"

"There are no precise records on that, Michael. This isn't baseball, where statistics and records are memorialized into infinity. What's the number one reason you shouldn't take the stand?"

Michael didn't respond, and Romano went into a lengthly dialogue on the merits of not testifying. "Kennedy will absolutely hammer you on cross on your relationship with Maureen. Other than that airhead from Georgia, he didn't bring in any witnesses to testify that they routinely saw you and Maureen in clubs and restaurants, because he figured you would take the stand. Then he would throw affidavit after affidavit at you from people questioning why a young black man had the attention of the best-looking woman this side of the Mississippi River. And what's your response going to be to the question if you ever spent the night at 14089 Meadowbrook Lane?"

"I have an answer for that, Anthony. I always slept in the guest bedroom."

Romano stared at Michael in disbelief. "Michael, that's the equivalent of saying, 'but I didn't inhale.' Your naivete is killing me, son. You want to testify before a national audience that a fricking Greek, or should I say Irish goddess, is sleeping naked across the hall and you're sacked out in the spare bedroom? The jury will convict you for being naive, not a killer. Every breathing male in Montgomery past the age of puberty wanted a piece of her."

"But doesn't the jury want to hear from me that I didn't commit this horrible crime?" Michael asked.

Romano was pacing the room like a caged tiger. "Yeah, they do, but in the end you can still look guilty while you're trying to tell the truth. You can't take the stand and do the old song and dance routine that 'I didn't do it' and expect the jury to believe you. You're it. From the very beginning, the police had you pegged as their only suspect. Sure, they interviewed other people, but even your friend Captain Rabas was only mildly convinced that you weren't the gunman. The only way you get convicted is to take the stand. That isn't a gamble you want to take."

"Well what about your cross of the Basch kid? You suggested he might have been the killer."

"That was just me deflecting the jury away from you. That crack-head couldn't step on a cockroach, much less kill another human being."

Michael was silent for a moment, trying to put everything in perspective. He then extended his hand to Romano and said, "We got a deal. I don't testify. Make it work Mr. Romano."

"We'll pull it off, Michael."

Michael had two days to reconsider his decision, but he never wavered as he immersed himself in card and video games with other residents in the city jail. He never let on to anyone, including his parents, that he wouldn't testify.

CHAPTER 40

Thursday morning brought bright sunshine and unseasonably warm temperatures for early December in Montgomery. Michael rose early, went through his daily workout in the yard, showered, and put on the repulsive orange jumpsuit Judge Brendle had ordered him to wear at all court appearances. At eight-thirty, two uniformed sheriff's deputies arrived, attached the cuffs and leg irons, and left for the short ride to the courthouse. It was only six blocks, but after one Birmingham newspaper had dubbed him "Alabama's Hannibal Lecter," he was surprised that there weren't armed police on each corner to protect Montgomery's citizens from this madman.

Anthony Romano was waiting for Michael in the conference room, nattily attired in one of his fashionable double-breasted Armani suits. Romano had worn a different version each day, and Michael wanted to ask him how many he owned. Romano gave Michael a firm handshake, and then reviewed the game plan they had agreed on. "After I rest, the judge will ask you if you were coerced into making this decision not to testify. And you will say ....?

Irritated at the suggestion, Michael said, "Christ, Tony, I'm not a child! Yes, I'll say it was my decision not to testify. Then you can say whatever you have to say, and I can go back to jail, get unchained, and watch *Days of Our Lives*. Just another normal day in the life of Michael Tyler."

Romano was apologetic. "I'm sorry, Michael. I know this last year has been tough on you. But the end is in sight. By this time next week, you'll be a free man, and, hopefully you can put this all behind you. Oprah will be calling, publishers and Hollywood will be throwing millions at you for your story. But most importantly, the State of Alabama will reluctantly have to say they prosecuted the wrong man, something they don't want to admit. Winston Kennedy will be mocked by his own peers, and any higher political ambitions he has, like a judgeship, will vanish. Now flash those pearly whites for me, and let's bring this nonsense to a close."

Michael shuffled into the courtroom, took his seat at the defense table and blew a kiss in the direction of his mother. Pastor Roberts was at her side, probably quoting some scripture that would proclaim his innocence. His father sat expressionless as he had throughout the entire trial, offering only a faint smile when his eyes connected with Michael.

After Judge Brendle had been announced and seated, he asked Romano if he was ready to proceed with the case for the defense. Romano turned to Michael and said, "You're all in?"

Michael nodded. "Yes, go for it."

Romano rose, the ever-commanding presence he struck in his thousand-dollar suits, ultra-expensive shoes, and tailored ties. "Your Honor, I have a motion before the court."

"And what might that be, Counselor?" Brendle asked.

"I respectfully ask that you dismiss all charges against Michael Tyler, because the State has failed to prove beyond a reasonable doubt that he took the life of Maureen O'Brien."

Brendle wasn't the least surprised that Romano would make such a request, because it's routinely done for show and to avoid a claim of ineffective counsel on appeal. He feigned a smile and offered, "Before I deny your motion, Counselor, what are your grounds for the motion?"

"Well, the evidence, Your Honor. Speculations, innuendoes, two defense witnesses committing perjury, a contaminated crime scene, and absolutely nobody who can place Mr. Tyler in the house at the exact time the crime was committed. Do I really need more, Your Honor?"

"No, Counselor, but your motion is denied anyway. Now would you like to proceed with the case for the defense?"

Romano paused briefly."Your Honor, the defense respectfully rests."

Other than a few gasps, the courtroom became deathly silent. Kennedy cast an inquiring look at Romano before Brendle ordered the two lawyers to chambers. "And bring the defendant with you, Mr. Romano."

Brendle gestured that the trio be seated. "I assume that if Judge Christian were here today, we would be having a drink while he asked the defendant if he fully agrees with his decision not to testify.

"Mr. Tyler, I have to assure the jury now and in my final instructions before they begin deliberations that you concurred with your attorney. So, Mr. Tyler, are you in full agreement that it is in your best interest not to testify? I assume that, as a law student, you know the risks involved in not taking the stand. Of course, the same risks apply when a defendant wishes to testify. Are we clear on that, Mr. Tyler?"

"Yes, Your Honor. In fact, it was my decision."

Romano turned toward Michael with a curious expression and said, "We're ready to go to closing arguments, Your Honor." *Somewhere, The Honorable Harold Baines Christian was smiling.*

"So be it," Brendle ordered. "As far as schedules go, I have a personal matter I need to attend to in Birmingham, so let's plan on next Tuesday morning at ten o'clock for closings. Any problems with that?"

There were none, and they returned to the courtroom. Brendle instructed the jury that Michael's decision not to take the stand was his and his alone. "Do not infer that he has anything to hide by not testifying. It is a constitutional right that all defendants have, regardless of the charges. You are excused until Tuesday. Court is in recess until then."

The jury seemed relieved that they would have a long weekend off, especially Morgan Franklin, the restless one of the panel.

CHAPTER 41

Tuesday was ushered in by light rain and a dense fog that police hoped would cut down the legion of spectators that had encircled the courthouse for the last ten days. The mayor had growled for a month about the city's cost to provide security, and had instructed his officers to write citations for anybody causing even the slightest problem. Inside the courtroom, the mood was tense as the winners of the spectators' lottery found their seats in the gallery. Michael's parents took their usual places behind the defense table, where their son was already seated in the court-mandated leg irons and hand cuffs.

Judge Brendle instructed the bailiff to bring the jury in, and after they were seated asked Mr. Kennedy if he was ready to give his closing argument.

Winston Kennedy's options were limited and he knew it. Two of his witnesses, the mail carrier and the sportswriter, were absolute train-wrecks, and Mrs. Carmichael was – and then wasn't sure – that the TV van in the O'Brien driveway belonged to Channel 10. He would keep it short.

The gun had its flaws, too, but the defendant's fingerprints and the victim's blood were a perfect match, and moreover, ballistics claimed that it had been fired recently, but could not offer any specific time frame. The victim's will, however eccentric, didn't include Michael, which was presumably why she had made him the beneficiary of her life insurance policy.

He stated that his detectives had conducted an extensive investigation, denying that they had zeroed in on Michael from the beginning, and had ignored suggestions that Maureen had a promiscuous lifestyle that didn't include Michael.

"We have the man who brutally ended Maureen O'Brien's life, and he sits there at the defense table. Find this man guilty and send the public a message that he be held accountable for his actions. He slaughtered her, then ran like a coward when the evidence linked him to this gruesome killing. He deserves the ultimate punishment the State of Alabama administers, and that ladies and gentlemen, is the death penalty – 2,000 volts of electricity."

The Attorney General's comments brought an angry response from Romano. "Objection, Your Honor! We don't have a verdict, and Mr. Kennedy is already advocating the penalty. I call for an immediate mistrial."

Brendle jumped into the spat quickly. "Hold on there, Mr. Romano. First of all, your objection to Mr. Kennedy's remarks are sustained, however there will be no mistrial. And Mr. Kennedy, we will have a short counseling session in chambers when we adjourn."

Kennedy might have had additional comments to make, but he knew possible sanctions were coming from Judge Brendle, and he wisely took a seat and meekly offered, "I'm through with my closing."

Brendle smiled briefly, obviously agreeing with the Attorney General, then asked Anthony Romano if was ready to proceed with his closing remarks. "Yes, Your Honor."

Romano, as usual, was impeccably dressed in

yet another Armani suit that he bragged was number eleven in his wardrobe. He walked to the jury box with hands clasped and a friendly smile. "The case the State of Alabama has brought against Mr. Tyler is all about suppositions and little fact, other than a relationship existed between my client and the deceased. The State would have you believe their relationship was more than professional, and that Michael acted out of rage when Maureen tried to suppress his sexual advances. That's it. That's all they have.

"Then they bring in a witness across the street from the O'Brien home, who as we speak today, *still* isn't sure what TV van was parked in the driveway the night of the murder. The detective in charge of the investigation didn't have to admit the early hours of it were tainted, because you saw the photos of the crime scene which showed that it was. It was typical police overkill; people were in the house who didn't belong there. Then the State brings in a former football player – and boy, was that a stretch – who perjures himself on the stand.

"And they produce a gun found in Michael's father's shed that was obviously planted by someone wanting to incriminate my client. Yes, the fingerprints matched those of Mr. Tyler because he owned the gun, but the forensics expert couldn't say for sure it was the actual weapon used to kill Miss O'Brien. Why? Because the killer left the scene with the spent bullets that were embedded in the victim's headboard. The gun and bullets have to match, and there are none to match here, ladies and gentlemen. Let me say it again: a gun with no bullets to match. Too much has been made of Michael and his relationship with Maureen because that's what people do when they don't mind their own business. Or was it, because they just happened to be of different races? Maureen O'Brien, a stunning Caucasian woman and Michael Tyler, a handsome black man. People of my color still get riled at the thought of blacks and whites being together in social settings, much less showing any affection for each other. You know what? The civil rights laws never changed anything in the South, they only enhanced our racist past. Jim Crow is alive and well, ladies and gentlemen. And that's why Michael Tyler is sitting at the defense table charged with an unspeakable crime he didn't commit."

Romano walked back to the defense table and stood behind Michael. "Let's talk about his flight from Montgomery after the gun was discovered. A poor decision? Not if you think you're about to be charged for a murder in which you had no part of. But he did return when he decided he would try to clear his name of this bogus charge. Can you believe it? A black man thinking he could beat a rap like this in the South?

"Now let's talk motive. The state flashes around an insurance policy that names Michael as the sole beneficiary of a million-dollar policy with a double indemnity clause. The insurance agent said it wasn't unusual for the insured not to tell the beneficiary he or she would benefit financially down the road someday. What if I told you that Michael didn't know he was the beneficiary?"

Kennedy was on his feet objecting. "Your Honor! If Mr. Romano wants to admit new evidence, he should should have done that when he had a chance to present his case. He can't just ...."

Brendle agreed. "Nice try, Mr. Romano. You do it again and you'll be writing me a big check with a lot zeroes before the decimal sign."

But Kennedy wasn't finished with his objection. "Thank you, Your Honor. However, it doesn't undo the comment."

"I understand, Mr. Kennedy, but it's the best the system can provide. Turning towards the jury box Brendle said, "You must disregard Mr. Romano's statement about the policy's beneficiary." Brendle then motioned to Romano to continue. "I urge you to use caution, Counselor."

"If you buy the beneficiary theory ...."

The judge had heard enough. "Chambers."

Brendle was wishing there was a bottle of Southern Comfort left behind by Christian and he railed at the defense attorney. "The beneficiary talk is off limits, Mr. Romano. I thought I made that crystal clear just a few minutes ago. You've used up two strikes, the third will cost you dearly."

"But Your Honor, the State's entire case is based on a long grocery list of suppositions and perjured testimony. Aren't we allowed to even the scorecard a little?"

"Mr. Romano, you had that chance during the trial, which you ignored. If I recall, you rested without calling any witnesses."

"I agree, Your Honor," Kennedy added.

"Shut up," Brendle snapped. "You brought in the life insurance policy as motive, not even considering the possibility that Mr. Tyler wasn't aware that he was the beneficiary."

Romano judged that it was safe to speak. "That's entirely my point, Your Honor."

"So noted, Mr. Romano. We will return to the courtroom, and you will finish your closing with no more references to the life insurance policy, since we don't know whether Miss O'Brien had informed the defendant he was the beneficiary. Now let's be good boy scouts, go out, and put a wrap on it for today."

Romano finished his closing, chronicling his client's exemplary life as a student-athlete, admittance to law school, and his dream as an attorney helping those wrongfully convicted of crimes. "Here sits a young man any parent would be proud to call their son. Release him from the shackles of imprisonment and allow him to leave this courtroom a free man. Thank you."

CHAPTER 42

Michael's parents received permission from Captain Rabas to join their son for dinner on Thursday evening. Instead of the jail menu, they were allowed to bring in dinner from the Sahara Restaurant, a well-known eating establishment that bordered the Old Cloverdale neighborhood.

Over fried shrimp and prime rib, the family reminisced about Margaret and Ralph's monthly trip to Montgomery to have dinner with Michael. On one such occasion, Michael had invited Maureen to join them for ribs at one of the Romano restaurants. His parents had seen some of Maureen's Sunday shows and remarked how attractive she was. But for Ralph, sitting across the table from Michael's new friend, it was difficult to concentrate on dinner, and Margaret was nervous throughout the evening, as all eyes in the packed restaurant were focused on this unusual four-some.

"You remember that night, Michael?" his father asked.

"Every day was special when Maureen was part of it," Michael said. "Why do some people think I had anything to do with her death?"

"Everything will work out just fine, Michael," his mother assured him. "This weekend we'll be back in Greenville as a family again. I"ll make you your favorite friend chicken, mashed potatoes, gravy and turnip greens. And Hercules will be so happy to see you. He's missed you so much."

"Thanks, mom. I'm already looking forward to it."

The courtroom was filled to near capacity when Michael arrived in his customary court-ordered jump-suit and restraints. A bailiff escorted the jury to its box and called the court to order after Judge Brendle took his seat on the bench.

The judge's jury instructions were short and to the point. "You are to find the defendant guilty or not guilty of first-degree murder beyond a reasonable doubt, which in legal terms means the prosecution has presented evidence that supports the charge of first degree murder. There can still be doubt, but only to the extent that it would *not* affect a reasonable person's belief regarding whether or not the defendant is guilty. And may I remind you again that the defendant's decision not to testify should not in any way affect your verdict. I cannot make that any clearer. Is that under-stood?" They all nodded in the affirmative. "Good. You may now retire to deliberate."

As Brendle left the bench, he said loud enough for Jennifer Dempsey, the court reporter, to hear, "And that shouldn't take too long for a conviction." This was Dempsey's first trial and she quizzed the judge about his remark. He angrily replied, "No, it's not part of the record. Forget I ever said it." Fortunately for Brendle, the jury was out of hearing range, as it would have been grounds for a mistrial.

Sam Hoskins, the life insurance salesman who had been elected jury foreman, was not relishing the task ahead. The few times the jury had been together in the deliberation room had been chaotic, as the bickering between Morgan Franklin and Debbie Finkel had consumed more attention than the testimony in the case. Franklin was upset that he was losing twenty-two dollars an hour on a downtown building project. Finkel couldn't have cared less, since the temporary day job as a juror didn't prevent her from her nightly tips at the Starlight Lounge.

"Let's get on with it!" shouted Franklin when they began to deliberate Michael's fate. "Let's take a vote, so we can all get on with our lives."

But Finkel couldn't resist needling Franklin, who always seemed in a hurry to be somewhere else. "You don't have a life," Finkel shot back, much to the delight of the other jurors who disliked the abrasive Franklin.

Hoskins, a diminutive man in his early fifties, hadn't solicited the foreman's job, but after four ballots had failed to select one, Finkel had called for a unanimous vote to give Hoskins the job. Only Franklin had objected.

"There'll be no quick vote," Hoskins warned, directing his stare at Franklin, who was gazing out a window overlooking the crowded courtyard below. "We'll take whatever time we need to give Mr. Tyler a fair and impartial verdict. If you're not pleased with the process, there are two alternate jurors who are available to take your place. Consider yourself lucky that we aren't sequestered, locked up in some motel room with only a radio to listen to. That being said, sit down and shut up.

"Now, let's review the jury instructions the judge gave us. We can find Mr. Tyler guilty or not guilty of first-degree murder. A guilty verdict makes him eligible for the death penalty. Of course, we can choose not to impose the death penalty, even though when asked in *voir dire* if we would have a problem voting for death, we all said no."

This brought a sharp response from Margaret Jay, the Alabama State librarian, who had said little during the course of the trial. "Mr. Hoskins, I don't think we should get ahead of ourselves regarding the punishment As you know, a guilty verdict must then go through the punishment phase, and we're still a long way from there."

"The quicker the better," argued Franklin.

"What is the state's most compelling evidence?" asked Dennis Graham, an apartment manager of a low-income housing project. "They have a delightful, but obviously senile, eighty-three-year-old grandmother who happens to enjoy moon-watching and believes – she thinks – she saw the Channel 10 van parked in the O'Brien driveway shortly after the ten o'clock news. Plus the insurance policy, which Mr. Tyler's attorney says his client had no knowledge of."

"Well, that's the problem, isn't it?" chimed in Chris Darvin, the retired plumber. "His attorney said it for him. Remember, Mr. Tyler didn't take the stand on his own behalf. His entire defense was included in his attorney's closing statement, which didn't impress me."

But Hoskins was quick to remind everyone that Michael's decision not to take the stand could not be held against him. "Remember the judge's instructions on that point. He was very clear on that."

Ken Myers, the electrical contractor had issues with the gun. "Even though it had the defendant's fingerprints and victim's blood on it, it can't be positively identified as the gun that killed the victim. And remember, he owned the gun, which explains his fingerprints. There could have been a second gun that was used and disposed of by the real killer. However, he should have taken the stand to explain how his own gun was involved in the crime, and he wasn't aware of it. And, if the gun was stolen before the murder, did he notify the police?"

"You're right, he did it," grumbled Franklin. "He owned the damn gun. Are you really suggesting somebody other than Tyler snuck down to Greenville to plant it and frame him?"

"Possibly," Myers countered. "If you were going to hide the gun, you surely wouldn't hide it on your own property, would you?"

But the irritable Franklin wouldn't let up. "What more do you need to convict him?"

"How about a motive?" Hoskins asked.

"Screw the motive," Franklin shouted. "Lots of people have been convicted without one."

The hour was approaching five o'clock, and Hoskins informed the bailiff that they were quitting for the day.

CHAPTER 43

On Friday morning at ten o'clock, the jurors were back to work. The early consensus was that a verdict determining the future of Michael Tyler would be reached today. They should have checked with Roscoe Jenkins, who said the jury reaching a verdict within two days was ten-to-one against.

"Let's do it," demanded Morgan Franklin. "I don't want to waste the entire freaking weekend thinking about it."

"I can't believe you and I agree on anything," quipped Debbie Finkel.

Sam Hoskins had heard enough. "I believe I speak for the other jurors who are fed up with your constant bickering. If you continue, I will ask Judge Brendle to release you from further deliberations. That is my call, you know. I would suggest that we put aside any differences and perform the job when chosen for what some people are calling a landmark case."

Hoskins then cautioned the jurors. "Last night I thought about the first day of deliberations, and my conclusion is that we are ignoring the judge's order regarding the defendant's decision not to testify. I know that's difficult to put behind us, but we can't convict someone with death penalty implications just because we think Mr. Tyler had something to hide, or that he was afraid he would come unraveled on cross examination. He's a second-year student at the Law

Center and apparently one of the brightest in his class I'm told. Personally, I think Tyler's got a lot of savvy and that he carefully deliberated whether or not to testify. And there's also several statements his defense attorney made that were ruled not admissible, but here again we heard them.

"Some of you seem in a hurry to call for a vote. Miss Jay, if you will distribute the ballots, we will have our first vote. Take your time. We don't want anybody thinking we were in a hurry to get out of here. Mark your ballots with an X in the appropriate spot – guilty or not guilty. If we don't have a unanimous decision, we'll have to discuss why there's a split in the voting."

Margaret Jay collected the ballots, and, with Hoskins' assistance, they tallied the votes; seven to five for a guilty verdict. The rest of the day produced two more votes with no change in the split. Hoskins informed the bailiff they hadn't reached a verdict, and Judge Brendle reluctantly excused the panel for the weekend after exchanging notes with Hoskins, who indicated they were making progress and assured the judge they would do everything to avoid a mistrial. "We will have you a verdict next week, Your Honor."

The case took a bizarre turn over the weekend, when Morgan Franklin made a visit to the Starlight Lounge where jury adversary Debbie Finkel worked. According to an off-duty Montgomery policeman who worked security in the lounge, the two got into a shouting match over the stalled deliberations, and Franklin said loud enough for everyone to hear that "the black bastard is headed to death row" if he had anything to do with it.

The conversation was relayed to Judge Brendle, and after a contentious Monday morning meeting with the judge, the two were dismissed from the jury; replaced by the two alternates – a retired meter reader for the city of Montgomery and a grocery store clerk. Brendle said he would give the new jurists until Wednesday afternoon to get up to speed and resume their deliberations.

Despite a new air of civility in the jury room, they were only marginally closer to a verdict than they were on the previous Friday. Six more votes over the next two days cost Michael two votes, as the margin for a guilty verdict increased to six, and he was within three votes of being convicted. Following lunch on Friday, they discussed the believability of Mrs. Carmichael's rambling testimony, but agreed that the Channel 10 truck she claimed to have seen in the O'Brien driveway was shaky but believable.

Midway through the afternoon, Hoskins asked the jurors if there was a need for another vote, and when they said a resounding no, he informed the bailiff that they were through for the day. When Harold Christian's clerk, Thomas Hagan, notified Brendle of the impasse, the judge was furious. "What the hell is their problem, Hagan? We should have had a verdict the first day. Notify the bailiff that I want them back in court immediately."

Brendle showed his impatience with the jury when he returned to the bench and asked Mr. Hoskins if the deadlock was "sealed in stone."

"I don't think so, Your Honor," Hoskins replied. "We believe a break in the deliberations would be beneficial at this time.

However, Brendle didn't agree. "I'm not in favor of weekend deliberations, but with the holidays nearing, I want you all back here at ten o'clock tomorrow morning to continue your work. Please resolve any issues you have and bring this case to a successful conclusion. Thank you."

CHAPTER 44

Anthony Romano was conferring with Michael in the jail lounge Saturday morning, concerned that weekend deliberations were a total waste of time. "The holidays are approaching and they'll be in a foul mood for having to work on the weekend. They won't get anything accomplished," he offered, as he sipped his coffee and munched on some of his favorite Krispy Kreme doughnuts.

Michael was in a reflective mood as he weighed the odds of lengthy or short deliberations being in favor of the defendant. "Remember the Rogalski case two years ago, Tony? He was dead-in-the-water guilty, and it took the jury a little more than two hours to say *not guilty.*"

"I've got a good one, too, Michael. In my last year at Duke we sat in on a murder case that had not guilty written all over it. The defendant was a nightmare on the stand, but the jury is out for six days before a mistrial is declared. Then a second jury acquits the guy over lunch on the first day of deliberations. Our jury is better with those two whack jobs gone, but I don't have a good feeling for our jury. I gave up predicting what juries would do a long time ago."

Romano's pocket pager interrupted their jury reminiscing, and he excused himself to return the call in another room. He returned shortly after with a grim look on his face. "I don't believe it, Michael. They've reached a verdict. They want us back at the courthouse at noon."

It took two hours for everyone to be in place after word spread throughout the courthouse that the most anticipated ending to a trial since the Scottsboro Boys case in 1932 was near. Michael's parents were home in Greenville when they received Romano's call, and received a police escort from the Greenville Police Department.

Brendle, who had been staying at a local motel, returned to the courthouse and ordered the bailiff to summon the jury. They entered the courtroom, walking solemnly to their seats in the jury box.

After Brendle arranged some papers on the bench, he addressed the packed courtroom. "There will be no outbursts or demonstrations of any kind when the verdict is read. I will make room in the county jail for anyone who disrupts my courtroom. Turning his attention to the jury foreman, Sam Hoskins, he asked, "Has the jury reached a unanimous decision?"

"Yes, Your Honor, we have."

Hoskins gave the verdict form to the bailiff, who handed it to the judge. After looking at the verdict, Brendle nodded as if in agreement, then handed the form back to the bailiff.

"Will the defendant please rise. Mr. Foreman, please read the verdict."

Hoskins' voice wavered as he announced the verdict. "On the charge of murder in the first degree, we find the defendant, Michael Tyler, guilty."

Despite the orders of the Judge, the courtroom erupted as spectators voiced their opinions, the majority of whom were pleased with the verdict. A few racial insults were hurled in Michael's direction, implying that Michael got what he deserved for "violating our white women."

"Order, order! Brendle bellowed. "I will not allow this kind of behavior! Deputies, take anyone into custody who is causing a disturbance." When order had finally been restored, Brendle thanked the jury for their work and told them to be back on Monday morning at nine to begin the penalty phase.

Michael turned to his parents for moral support, but a deputy blocked their path when his mother reached out to her son. Michael, who had inherited his mother's stoic composure, seemed resigned to the verdict. He wondered, too, if the real killer or killers were in the courtroom, knowing the verdict absolved them of any complicity in the crime. His thoughts also went back to his initial meeting with Anthony Romano, and why he had offered his services *pro bono* – effectively shutting the door on more experienced criminal defense lawyers who were now privately questioning Romano's strategy of resting without calling any witnesses who could refute the theory Michael was romantically involved with Maureen. And that included the most important witness, the defendant, Michael Tyler.

Romano, tossed out some expletives on the jury, which was now only a useless penalty phase from sending Michael to the electric chair. He patted him on the back and uttered the words defendants have little faith in: "We'll appeal Michael. We'll appeal."

CHAPTER 45

Michael spent an emotional weekend in lockup, realizing that he was headed to prison for the rest of his life, or worse, to death row. But with Brendle's history of sentencing overrides, especially those involving black defendants, there were no guarantees that his life would be spared. The aggravating factors of Maureen's death were blatantly repulsive, and now that the jury had found him guilty, his only hope was mercy from the jurors in the form of life without parole.

The penalty phase would offer Michael the opportunity to show any mitigating factors that might serve as a basis for a sentence less than death. There was little more Romano could present than he already had in his closing argument. He would rely on family and friends to attest to Michael's outstanding moral character and disciplined upbringing and that he was not, under any possible circumstances, capable of taking another person's life.

Monday morning came all too soon. Michael changed his morning routine of a run through the jail yard, opting instead to write a few letters and listening to the blow bag on a local radio station who advocated a public stoning in the downtown fountain. Seven of the eight callers agreed with him.

At eight-thirty, his two escorts chained and shackled him for the trip to the courthouse. After the sentencing, he would be returning for an undetermined period before being transferred to a maximum security prison in South Alabama. Would it be in general population or death row? He noticed from the police van windows that the crowds that had filled the block around the courthouse during the trial had dwindled, and the police presence was only minimal.

Anthony Romano was already seated at the defense table when Michael shuffled into the courtroom. His voice betrayed his resignation as he went over the list of people he would be calling to testify on behalf of Michael. Beside Michael's parents, there was Pastor Roberts, who undoubtedly would present a scathing rebuke of the death penalty, three former coaches, Professor Robert Mullins of the Law Center, two former Auburn players, and several employees of Channel 10. Twelve people who would testify that Michael Tyler wasn't some deranged man capable of committing this disturbing crime.

Winston Kennedy would probably drag out Dr. Jacobsen, the county pathologist, again to describe the graphic details of Maureen's ghastly death. While Dr. Jacobsen's original testimony couldn't tie any specific person or persons to the crime scene, the jurors' eyes had been fixated on Michael after looking at the photos of this indescribable horror. He would be Kennedy's only witness, presenting the State's one aggravating factor in the penalty phase. And it was a powerful one.

Professor Mullins was the first to take the stand, calling Michael an excellent student who was looking forward to a career in law. "With his knowledge of the law, he can provide legal counsel to inmates who have inadequate legal representation. Spare his life."

His former high school coach, Walter Lerner,

related his former experiences with Michael. He also used his time on the stand to question the jury's verdict which brought a mild rebuke from Judge Brendle.

"That issue can be taken up on appeal, sir, but not here. Are we clear on that?"

"Yes, Your Honor." Coach Lerner concluded, "It would be wrong to execute one of the finest young men I have ever been associated with."

After the next four witnesses spoke highly of Michael's good character, Brendle asked Romano if the remaining eight witnesses would be echoing the same sentiments.

Romano objected without leaving his chair. "Does it really matter, Your Honor? Are we on some kind of schedule that we can't give Mr. Tyler the time to hear from his family, friends and peers? I'm a little offended by your lack of sensitivity."

"Watch it Counselor," Brendle warned.

Pastor Roberts took the stand with the same ministerial presence he did in his Sunday sermons. After speaking highly of Michael, he launched into a scorching attack of the death penalty, and specifically how it was administered in Alabama. He came prepared with facts and figures to show how blacks were more likely to receive the death penalty than whites, and why this sentencing phase was only a ruse to send Michael to the electric chair. Clutching his cross, Pastor Roberts said, "You, Your Honor, will answer to a higher authority someday, a God who doesn't judge people by the color of their skin, and ...."

It was all Judge Brendle would tolerate. "You are excused, Pastor Roberts. Save it for Sunday."

Ralph Tyler declined to speak, because he surely would have been handed a contempt of court charge, expanding on the Pastor's comments on the sentencing of blacks. This left Michael's mother the last to speak. A woman whose composure never wavered in the face of adversity, she spoke passionately about her only child. "God gave us this wonderful son twenty-five years ago to love and nurture, and we have done that, Your Honor. I'm sorry, sir, but there is no power on this earth, including anyone in this courtroom, that can substitute God's will. I ask that the jury spare my son's life."

Brendle called for a short recess before Winston Kennedy would counter with the State's aggravating factors.

Kennedy spoke with the same venom he'd displayed in his closing remarks, calling Michael Tyler "an opportunistic devil who crossed the line of racial boundaries, and when Miss O'Brien rejected his sexual fantasies, he cracked. He took the life of a beautiful human being because he couldn't have her for himself. Look past his academic and athletic achievements and look into the eyes of a calculating and manipulative cold-blooded killer."

Dr. Jacobsen was prepared to repeat his trial testimony, but the Attorney General wanted a more powerful graphic to show the jurors the horror of this macabre slaying. With the help of a slide show presentation, the images of Maureen O'Brien's lifeless body on a bloody bed were magnified on a much larger scale than the photos Jacobsen had provided the jury. Most of the people in the courtroom covered their faces when the screen lit up.

Romano vigorously objected to the enlargement and directed his anger at Kennedy. "Do you have no shame, Counselor? Right now, I can't find the words to express my feelings for your behavior. Your Honor, are you not appalled?"

Brendle seemed momentarily out of sync, as if he had lost fucus during Romano's lambasting of the Attorney General. With nothing to say to Romano, Kennedy looked upward and shouted. "There is only one sentence, and it is death by electrocution! Maybe Pastor Roberts purposely overlooked Exodus 21:24 which advocates an "eye for an eye."

Ralph Tyler used all his 250 pounds to hold down the Pastor seated next to him who always had his own proverb ready to answer any argument over Bible interpretations.

Kennedy didn't escape the glare of the Pastor and said solemnly, "The State rests."

CHAPTER 46

The first decision the jurors had to make was lunch. The clock was nearing noon, and the menus from a nearby restaurant that serviced the jurors were being distributed.

Sam Hoskins thanked his fellow jurors for their service and asked them to consider the mitigating and aggravating circumstances in deliberating the proper sentence. "Although we're glad to put these past two weeks behind us, take your time and privately consider the two options: life without the possibility of parole, or death."

After a brief lunch, the jury, with only minimal discussion, unanimously agreed that life without parole was the appropriate sentence. A death sentence would take a unanimous vote, but any verdict less than death would only require a simple majority.

At two-thirty, the court was called to order, and the jury was seated. Judge Brendle then warned the spectators to keep their opinions to themselves and asked Sam Hoskins if they had reached a decision.

"Yes, Your Honor. we have."

"And your sentence is?"

"We unanimously agree that the defendant, Michael Tyler, be sentenced to life in prison without the possibility of parole."

There was a collective sigh from the Tyler clan until Brendle interrupted the proceedings with a bang of his gavel. "While I respect the jury's sentence, I am overriding the life without parole recommendation, and, as Alabama law provides, ordering a sentence of death by electrocution."

There was an eerie silence, as if the people in the courtroom hadn't heard the judge's order. It caught Brendle by surprise, too, but he recovered and ordered Michael to stand. Michael needed the help of Anthony Romano to stand erect, then heard the bleak words, "I sentence you to death at a time to be determined by the Supreme Court of the State of Alabama. May God have mercy on your soul. This court is adjourned."

Winston Kennedy reached across the isle to shake Anthony Romano's hand, but Romano declined, and offered Michael his condolences. "We'll beat this, Michael. Keep the faith."

Michael turned to his family for reassurance, but two bailiffs were already ushering him out of the courtroom. They were all too dazed to speak, but Pastor Roberts asked them to join him in prayer. His words, though, seemed lost on everyone and he closed with a simple "Amen."

CHAPTER 47

Nothing could have prepared Michael for life on Alabama's death row. Because of Captain Rabas, time in the city jail had been a paradise compared to what awaited him in the South Alabama Correctional Center near Mobile.

Shortly after his conviction, Michael received a special delivery mailing from the Alabama Corrections System, which described in meticulous detail the policies and provisions of death row. They included the daily activities that began with a five o'clock breakfast and concluded with lights out at midnight. They also dealt with family visits, telephone privileges, incoming and outgoing mail, and canteen services. Michael was to sign in triplicate that he would adhere to the State's rules and regulations for death row inmates. *Be a good boy, and they'll reward you with a Snickers bar on the first of each month.*

Michael was first on the waiting list to call death row his new home, taking up the vacancy left by Rollie Johnson of Phenix City, who was scheduled to be executed in mid-March. It didn't take a home cleaning service to prepare his old cell for a new tenant, but the prison bureaucracy operated at a snail's pace on inmate transfers, especially those to death row.

There was no advance notice as to when Michael would be leaving for SACC; neither was he surprised when a guard interrupted a Monday afternoon card game three months later in the prisoners' lounge with a note that he would be leaving the following morning. "Have your bags packed for the eight o'clock trip to South Alabama."

Captain Rabas stopped by Michael's cell later that night to wish him well on his next "journey of life" as he called it. They reminisced on their own football careers, which had been so parallel, and what life might have been for Michael if it hadn't been for some deranged psychopath who had brutally ended Maureen O'Brien's life.

After an hour or so, they embraced and Rabas kissed Michael's cheek with a promise to visit him regularly on the row. "Don't let the system beat you down," were his final words.

With the exception of a few letters over the next ten years, the Captain never came to visit him. Michael heard that he had retired to New Mexico after a thirty-two-year career with the Montgomery Police Department.

On April Fools' Day, shortly after eight o'clock, Michael was handcuffed and shackled for the two-hour drive south in an air-conditioned van, a luxury he tried to enjoy, because there was none waiting him on death row. The van was part of a convoy that included three state patrol cars. It was overkill, but Michael Tyler was a convicted killer, and the State was only following procedures on death row transfers.

He tried to interject a little conversation during the ride, but since there was no response from the escort service, he surmised the two officers had lost the draw for his transfer, or maybe they were die-hard Alabama fans.

It was a beautiful spring morning, and the Alabama landscape was slowly coming to life after an unusually harsh winter. As they passed the first Greenville exit, Michael noticed the new shopping center his parents had talked about. A Pizza Hut, McDonald's, and Kentucky Fried Chicken food outlets were part of a complex that also included a Winn-Dixie food store, post office, and an Exxon station.

As we sped south to a place in the absolute middle of nowhere, my thoughts focused on the life I had planned to the one the State of Alabama was now charged with. I had lived a charmed life for a young black man in Alabama, but momentarily I felt I was on the same level with the impoverished inner-city youth the government housing projects fostered, then turned over to society to mend.

Two hours later, we exited off the interstate and turned right onto a narrow service road that led to the sprawling SACC complex. Situated on 1,500 acres of wasteland in Mobile County, the state's sixth maximum security facility was built in the late 1950s at a cost of seven million dollars to the Alabama taxpayers. Architecturally, it left everything to be desired. A mass of grey concrete buildings dotted the landscape, which was enclosed with what seemed like miles of chain link fencing, topped by two rows of razor wire, the last physical barrier to anyone entertaining thoughts of taking a leave of absence without prior approval.

CHAPTER 48

Michael was hustled out of the patrol car and into a building that served as the reception center for death row. There were some forms for his escorts to sign, and before they left, one of them wished him well. He thanked them for the ride and turned his attention to a guard, who gave him a quick pat-down for any contraband the deputies might have missed.

He was ushered into a smaller room where he was issued the standard death row clothing attire: two white jumpsuits, two pairs of white boxer shorts, socks, t-shirts, and a scarred pair of tennis shoes, probably the ones' Rollie Johnson wore when he took his seat in the chair. The shoes were optional, so he declined their offer in favor of his Nike Runners.

He thought to ask when he might be free of the chains that clung to his sides and feet, but the four guards who encircled him as if he were a trapped animal, had said little since he'd arrived. After signing some papers confirming that he had received the prison wear, Michael was led down a flight of steps to a dark corridor void of any substantial light, other than a few dimly lit light bulbs. He counted twelve cells, one of which was occupied by a slim black man who was curled up in a corner of his cell, oblivious to the group's presence.

"This is your new home for the next thirty days," shouted one of the guards. "It's part of the orientation process to prepare you for life on death row. It also serves as a reminder where you can land for thirty or sixty days if you don't follow the rules here. Understand?"

"I guess, but I want to know if death row is an upgrade? What did I do in the first fifteen minutes since arriving here to deserve this?"

"You're a convicted killer, Tyler," snapped one of the guards whose uniform sported the name Kevin Johnson. "Everyone comes here first. I don't make the rules, I just follow them."

"Well, if you'll get me unchained, I'd like to take an afternoon nap," Michael suggested.

As the guards prepared to leave, Michael asked what was on the dinner menu. He got no response, but it did pique the interest of the guy two cells down. "Food ain't worth a shit down here, so you better get used to it." He spoke little else over the next ten days before he was chained for his walk to death row. Michael never got his name.

The conditions in administrative segregation, or better known as solitary confinement, were spartan, to say the least. There was a bloodstained mattress and pillow that even Hercules would have declined to sleep on, and a frayed wool blanket that had absorbed the sweat of how many visitors before him? The toilet and sink reminded him of some Alabama backwoods gas stations where sanitation wasn't a priority. A twenty-five watt light bulb in the ceiling would stay lit 24/7, and for entertainment purposes there was an AM-FM radio whose main feature was static.

One week into his confinement, Michael had a visitor. Dr. James Fellows, one of the prison's two psychologists, showed up at his cell unannounced and asked if he would answer a series of questions. A short, stocky man with a scruffy salt-and-pepper beard meant to cover up the scars of teenage acne, Fellows extended his right hand through the bars of the cell, a gesture Michael declined.

"I'm here to determine your mental status, Mr. Tyler."

"Are you kidding? I've been caged up, for what, a week now, in conditions to which I wouldn't subject our family dog. The cockroaches have free run of the place, but that's understandable, considering the filth and stench they enjoy roaming through twenty-fours a day. I even have names for a few of them. Now you said you have some questions for me?"

"Yes sir, I do."

Before the doctor could ask his first question, Michael interrupted him with the first of several coarse verbal jabs over the next five minutes. "First of all, don't address me as 'sir' or 'Mr. Tyler,' now or anytime in the future, and hopefully, that doesn't include you or any other shrink who wants to screw with my mind. The state's only purpose here is to keep me alive for maybe fifteen years before they strap me into a chair and send enough electricity through me to kill a baby rhinoceros. And I assume you want to know how I feel about that?"

"I just want to get some insight on you, Mr. Tyler, excuse me, Michael."

"Here's the lowdown on Michael Tyler, doc. Two years ago, I was a second-year law student at the Clarence Darrow Law Center in Montgomery, looking forward to a career of helping wrongfully convicted people in overturning their guilty verdicts. I worked part-time for a Montgomery TV station as a cameraman for news and sports reporters. One day, a gorgeous redhead from Chicago walked into our station, and within a year, I was wrongfully accused of her murder, subsequently arrested, tried, convicted, and sentenced to death. If I'm going too fast, let me know.

"Physically, I have constant pain from my right knee, which required reconstructive surgery after a football injury ended my career during my sophomore season at Auburn. I'm told I need more surgery to alleviate the pain and to assure me that I won't be a cripple by the time I reach forty. It's unlikely that I will get that type of medical care here, or for that matter, reach my fortieth birthday, so I'll just take my daily dose of Tylenol and do the best I can. I'm sure you have my bio on your clipboard, so spare me any additional questions and leave me to the peace and solitude that I've actually come to enjoy down here. Good day."

"Michael, I only have a few more questions for you. I'm just doing my job."

"Again, good day, Dr. Fellows." Michael turned away and refused to further acknowledge the doctor's presence.

CHAPTER 49

Michael's move to death row came without any prior warning. The only source of communication with anyone was Willie Williams, the ad seg guard, who brought Michael his three meals each day. With no newspapers or television, and a radio that was barely audible, Michael had lost track of time. A classic introvert whose conversation was limited to an occasional "yes sir" and "no sir," Willie surprised Michael one morning when he said something that made him believe that there was at least one person at SACC who was concerned about his well being.

"Iz thinks you got a raw deal up in Montgomery, Mr. Tyler. You's not the kind of guy who would kill somebody. I hopes you can get free someday. And even though you beat my Crimson Tide with that kickoff return at the end of the game in your freshman year, I kinda likes you."

"Thank you, Willie. I won't complain to you any more about the lousy food or anything else down here. I know, you're just doing your job, but I'm not sorry about that touchdown. Agreed?

"Thass right, Mr. Tyler, but I agree, the food is worse than lousy. I wouldn't serve it to my huntin' dawgs."

That evening Willie told Michael that he would probably be going to death row the next day. He was right. Around noon on May 1, a posse of guards, led by the warden himself, Samuel Gus Wiegert, showed up at Michael's cell door.

"It's time to go," shouted one of the four guards, who all had the features of the cuddly Pillsbury Dough Boy.

"So you're the wise-cracking asshole who gave one of my psychologists a hard time a few days ago," Wiegert said without any formal introduction. "The next time you disrespect one of my staff, you'll find your black ass down here for sixty days or more. Is that understood?"

Michael nodded, but Wiegert wanted more, the self-anointed dictator of this hellhole. "Do you understand, boy?"

"Yes, Warden, I understand. And for the record, my name is Michael, not boy."

"Okay, get your shit together and get a move on. Time to meet your new family on the row." It was then that Michael learned that Cell Block C, which housed one hundred and sixty-eight death row inmates was simply called the "The Row." He also learned that anytime they left their cell, they were hand-cuffed and chained, no matter how short the trip.

After navigating two flights of stairs, which is no easy task with leg irons, they reached tier two of The Row. A badly-contrived chorus of "Dead Man Walking" serenaded Michael's entrance, as all eyes followed the newest member of their fraternity. There were a few "War Eagle" and Roll Tide" chants amidst the ruckus, and even a "fuck you, Wiegert" or two, once the warden was out of sight, but not out of hearing range. It was nothing new to the warden, who seemed to enjoy the wrath of the men for whom he was charged to oversee their deaths someday.

The door to Cell 16 was opened and Michael stepped into his meager surroundings. It was home now, and the stark reality that he would probably die here someday hit him like a thunderbolt. As Grandpa Tyler used to say,"Good or bad, do the best with what you got."

CHAPTER 50

Michael scribbled his name on a form for the warden indicating that the necessities of the cell were there as promised: one cot-sized bed with a three-inch mattress, a lumpy pillow, stainless steel commode and sink, an overhead mirror, a metal table and chair, 12-inch fan, a 14-inch Zenith color TV, and an AM-FM radio. The electronics had been provided by Michael's parents, purchased through his prison bank account, which they had funded with five hundred dollars.

The warden was running his mouth about rules and regulations on The Row, as well as how discipline was enforced when they were broken. Michael's mind was numb from the previous thirty days in ad seg, and the best he could do was nod his head in response to the litany.

He didn't look up as Sam Wiegert and his four lackeys left the cell and endured more insults on their way out. The door to his cell didn't close immediately, so Michael stood in the doorway just enough to block the electronic door from making the connection it needed to let the door close. Michael's neighbor to the right, in Cell 18 said, "If you don't want another thirty days in the hole, it would be wise to step back and let the door close." His name was Frederick Giles, an eleven-year veteran of The Row, who Michael later learned had killed three cops during a drug sting in Birmingham. Cop killers have the shortest life span once they reach The Row, and his appeals were in their final stages. Six months from now, some unfortunate new soul would take his place.

The inmate to Michael's left, in Cell 14, Walter Conway, was the poster child for delayed justice. Conway, who in two weeks would celebrate his twenty-fifth anniversary on death row, had killed an elderly couple in Montgomery, and nobody in the system seemed in a hurry to execute the sixty-five year-old farm laborer. Maybe because both he and the victims were black, or maybe the system had conveniently forgotten about him.

Conway informed Michael he was fortunate he had missed Wednesday's sorry lunch of macaroni and cheese, lukewarm tea, and one slice of stale bread. Among the maze of papers the warden had left behind, Michael found the daily menu for April. May's hadn't been posted yet, but Conway said it seldom, if ever changed.

"Same shit every month, except when there's a holiday, and there ain't enough of those," Conway informed Michael through the bars to his cell. "If you gots some money in your food account, you can get some decent microwaved sandwiches. The sodas are the cheap brands the big grocery chains sell, but at least they're cold and got plenty of sugar in them. Once in a while we can get the better brands, but they cost more."

Michael checked tonight's dinner offering – spaghetti with tomato sauce, one hard roll, and the usual beverages: tea, coffee, or powdered milk. He asked Conway if they could expect the same meal next Thursday.

"And the following Thursday, too."

A prison trustee from general population tossed Michael a backlog of mail through the bars he hadn't been privileged to receive during his first thirty days in solitary confinement and mumbled something about mail regulations. "Read the rules about what kind of mail you can get," was all the gangly con with grotesque arm tattoos had to say. There were a few rejection slips in the packet informing Michael that all magazines had to be ordered through a special mail-order clearing house – just another scheme for the system to make money off its twenty thousand inmates.

Michael made a half-hearted attempt to pore through the list of mail regulations, then tossed it aside and decided that an afternoon nap might improve his spirits.

"Screw the damn rules and screw the State of Alabama."

CHAPTER 51

There is nothing complex about life on death row. Spending twenty-three hours a day in a six by eight cell requires little imagination or planning. The small desk in each cell is bolted to the floor, so rearranging the bed, table, or chair to give one's home a fresh look each spring is negated. Everyone's day is dominated by sleep, watching TV, listening to the radio, reading, letter-writing, and the one hour in the recreation yard. Not a lot of options, and they're the same every day.

Sleep at any time is a monumental challenge. Concrete walls and steel bars do nothing to cushion the noise ricocheting through the tiers from loud music or the shouts and screams of despairing men railing at the system that has them marked for death. The prison cuts the power to the TVs at midnight, but the radios are allowed to play throughout the night. Guards are supposed to patrol the tiers, threatening ad seg time for loud music, but enforcement entails mountains of paperwork they'd rather not have to deal with. And who could blame them?

Death row is special in another way: while the great majority of the condemned men openly admitted their guilt, the common denominator among them was their unwillingness to discuss the details of their crimes. Walter Conway explained it to Michael in the simplest terms. "We all know you killed somebody, we just don't need to hear the sordid details. It ain't nothing to be proud of." In Michael Tyler's case, since he was a former football star at Auburn, everybody knew the details without his telling them.

Talking through the bars one day, Conway said, "Once you beat the mental aspect of The Row – and hopefully you will – how you handle it physically doesn't matter. Take Jimmy Collins, the fat slob three cells down from me. Ole' Jimmy weighs 350 pounds, seldom goes out for exercise, stuffs his mouth with candy bars every day, immerses himself in soap operas and comic books, and is the most docile guy on The Row. He says that even if the State kills him, which they will, they haven't beaten him. He's bragged that he hasn't shed a tear in here. Wanna know what he did to get here?"

"No."

"Okay, you wouldn't believe it anyway."

"Good."

Conway believed in Michael's innocence, but told him about a guy on row two of The Row who had proclaimed that the State had convicted the wrong guy. "They executed him two years ago, and a month later the real killer broke his fifteen-year silence. He's up on row three, a real asswipe if there ever was one. Let me say this, Michael. He's really fortunate he's not in my rec yard group, because I'd dice him up like cubed ham. And then there's nice guys like you and me."

With Walter's daily philosophical tidbits, Michael managed to make it through the first year in better mental shape than he could have ever imagined. Walter's favorite saying was straight out of the movie *Shawshank Redemption:* "Get busy living, or get busy dying."

Another bond the fraternity shared on The Row was poverty. "Ain't no wealthy folks in here," Walter lamented one day. "The brothers might think they're special with all them cheap-ass gold-plated rings and earrings they sport, but none of us got a portfolio of Fortune 500 stocks."

Michael was thankful his parents had supported him financially, which made him the exception to almost everyone else. He did his best to get in a daily routine of calisthenics: push-ups, sit-ups, anything to stretch his physically impaired knee. He was never big into rep counting, like his teammates in high school did, so when he tired of them, he just quit. One of the guys on The Row claimed to have done 258 push-ups in one day – an odd number – and boasted that it was a Row record. Walter's reply was: "He killed three people, lied about it at his trial, and still does today." Walter had an answer and opinion for anything and everything.

Letter-writing became a passion to pass the time. The inmates get all kinds of mail from people wanting to be their pen pals, a favorable practice that most guys accepted, because it's just more people from whom they could beg stamps, money, books, and magazines. They couldn't have cared less about the writers' lives on the outside, and how sorry they felt about the inmates' situations. Of course, nobody ever wanted to trade places with them.

Michael's parents and Pastor Roberts were avid letter-writers, and they kept him well supplied with stamps, some of which he gave to other guys who were fortunate to receive a dozen a year. Other friends from the Law Center and Channel 10 wrote occasional letters wishing him the best on his appeals.

All incoming mail went through a small post office in the administration building, where it was opened, checked for contraband, and briefly scanned by a clerk for inappropriate language, sexual messages or photos, threats to staff, and even bizarre plans to rescue someone from The Row. Some first-time letter writers weren't aware that their mail was censored before being delivered to the inmates, so it wasn't unusual that an occasional letter reached the prison promoting an escape plan. Such letters are taken seriously, and the plotters receive a visit from their local sheriff that any future letters of this kind could result in jail time. The inappropriate letters were returned to the sender with a "rejection" notice and an explanation for the rejection.

The irony of letter-writing was that outgoing mail was not censored, and the envelope carried a disclaimer that the SACC believed in at least one premise of the First Amendment. To the inmates, the mail clerk was just another in a long line of faceless people who dealt with their dismal existence.

CHAPTER 52

Six months to the day he spent his first night in ad seg, Michael's parents, and Pastor Roberts made the trip south for their initial visit. Ralph could have done without the Lord's messenger, but he accepted the ride the preacher offered in the new Cadillac the church had given him on his twenty-fifth anniversary as Pastor. Ralph had suggested giving the Pastor his rusted-out Pontiac Chieftain as a substitute to the Caddy, but Margaret had scolded him for his lack of respect for the clergy.

The visitors' meeting area, which had been nicknamed the "Dead-End Lounge," was a bland, unappealing room large enough to accommodate eight standard picnic tables. The walls were painted the prison's favorite color, mint green, and there was nothing to suggest the decorator had wasted any time or imagination in creating a sense of warmth for the condemned men and their special guests.

Margaret's hug reminded Michael of the time he'd left her side at a Fourth of July parade in Greenville, when he was only four. After a frantic thirty-minute search, he was discovered sound asleep under the bandstand. Given a minor reprimand, she'd swept him into her arms, nearly suffocating him and then rewarding him with a two-scoop ice cream cone. Michael had thought that if this was the prize for an afternoon nap, he would gladly take more of them.

Pastor Roberts was a step ahead of Ralph and whispered some scripture about the Lord's plan to save Michael. Ralph was last in the receiving line, and he gave Michael his usual firm handshake and a pat on the back, as he'd done the first time Michael scored a touchdown in a youth football game. He was irritated that he had take off his shoes for the contraband check, and Pastor Roberts thought the clergy should be exempt from this minor intrusion. Margaret was in flip-flops and offered a polite "thank you" to the guard after they all had passed inspection.

Visits were limited to three hours, but Michael was told that a ten-dollar tip to the captain of the guard detail would get an extra hour. There were four guards in the room, all armed with enough fire power to thwart any plans to bolt through the front door, which was surprisingly, just a hundred feet away. The ever-observant Pastor, who always spoke in whispers, said, "Don't they ever smile?"

"I don't know, Pastor Roberts, this is my first time in the room." And no, they didn't smile for the entire three hours that his guests were there, pestering Michael with questions about how he managed to keep his sanity for twenty-three hours a day in a six-by-eight cell. There were twelve other guys from The Row with their guests, two that Michael knew from his rec yard crew. Eddie Stevens, one of the few on The Row who passionately declared his innocence, came over to their table and asked Pastor Roberts to pray for him.

The activity in the room was closely observed when wives and girlfriends of their loved ones tried to share their affection with the men who had forever forfeited any heterosexual relationships on the day they walked through the front door to The Row. Michael was hoping the testosterone levels were low today, so Pastor Roberts wouldn't get new material for a Sunday sermon. Unfortunately, a couple next to them were engaging in under-the-table massaging that had caught the Pastor's attention, and he put his hand to a cross that hung from a gold chain that was always part of his wardrobe. He whispered again to Michael, "Does that go on all the time ?"

Michael responded as he had done the first time he was asked about the guards' demeanor. "I don't know Pastor Roberts, this is the ...."

"Yeah, I know. This is your first time here."

From time to time, a guard would shout, "Okay, everybody. Hands on top of the tables."

Michael apprised them of the appeals process, indicating that his first appeal to the Alabama Court of Criminal Appeals, was being prepared by Anthony Romano. His mother wondered why he would wait six months to file the first appeal, but he told her about Walter Conway. "I'm not in any hurry, mom, and the courts aren't either."

It was approaching late afternoon, and it was time for them to head back to Greenville. Pastor Roberts had to prepare for his Wednesday night prayer service and Margaret would have to change into her church clothes. Ralph's tattered blue jeans and orange golf shirt would have to do. They hugged, kissed, and shed a few tears as they left, a routine they would follow on all future visits.

CHAPTER 53

One of the few death row perks is the one hour each day the inmates spent in the recreation yard, or "the cage," as they referred to it. The area, which was enclosed by a sixteen-foot chain link fence with the usual forbidding razor wire, provided one half court for basketball and a second for volleyball. There was a walking area around the courts for the non-athletic types, of which there were many on The Row.

Michael was in a group of twenty-four that used the yard from two to three in the afternoon, rain or shine. Depending on the whim of the yard captain, the times could change every month or so, with no reason given for the change. They considered it a minor inconvenience, or just another change in their daily routine, over which the system had total control.

On Michael's first visit to the cage, he met Bobby Rae Quinton, a self-proclaimed redneck from North Alabama, who had hit The Row three years before Michael's arrival for the macabre killing of his parents one Christmas morning. Unrepentant and cavalier, Quinton was a basketball legend of sorts, leading his high school team to a pair of state basketball championships while setting Alabama career-scoring records in his senior season. He once scored 73 points in a single game, but for all his marvelous talents on the court, Bobby Rae was a hopeless, but likeable, screw-up off it. It all came honestly.

The last of eight children born to Elizabeth and William Quinton, Bobby Rae had endured mental and physical hardships from the dysfunctional Quinton gang that had ultimately driven him to a cell on The Row. A chronic bed-wetter until he was eight, which earned him countless trips to a dark closet and severe whippings for his problem, Bobby Rae was cursed by the family tree with intellectual incompetence. Only two of his older brothers had made it through high school, while the others set records for truancy and trouble before gladly accepting permanent suspension from school. Bobby Rae became the family whipping boy for anything that was wrong with the clan, and there was an ample supply of it. He was unmercifully taunted for a stuttering impediment that made it difficult for him to string together a coherent sentence of ten or more words.

Only one month after dropping out of an area junior college, where he had hoped to improve the academic deficiencies he needed to earn an athletic scholarship, Bobby Rae had calmly walked into his parents' bedroom and bludgeoned them to death with a Louisville Slugger – the same bat with which, he'd hit twelve home runs as a senior outfielder on his high school baseball team.

After a short two-day trial, when asked if he had anything to say before being sentenced to death, he boasted, "I should've killed all the sons of bitches in the family. If you let me out for twenty-four hours, I'll complete the job, Your Honor."

It wasn't difficult to notice his superb athletic talents as he gracefully drained three-point baskets with ease, or finished off a drive through the lane with an array of spectacular dunks that left his audience speechless.

"Ain't bad for a white dude," Michael thought. "Not bad at all."

Bobby Rae's six-foot-five frame was blessed with exceptional jumping ability and ball-handling skills that would have served him well at the collegiate level, but the scholarship offers waned when his social and academic shortcomings couldn't be overlooked.

CHAPTER 54

Michael and Bobby Rae became instant friends, and often treated the other inmates to the spectacle of one-on-one games where soda and candy bars were wagered on the outcome. Michael had been a better-than-average player in high school, making his mark on defense with his speed and quickness, and always pushed Bobby Rae to the limit. He just wished he could shoot better.

That winter, with three other marginal players, they won the 22nd Annual Death Row Tournament, beating off the challenges of twenty other teams. They wanted to play the champion of the general population league in a best-of-three playoff, but the warden nixed that idea, citing security reasons. Anything out of the ordinary always fell under the all-imposing security blanket.

Bobby Rae was the judicial victim of bad legal counsel for the first capital murder case in Sand Mountain in eighteen years. Johnny Shaw, a twenty-six-year-old litigator, who had finally passed the bar exam on his third attempt, and wasn't on any law firm's list of recruits, was assigned Quinton's trial, after reluctantly accepting a position in the newly-created Public Defender's Office, which served four counties in northeastern Alabama.

Shaw had convinced Quinton to plead guilty, which considering his confession and the bat with his bloody fingerprints on it, made it an impossible case to defend. I'll persuade the prosecutor to give you life without parole to escape the death penalty," Shaw boasted. "It's a slam-dunk."

"Yeah, man, I know all about dunks," Bobby Rae joked.

The jury complied with the request, but Circuit Court Judge Robert Donaldson had overridden the jury's sentence, and under Alabama's controversial law, said that Quinton deserved death.

Shaw had feebly raised Quinton's miserable upbringing as the one and only mitigating issue at trial, but the inexperienced and overworked lawyer had a backlog of cases that were easier to fix than a death penalty case. His only shining moment in the trial was his closing argument, when he said, "The parents of Bobby Rae deserved to be killed." That brought a strong rebuke from the judge, who cited Shaw for "outrageous courtroom behavior" and fined the young attorney five hundred dollars. He never paid it.

Bobby Rae said, "Going somewhere that I'll get at least three squares a day for maybe the next fifteen years ain't all that bad." He wasn't aware of the death row menus at SACC, as they weren't known for their Southern cuisine.

The word had spread quickly throughout The Row that Michael was a former law student, which, given the inadequate counsel most death row inmates experienced at trial, prompted some to seek out his advice as their hopeless appeals chugged their way through the tedious system.

Michael's first adventure into legal counseling involved his basketball teammate, Bobby Rae. When a defendant loses in court with a Public Defender, they generally lose them through the appeals process. Two factors work against them: first, the PD's case load is immense, and second, they have little or no experience in capital murder cases. Bobby Rae's case had no meaningful defense, other than the condemnation of his parents and wretched siblings for his loathsome upbringing.

Quinton's trial did have a few improprieties, and though there was never any question of his guilt, a new hearing could question the judge's sentence override and award the State of Alabama custody of Bobby Rae for the rest of his natural life. Michael said he would look into it.

Michael was in regular communication with Professor Robert Mullins at the Law Center, and he paid for and was sent a copy of Bobby Rae's trial transcript. For a trial that had lasted only two days, there were one hundred pages to the transcript which was replete with spelling errors. The professor made a rare visit to Michael and urged him to continue his law studies. "I will provide you with all the material you'll need, and when you're ready, let me know and I'll make the necessary arrangements for you to take the bar exam. We'll have to be creative and find a way to work around the law regarding convicted felons from taking the exam, but the fact that you'll be representing death row clients, and not appearing in court might be the exception you need. Boy, won't this turn the legal world upside down?"

After Mullins left, Michael returned to his cell, put out the "closed for business sign" and took a well-deserved nap. Another five-star dinner was only an hour away.

CHAPTER 55

Two years into Michael's incarceration, he was notified that the warden wished to see him in his office across the complex. It wasn't unusual for Sam Wiegert to visit The Row, but after his last trip to deliver a death warrant had resulted in the usual obscenities and chaos, he passed the duty on to an administrative assistant. And, as expected, he too incurred the same wrath of the fraternity.

Chained and shackled, Michael was escorted in a prison van to the warden's office for their first meeting since he had berated Michael on his last day in solitary. Then the first of several unusual events transpired. First Wiegert asked the guard to remove the chains, and then told him to leave the room, which brought a strong protest from Kevin Miller, The Row guard.

"But, sir, it's against prison policy, especially for someone from The Row not to have a guard present at all times."

"Thank you, Kevin, for your concern, but we'll be fine. I'll call you when Michael and I are finished here so you can take him back to The Row."

Then free of his chains, Michael was asked to take a seat across from the warden's expansive desk, which had all the trappings of a neatness freak. Family pictures, sports mementoes, and papers were all arraigned in a seemingly specific spot.

"Could I get you a cup of coffee, Michael? It's probably a little better than what you get on The Row."

Michael wisely let Wiegert's suggestion pass, not wanting to get into a discussion on the prison food, knowing it would never improve, but after a sip, he concurred, "Yes, it's a major upgrade, sir."

"Michael, there are several reasons for this visit. Your bio here says you have extensive knowledge of computers and their inner workings. Says you've built them from scratch with used parts that would make Compaq and IBM envious. Over the next six months, the entire prison system's computer division will undergo major changes, which we are told will save the ACS money and make the prisons more efficient. Can't promise it will improve the food service, but you never know.

"I can offer you a job, maybe two or three days a week, around fifteen hours or so. That's the good part. Now the not-so-good. I can only pay you the current federal minimum wage of $5.15 an hour, compared to the $25.00 an hour for the technicians that will be hired in the other prisons around the state. But you can milk the job for as long as it takes, because you'll have little or no supervision. I'll catch some flack from a few politicians, but it's nothing I can't handle."

Tossing several manuals across the desk, the warden said, "Please, look these over and let me know if you're interested."

Michael found it difficult to separate the man who had once told him that he would have his "black ass" back in the hole if he should disrespect his staff, from the one now basically kissing his ass to take his minimum wage job. Michael did the math quickly, and accepted without any reservations. State and Federal taxes would have to be withheld, but the two men shared a lighthearted moment when the warden said Social Security taxes would be waived. *Good point, Warden. Won't be around to collect, will I?*

"Secondly, you may have noticed that on the end of each tier, there are two cells that are slightly larger that than one you now occupy. Believe they're 8x10 which gives you ....?"

"Thirty-two more square feet of space," Michael interjected.

"Yeah, something like that. Anyway, they were built with the idea that model prisoners on The Row could occupy them after their first two years here. You have zero disciplinary reports, so you qualify. You can move into one of them this week if you'd like.

"One last thing. I hear you're helping some of the inmates with their appeals. You'll be glad to know that a group of defense lawyers around the state have donated $250,000 to build a law library adjacent to The Row, complete with legal case books and other reading material – novels and magazines. It should be completed in about three months, and after the ribbon-cutting, I'll give you a few extra hours on the weekends to help the guys with their appeals. For helping us install the new computer programs, I'll provide you one in your new cell, with limited internet access. Now, am I such a bad ass, Michael?"

"No, Warden, a good ass." They laughed again.

When Michael returned to his cell, there were letters from his attorney, his parents, and a woman in Arizona with a marriage proposal. Marilyn Williams had written Michael several times, but each letter had been ignored. Williams, a recent parolee for drug trafficking, demanded a response or said, "she would be searching for a new beau."

Death row inmates were the target of publicity-seeking women from around the world who had a fetish for seeking relationships with condemned men. There was a national website and a monthly magazine, *Connecting With Cons,* that consisted mostly of naked women showing off their wares to men who had no access to them through the mail in any of Alabama's prisons. But that didn't stop them from being brought in by other means – SACC staff or visitors.

Margaret's letters followed a familiar path. "Keep the faith, Michael, God will intervene. We all know you didn't commit this horrible crime."

Michael and his father had respectfully tolerated his mother's devotion to the church, and from the first day he could remember, they had always walked up the aisle to row three, seats one through three. A sizeable financial contribution to the church earned the parishioners reserved seating. Ralph never thought to ask what it had cost, and it wouldn't have mattered if he'd known. Even a kindly protest fell on deaf ears when it came to the church and what "God expected from the Tylers."

Anthony Romano's letter informed Michael that he would no longer be representing him through his appeals. "I regret that I will not be able to assist you in the future. My expertise, as you know, is in tort law, and I would be remiss to think that I can bring your case to a successful conclusion. If you like, I can refer you to several outstanding lawyers who have extensive experience in the appeals system. You have my best wishes."

Michael was expecting Romano's departure, if

for no other reason than a lack of communication between the two since his first appeal to the Alabama Court of Criminal Appeals in round one of the appeals, which questioned Judge Brendle's override of the jury's sentence with a not-so-subtle hint that his other reversals regarding black defendants were disturbing, if not downright racist. This wasn't the first appeal based on Brendle's sentencing history, and in each case his decision was upheld. The next steps in round one were to the Alabama Supreme Court and the United States Supreme Court.

CHAPTER 56

It took Michael all of thirty minutes to move his worldly possessions to his new home on the south end of row two. The first thing he noticed was a small window – maybe a foot square – that he could reach if he stood on his chair. The first night, he could see the moon passing by on its journey westward through the clear black sky. His mother was a moon-gazer, and he remembered the times when his dog Hercules would join them on the back porch, caught up in its wonder. "One of God's great gifts," Margaret reverently called it.

His new computer was delivered a week later, along with an extra table, a chair, and a small lamp. He'd been given limited internet access to reference material, but he was initially unable to send or receive email. The captain of The Row, Johnny Davis, whose hobby was woodworking, made a small sign that read "Michael Tyler, Attorney at Law." It wasn't wishful thinking.

Michael went to work on his next appeal, again citing the bias in jury overrides by Judge Brian Brendle. He figured he had a better chance of winning the lottery, which had finally been approved by a state referendum; the same people who keep one-third of Alabama's sixty-seven counties free of alcohol, but like the ridiculous odds of winning millions with a one-dollar investment that was theoretically designed to help the state's ailing public school system. The same dollar got you a cold can of beer and a better feeling for the moment.

About a month after moving in to his new "apartment", Michael looked up to see Captain Davis, who had stopped by and said he had a visitor – his new attorney. All visitors have to be pre-approved by the ACS, and this includes attorneys who are not assigned to a particular case. "I don't have an outside attorney," Michael told Davis. "You're looking at the only person close to being an attorney, Captain, and that's me."

"Well, Michael, a Mr. Bruno Romano is in the visitors' lounge wishing to speak with you. I checked with the warden, and he said he'd waive all the paperwork, so you could talk with him now."

Bruno Romano, founder of the Alabama Defense Project, and a first cousin to Anthony, stood to greet Michael when he entered the Dead-End Lounge. "Thank you, Michael, for seeing me on such short notice. I'm on my way to Mobile for a seminar on DNA tomorrow, and I was hoping we could talk about your case. I'd like the Defense Project to represent you through the rest of your appeals."

Michael reminded him that the first Romano defense strategy hadn't turned out too well, but said he would listen. He had plenty of time for that. "So what's your plan, Mr. Romano?"

"Look, Michael, Tony's defense wasn't one of his better courtroom moments. Not calling you to testify was a monumental error, and I still don't understand his motive for that. And, I've got a much better resume in criminal law."

If Bruno was fishing for a compliment, Michael didn't acknowledge it when Bruno told him about his most recent success story, rescuing a South Carolina woman from the electric chair just two weeks ago. He would pen another best-selling novel, traverse through the book signings and media interviews, and maybe find time for one of God's lost souls on death row.

"What do you have in mind, Mr. Romano?"

Bruno corrected him. "It's Bruno, Michael."

"Okay, Bruno, I'm all ears."

CHAPTER 57

Bruno suggested they sack the jury overriding issue and switch to ineffective counsel when round two in the Rule 32 hearing began.

Michael was surprised to hear this from a close family member who had once practiced law with Anthony before their career paths took them in different directions. "Bruno, you want to attack your first cousin for providing ineffective counsel? That should make for some interesting family gatherings, wouldn't you agree?"

Bruno laughed at the suggestion. "Neither Tony nor I make many of them, Michael. We're too busy running around the country saving or suing people. Why do you think I'm paying five thousand a month in alimony and support payments to an ex-wife? I spend more time in hotels and motels outside of Alabama than I do in my office, which is now my new home. I have enough frequent flyer miles to get me around the world a few times."

"Bruno, no disrespect intended here, but I've researched the ineffective counsel concept to death." He smiled at his own choice of words. "First we must show that counsel's errors were so egregious as to deprive me of a fair trial, and that his legal representation prejudiced my defense."

Bruno had heard the argument before. "Michael, first put aside the family ties. As people like to say, that train has already left the station. And don't worry about Tony. He's a big boy, and he can take the heat, even if it's from his own family. He tried to make his case in closing, calling no witnesses, in particular you. This isn't an old Perry Mason case where Raymond Burr points the finger at someone in the courtroom and says dramatically, "There's the guilty one."

Now, here's a little recent history on Brendle's jury overrides in the past two years. He's let the life without parole sentences of three black defendants cases stand. But he overrode two white defendants for the same exact sentences and sent them to death row: Ty Mitchell and Casper Williams from the Birmingham area. You know them?"

"No, Bruno, The Row doesn't sponsor afternoon socials where we sit around eating cake and ice cream, sharing our miserable stories, and wondering what we could have done to be anywhere but in this God-forsaken hole. I have daily contact with twenty or so guys in the rec yard, and six more I'm helping with their appeals." He paused. "Sorry for my attitude. It wasn't meant to be personal."

"No offense taken, Michael. Look, you're an extremely bright young man, and you and you alone will determine what course of action we take from this day on. Now that you have your computer, I want you to research the other two states, Delaware and Florida, that allow jury overrides. Look for any racial bias in the sentences, and if there are any, we'll take a realistic look at it. But let me caution you, Michael: Alabama judges don't like tossing their peers under the bus. Brendle knows it – not one of his fifteen overrides has been overturned, and there's no indication it will take a drastic change.

"The appellate courts are full of judges who enjoy their privacy and whose circle of friends are pretty much each other, and castigating one on a lower court – in effect calling one a racist – isn't going to happen. Since the mid-1970s, there have been close to ninety jury overrides in the state, and the vast majority of them have been upheld. However, Brendle is apparently checking his scorecard, and maybe that's the reason Mitchell and Williams are here. Take your time in preparing your next appeal. I hear the courts are backed up almost a year. And they call this a cost-effective program," he said cynically.

"Oh, and one other point. I talked with Professor Mullins at the Center about you taking the bar exam. He said he's working with a state representative from Montgomery to sneak in an amendment on the state budget bill to allow you special status to take the exam. Hell, half those clowns don't have a clue what they're voting on sometimes. We'll keep you posted."

Two weeks later, Bruno called Michael to inform him the amendment was one of one hundred and twenty-eight that were passed in the budget bill. Other than the representative who authored the amendment, neither member of the Alabama Senate or House of Representatives had questioned it, or even noticed it.

CHAPTER 58

Michael's initial appeals to the Alabama Court of Criminal Appeals, the Alabama Supreme Court, and the United States Supreme Court, took only three years to receive denials, but it was the dissenting opinion by the latter court in a five-to-four decision that may have offered hope for future appeals on jury overrides. The court's minority opinion, written by Justice Herman Rankowski, questioned the "power" of the Alabama Circuit Court judges in sentencing. He went on to say, "The fact that only three states allow this practice is very disturbing."

With all the books and materials he needed to complete the remaining year of his studies at the Center, Michael spent days and nights studying, and taking quizzes that were available on the Center's web site. Captain Davis would be present for the tests, assuring the Center that Michael had no access to notes or books. Whatever else anybody thought of him, nobody could label him a cheater.

In May, Michael notified Professor Mullins that he was ready to take the bar exam. Mullins then wrote Warden Wiegert, asking that Michael be allowed to return to Montgomery to take the test with thirty other applicants. Wiegert gave his approval, but the ACS said no, claiming security reasons that might arise if the public were made aware of the plan. The ACS believed that all death row inmates were the pitiful rabble of society, and were embarrassed to admit that Michael Tyler was an exception to their cast of misfits on The Row.

Later in the summer, Professor Mullins and two attorneys of the examining board arrived at SACC at 10:00 a.m. to administer the three-day, fifteen-hour exam in the law library that would encompass areas of family, criminal and constitutional law, arbitration, contracts, evidence, torts, and other subjects.

Professor Mullins was accustomed to seeing Michael in chains and shackles, but his associates were taken aback when he shuffled into the room with two armed guards at his side. Michael assured them that they were in no danger of harm in the presence of a convicted killer, and if they felt uncomfortable, Captain Jackson would give them the ten-dollar tour of The Row. They declined the invitation, indicating they had brought enough reading material to pass the time while he took the exam, which consisted of ten different segments. They took a break for lunch at 1:30, and through the generosity of Warden Wiegert, didn't have to endure the overcooked grilled cheese sandwiches, which were on the lunch menu every other Wednesday. Wiegert had some barbecue sandwiches delivered from Sammy's Grill down the road from the complex, along with strong iced tea, not the watered-down version the prison kitchen served.

Michael finished the first three segments in a little less than five hours, confident that his strict preparation had served him well. The final two days took all the time that was allotted – ten hours – and he signed all the documents attesting that he, Michael Cummings Tyler, had taken the exam in the presence of Professor Mullins and the two attorneys from the examining board. They said their goodbyes, wished him well, and went back to their normal lives. Michael went back to cell 24.

One month later, Professor Mullins informed Michael that he'd posted the third-highest score of the thirty-one who had taken the test. Michael was now licensed to practice law in the State of Alabama, or was he?

A state representative who practiced law in north Alabama and needed two attempts to pass the Bar screamed to anyone willing to listen that it was a travesty and a disgrace to the state of Alabama to have a death row prisoner admitted to the Bar. But when it was revealed that the representative's two DUI's and numerous speeding tickets had been squashed by a local judge, he shut up. In the fall elections, he was voted out of office by a constituency, who instead favored a former classmate of Michael's at the Center. Justice had been served.

Any attempts to bill the state for Michael's legal work were suppressed when the new Attorney General, whom he would meet later down the legal road, ruled what kind of money an inmate could earn as a ward of the state. He quoted some obscure rule written back in the 1930s that limited what inmates could make in the prison system. Making license plates and working on chain gangs qualified for a dollar-a-day in wages, but not a con asking for fifty dollars an hour – a pittance as legal fees went – to help his brothers on The Row.

Michael suspected, and he was right, that his law degree would come back to haunt him. He had become a national news story, and the legal minds in the state were tiring of the publicity a death row inmate had generated. Warden Wiegert had reluctantly paved the way for the popular Legal News Channel, *On Trial*, that had covered Michael's trial for a follow-up story, and *MSNBC* and *FOX* were waiting in the wings.

The patience of the ACS and the Attorney General's office was also wearing thin, as Michael's notoriety continued after passing the bar exam. An outspoken Montgomery radio station talk show host, who advocated that the death penalty should be carried out twenty-four hours after conviction, was critical of the ACS, and, in particular, of Warden Wiegert, for allowing the media access to Michael. But the warden had too many allies in the Prison Oversight Commission, who were overly impressed with his fiscal and organizational management skills. SACC was the most cost-effective prison of the six maximum prisons in the state, and the prevailing opinion was that Grover Hersbacher, the ACS Commissioner, took his orders from Sam Wiegert.

Michael's research into judicial overrides in Delaware and Florida confirmed that the two differed greatly from Alabama, and were rarely used. He was convinced that if enough of these appeals reached the high court, the practice would, at last, face the scrutiny it deserved.

Michael's first case as an attorney was a Rule 32 hearing that sought relief for Travis Mulhaney, a 35-year-old black man convicted in the death of a convenience store clerk during a robbery attempt in Hoover, Alabama. Mulhaney was an accomplice in the robbery and shooting death of a high school cheer-leader, but wasn't in the store at the time of the shooting. Mulhaney was waiting in the getaway car while a friend from high school shot the clerk when she refused to open a small safe behind the counter.

As his attorney, Michael requested the Attorney General's permission to represent Mulhaney in the Birmingham Circuit Court, where Judge Brian Brendle had overriden his life without parole sentence. Randall Simmons, who had succeeded Winston Kennedy as Attorney General, thought the idea was novel to have one convicted killer represent another. Brendle, though, wanted no part of what he thought was a publicity stunt, and asked the State Supreme Court to step in and keep Tyler on the sidelines. They agreed, citing the standard ACS policy of security reasons. Michael handed off the appeal to Professor Mullins, who eloquently, but unsuccessfully, argued his brief.

CHAPTER 59

In any of the thirty-two states that use the death penalty as the ultimate punishment for specific crimes, there is no practical rationale in its application. In Alabama, some defendants spend less than ten years on The Row, while others, like Walter Conway, occupy a cell for twenty-five years or longer before being executed, or having their sentences commuted to life without parole. One of Conway's briefs in the second phase of his appeals was hung up for seven years before it was denied.

Michael wasn't experiencing the same good fortune, and he knew why. The appellate court system was punishing him for his relentless opposition to the jury overrides he was using on six different cases by rushing through his own appeals with uncanny speed. He ignored Bruno Romano's suggestion to sack the override issue, and started the second round of his own appeals at the Rule 32 hearing, determined that he could either change the law or die trying.

Shortly after the Mulhaney appeals to the Circuit Court, Michael received a letter from Professor Mullins and Bruno, requesting an emergency meeting. This was no ordinary visit.

"They're out to get you, Michael," Bruno said after barely taking a seat in the new law library.

"He means the Alabama Appellate court system, Michael," Professor Mullins added.

"You mean a conspiracy," Michael asked.

"Yes, Bruno assured him. "Last week, a law clerk from one of the Alabama appellate courts, who will remain anonymous, visited me in Montgomery. He was disturbed, and rightly so, about several emails circulating between the justices of the courts that suggested Michael Tyler's own appeals, and those of the death row inmates he was representing be handled expeditiously."

"Bottom line, gentlemen," Michael said, "they want me dead?"

"I wouldn't go quite that far, Michael," Bruno explained. "To the appellate courts, there's a difference between a lawyer on death row and one in private practice questioning judicial overrides. Is it right? No. But that's what you're facing here. The Mulhaney decision took only two months before Judge Brendle denied the appeal. Your latest appeal for Bobby Rae Quinton to the Alabama Supreme Court was turned down six months after the appeal was argued. The average time between the oral arguments and the court's decision is one to three years, but the clerk said Quinton's denial was released ahead of six other cases that were argued two years before his."

Michael inquired, "And how long will the law clerk remain anonymous?"

"Forever," Bruno said. "For an appellate clerk to divulge highly privileged communications between justices is a career-ending move, should it ever be revealed he ratted out his superiors. It's incredible to believe that the internet was used for these communications, but then nothing surprises me anymore in our profession."

Michael smiled briefly, and Professor Mullins

inquired what he found so amusing about the latest developments.

"Well," he said jokingly, "in lieu of taking a seat in the Yellow Mama, we'd better find a way to get me out of here by unconventional means."

"Michael, before you try walking out the front door, get to work on your Rule 32 hearing," Mullins suggested. "Whether you go with ineffective counsel or jury overrides, the success rate is almost nil. The Cubs have a better chance of winning the World Series, but it's a necessary step in the exhausting process. The clock is running, young man; a lot faster than the day you first walked in here."

Michael, however, wouldn't be deterred. Recent studies showed that ineffective counsel appeals were wearing thin at the Federal level because of their frequent use. Appellate judges were concerned that their use was damaging to the legal profession, and they showed their hostility to them with routine denials.

The professor was right. The clock was running faster, and his appeals were zipping through the system with alarming efficiency. Over the next four years, he had concluded his second trip to the U.S. Supreme Court. The Court concurred with their first opinion with one less vote in Michael's favor. Judge Rankowski had since retired, and his successor was a conservative Federal judge from New York, who in his confirmation hearings before Congress, steadfastly testified he was pro-death penalty.

CHAPTER 60

One month after Michael's appeal to the U.S. Supreme Court was denied, he received a letter from a Mississippi man who professed to be a journalist, wanting to visit him under the premise of writing a book on Michael's life, and others on The Row. John Wilheim had received Sam Wiegert's approval, and in early February, Wilheim and a photographer, Marcus Archer, showed up at The Row shortly after lunch.

Wilheim had requested that the interviews be done without the intimidating presence of the guards, citing the reluctance of Michael and other inmates to tell it like it is on The Row. Wiegert had acquiesced and had made arrangements for them to meet in the law library for three hours. They would be allowed to tour The Row for one hour, take pictures and interview a sampling of inmates, including Bobby Rae, who, like Michael, was running out of appeals.

Wilheim was an engaging "good ole' boy" from the South, who embraced the charm and history of his upbringing in the Mississippi Delta. He was a third-generation cotton farmer-turned-author, who had left the cotton fields to his younger brothers and their offspring to carry on the family tradition. Wilheim's first adventure in publishing was a classic bomb on the history of cotton farming in the South, which had sold all of 867 books. But his second effort, "*The Killing of James Dawson,*" a black man from Pass Christian,

Mississippi, wrongfully executed for a double homicide he didn't commit, made the *New York Times* Best Seller List, where it remained for five weeks. Michael Tyler and his life on Alabama's death row would be his third editorial endeavor.

He had explained in his letter that he was an Auburn alumnus from the class of 1970, which put him in his early fifties. A slender man with dark, horn-rimmed glasses and boyish features, Wilheim had made a good trade when he swapped farming for writing.

While the warden was personally giving Marcus Archer and his camera the grand tour of death row, including the death chamber where the executions were carried out, Wilheim was peppering Michael with questions that had no limitations. They talked about the conditions on The Row: the food; the monotony of being caged in a cell for twenty-three hours a day; the oppressive heat from May through September; the indifference of some of the guards; the inadequate medical care; and, at the top of the list, the separation from family and friends. Michael took him on a trip through the frustrating appeals system, as well as a few of the cases he was working on for some of his friends on The Row. Wilheim was particularly impressed with Michael's passing the bar exam on his first attempt, even though his practice was limited to death row inmates. A recording device which separated them across the table and could record three hours of conversation was now in its second hour.

They left the room to visit The Row, where they would talk with the six inmates Michael had chosen to be interviewed. Bobby Rae, as expected, was the undisputed jewel of the six that Wilheim interviewed.

Despite his life-long stammering, he took Wilheim on a painstaking journey through his persecuted life that had concluded with own death wish when he had sent his tormenting parents off to hell, courtesy of a Louisville Slugger. Wilheim was surprised that Bobby Rae had found peace on The Row, and given the choice between life or death, the latter was acceptable. Bobby Rae embraced Michael warmly when Marcus took pictures of them on the basketball court where they had first met and had become inseparable friends.

"Hey, guys, I can still dunk the dang basketball," Quinton bragged to Marcus. "How about one for the book?" Bobby Rae started at half-court, doing three crossover dribbles before unmercifully ramming the ball through the worn-out hoop with a dazzling two-handed reverse dunk that left the visitors in awe.

Wilheim seemed mesmerized by Bobby's effortless talent and whispered to Michael, "He's something special. Didn't think white guys could jump like that."

Michael whispered back, "Maybe he has some bloodlines we're not aware of."

Wilheim asked Bobby Rae if he wanted some of Archer's pictures sent home to his family. "The only family I have is here on The Row, Mr. Wilheim. I've been here for twelve years, and not one of those sons of bitches up north has ever written or visited me. 'Scuse my language, gentlemen, but fuck 'em. And the bat I used to kill my momma and daddy should be in Cooperstown."

Before they left, Wilheim slipped a small cell phone into Michael's pants pocket and instructed him on its use. "Outgoing calls have been blocked; the phone will vibrate when you have an incoming call. A battery charger will be delivered to you in a few days by a prison guard. There is a plan in motion to get you out of here sometime later this year, but we know nothing about the details."

Michael didn't respond at first, and Wilheim asked Michael if he had heard him correctly. "I don't know what to say. How do you expect to pull that off? Nobody's ever come close to escaping The Row. We all like to think it's a far-fetched possibility, but how?"

Wilheim insisted he knew nothing of the plan or anybody behind it. "Our only role was to give you this cell phone. Captain Davis is the only person on The Row that knows you have one. Be careful, don't let the other guards see you with it. Okay?"

"Yeah, I've got a good place to conceal it."

That concluded the first of two visits they would make to The Row, and three days later as promised, Captain Davis delivered a battery charger to Michael. The Captain treated his wife to dinner in one of Mobile's fine seafood restaurants, and a thousand dollar gift card to a pricey department store, courtesy of John Wilheim.

After the author's visit, and the startling news about an escape plan, Michael went to work on his appeal to the U.S. Federal Court in Atlanta – the same court his great-grandfather once served on. Only three stops and three denials remained before a clemency hearing, at which time the Governor would find him unfit for society, and order the Alabama Supreme Court to set an execution date. He surmised, too, that he might be one of the early casualties of AEDPA.

CHAPTER 61

AEDPA, the acronym for the "Antiterrorism and Effective Death Penalty Act," was enacted in 1996 to impose a strict time line on the filing of federal *habeas corpus* petitions after all other claims in the state court system have been exhausted.

One year after Michael's second appeal to the U.S. Supreme Court was denied, his next appeal was presented by Bruno Romano before the U.S. Federal District Court. Predictably, it was rejected, and so were the last two stops at the 11th Circuit Court of Criminal Appeals, and finally, the U.S. Supreme Court that denied his final Petition for Writ of Certiorari. All that remained now was a clemency hearing before the Governor and the State's Pardon and Parole Board.

It was now 2005. In ten years, Michael was out of appeals and resigned to the fact that he was going to die, courtesy of the State of Alabama. He was working on an appeal for Josh Daniels, a member of his rec yard basketball team, when Captain Davis stopped by his cell to say he had a call on the tier phone from Bruno Romano. He knew what the message was without even taking the call.

"Michael, Bruno here. How are you doing?"

"Keeping busy, Bruno. Work is the best medicine for me right now. Remember those two guys from Birmingham? Mitchell and Williams?"

"Let me guess, Michael. Jury overrides by Judge

Brendle will be the focus in their appeals?"

"You know me all too well, Bruno."

"Michael, all kidding aside. A date has been scheduled for your clemency hearing in Montgomery before the Governor and the State Parole and Pardons Board. We're looking at Monday, August 15."

There was silence as Michael reflected on the date. Finally he spoke. "Ironic heh, Mom and Dad's wedding anniversary, Bruno."

"I'm sorry, Michael. I can ask for another date if you'd like."

"No, Bruno. Maybe the Governor will be moved by the occasion." Attempting to make light of the awkward moment, Michael said, "Bruno, check with my buddy Roscoe Jenkins and see what the odds are for a commutation?"

"That's the spirit, Michael. Look, I'll get back to you in a few days on the procedures. I believe you're allowed four or five witnesses. There are some obvious people, like your family, that you will want to speak on your behalf, but you might consider asking Warden Wiegert."

"The Warden, Bruno?"

"Yes, a little unusual, but you seem to have created a special bond that might be to your advantage. Shoot, where's he going to find another computer expert to work for the minimum wage?"

"Love your sense of humor, Bruno."

"Think about it, Michael. I'll get back with you in a few days. And check your cell phone; think the batteries need recharging. Had to go through the switchboard today, which I don't trust."

CHAPTER 62

Michael wasn't the least surprised when Sam Wiegert agreed to be a character witness for him. In a memo to him he said, "I'd be honored, Michael. The damn press will have another field day hammering their favorite warden, but it's been a while since I've given them any material for a new story. Actually, I'm looking forward to it." In addition to Wiegert, Michael added his mother and Professor Mullins.

A week after speaking with Bruno, Michael received a copy of the clemency hearing procedures. His attorney and three other witnesses would each be allowed to speak for five minutes, but there was no time limit for the condemned seeking commutation. Usually, they had little to say other than that they were sorry for their crime and didn't want to die.

Bruno pleaded with the governor's office to allow Michael to wear something other than the dreadful white jumpsuit for the hearing, but, as expected, they denied the request. He would also be cuffed and shackled for the hearing, which would take no longer than two hours. After both sides had spoken, the Governor and the board would retreat to another room and make their decision. If this were a game of poker, Michael would be holding a pair of deuces to the board's three aces.

His clemency hearing commanded page one headlines in the *Montgomery Reporter:* "The Michael

Tyler Circus is Coming to Town." The state could have leased out the Montgomery Civic Center and sold it out in an hour.

The hearing was just another sham in the disingenuous system. The Governor would pose for the cameras with his annoying grin, adding some level of authenticity in the grinding wheels of justice, while exercising his power to veto a favorable decision the board might make on behalf of the condemned – which was rare. Why were they even there? It couldn't be for the hundred bucks, gas mileage, and the fifteen-dollar meal allowance.

An early morning fog was burning off as they departed for Montgomery and the ten o'clock hearing. The escort service included three state patrol cars and six officers for the trip north on I-65. They arrived in the capital city thirty minutes early and headed directly to the State Capitol building where the hearing was scheduled to take place. As the cars turned onto Dexter Avenue leading to the building, Montgomery's sign writers had lined the street with various greetings for the State's most prominent death row resident. They parked in an area beneath the capitol complex and took an elevator to the third floor, and a large conference room that could seat about one hundred people.

Michael's parents, Pastor Roberts, and other friends were already seated when he entered the room, and made his way to the table where Bruno Romano was waiting for him. Randall Simmons, the Attorney General, and two aides were only a few feet to their left, and barely acknowledged Michael's entry, which was difficult, given the noise the chains made when making the short, choppy steps across the hardwood floor.

At ten o'clock, Governor William Bubba Levens entered the room with the five-member State Pardon and Paroles Board, and took their seats at a table in the front of the room. Only twenty-five feet separated Michael from the man, who, most likely, would deny his plea to commute his sentence to life without parole, and then instruct the Alabama Supreme Court to set an execution date. During his six years in office, Levens and the board had turned down thirty-five similar appeals, so the odds that Michael would be his first commutation were monumental.

After a courtroom reporter indicated that she was ready to record the hearing, the Governor nodded to Simmons to state his case for denial. Simmons lacked his predecessor's style, and they weren't treated to a fire and brimstone homily as to why Michael's life shouldn't be spared. He categorically traced Michael's case's long journey through the appellate system, emphasizing the denials at each court. "Mr. Tyler has been afforded the best legal representation, including his own as a member of the Bar. It is time to put this case to rest and carry out the wishes of our state as the law provides. The sheer gravity of the murder speaks for itself."

There were no victim's family members to call on, as they had long ago erased Maureen O'Brien from their memories. The few distant cousins who had received a few scraps from her mammoth estate didn't even respond to appear. Maureen's closest friends were also Michael's friends, and, though some were present at the hearing, none had expressed their feelings for or against Michael.

"Governor, that concludes our argument against clemency in the case of Michael Tyler."

That was it! A whole fifteen minutes. Michael glanced at his watch. If Bruno and his three witnesses stayed on schedule, he'd be back at SACC in time for his three o'clock rec yard time.

Before Bruno rose to address the Governor, he whispered in Michael's ear. "Roscoe says there's no line on this hearing, but he wishes you the best." Then he faced the panel.

"Governor, Michael Tyler and I thank you for the opportunity to hear our request for clemency on his wrongful conviction in 1995. This case is about more than just guilt and innocence, Governor. It's about a system that allows Alabama judges to override the good intentions of twelve people sworn to offer an impartial sentence based on the evidence in the case. The jury in Michael's case did just that, and then a Circuit Court judge dismissed their work as if they had slept throughout the trial. And the history of Brian Brendle's overrides is shocking as it pertains to race. I can assure you, Governor, if the Honorable Harold Christian were alive, we wouldn't be here today seeking clemency for his death sentence. And no, not because Judge Christian and Michael Tyler are black. Harold Christian was a man of honor and principle, and his reputation for acknowledging the work of jurors is well documented. Not once in the judge's three decades on the bench did he ever override a jury decision. Not one!

"And now the State of Alabama wants to end the life of a young man who earned his law degree and passed the bar in an eight-by-ten cell, and who, over the last eight years, has helped men on death row with legal representation they can't afford. Michael Tyler can't bill the State for his work, so why kill the man who has saved the system thousands of dollars in legal fees? His fee for an appeal is half a dozen Snickers and Mountain Dews. And he shares those with inmates who can't afford them. He has been a Godsend to the State of Alabama.

"Governor, Michael Tyler did not kill Maureen O'Brien, and, he doesn't deserve to die. A jury of his peers said so. Don't accept the word of a racist judge whose record in jury overrides is appalling and has been questioned by his own peers, including four members of the United States Supreme Court. Thank you, sir."

Michael's mother and Professor Mullins all gave moving appeals on his behalf, but it was Warden Sam Wiegert who offered a different perspective on inmate 234765A.

"Governor, I have been in contact with over two hundred different death row inmates over the last decade, and I can unequivocally say that Michael Tyler doesn't fit the persona of anybody else on The Row. He is a model prisoner, and, given the opportunity to live out his life at SACC, will be far more valuable to the State than taking his life. The judge who overrode his sentence got it wrong. And so did all the appellate courts. Michael Tyler does not possess the heart of a killer. Thank you."

The Governor ordered a short ten-minute break before Michael spoke.

CHAPTER 63

Michael rose slowly, his chains clanking loudly on the metal table."Governor, I don't know what I can say that hasn't already been said for me by my family, friends, and peers in the legal community. Maureen and I had an extremely meaningful relationship during the short time we worked together at Channel 10 here in Montgomery. I cherished her professionalism, loyal friendship and love of life. I can't imagine anyone believing that I would take the life of this remarkable young lady. I accomplished my life's goals under rather unusual circumstances: earning my law degree and passing the Bar, while incarcerated on death row – and I now find satisfaction in helping other death row inmates with their appeals. Their situations are unique, to say the least, and it motivates me every day to offer help to those who feel the legal system has left them with no recourse in the appeals process. This is my life now, and I hope you can find it in your heart to let me live it by helping those who really don't have one. Thank you."

Governor Levens thanked the opposing counsels and said he would have a decision after conferring with the Parole and Pardons Board. It didn't take long. Fifteen minutes later, they returned and the Governor addressed the room. "While I am impressed with Mr. Tyler's record on death row, I can't usurp the system that gives every defendant the opportunity of due process. It has been served in this case and the board and I concur that Michael Tyler should be returned to prison to complete the sentence of the court. This clemency hearing is adjourned."

Michael was back at SACC at two-thirty, just in time for his one hour of recreation. His competitive attitude was evident as he "schooled" Bobby Rae in a fierce one-on-one game; the first time in ten years he had beaten the Sand Mountain legend. The rec yard playmates were shocked, as was Bobby Rae.

"What the hell got into you today?" Bobby Rae asked.

"The Governor."

"Maybe you should see him more often."

"Once was enough, Bobby."

One week after the clemency hearing, Captain Davis interrupted Michael from an early afternoon nap, indicating he wished to speak with him. Guards don't normally interfere with inmates' naps, but he said he had an important letter from the warden that needed his signature. Davis offered his apologies and said, "I'm sorry, Michael, I know how you value your rest."

Michael knew what the contents of the letter were without opening the envelope marked personal. "My execution date. Right, Captain?"

I'm afraid so, Michael."

"What, the warden is too busy with other things to deliver it himself?"

"He's on vacation this week, Michael, and state law says it must be delivered to you within five days after the Alabama Supreme Court has posted a date. I'll leave it with you and pick it up later."

Michael relaxed on the edge of his cot and slowly

opened the envelope. The letter was the final legal dagger in his ten-year battle against the system that had brought nothing but denials from six different courts. Michael understood why it was probably difficult for the man who believed in his innocence to tell him in person.

"Dear Michael. This isn't part of my job that I necessarily enjoy doing – notifying a death row inmate of his execution date. Following your rejection of clemency, the Alabama Supreme Court has set a date of Thursday, January 15 for your execution. I don't know how many I have supervised since I arrived here, but the notion that they become routine and impersonal is far from the truth. I don't look forward to seeing you die for a crime you adamantly deny committing, but the courts have spoken, and the system, however flawed at times, is what we abide by. When I return from my vacation, we'll discuss your work status. I have no problem if you'd like to continue, but it will have to be under the strict supervision of a guard. I think it would be good therapy for you." Yours truly, Sam Wiegert.

Michael looked at the calendar and smiled briefly. At least the court waited until after the Super Bowl was played. He also thought how his legal skills and those at Bruno Romano's Defense Project would be tested as they filed new motions and petitions over the next five months to save his life. It would be a daunting task, but one he was prepared for.

CHAPTER 64

Sam Wiegert couldn't have envisioned the week in store for him one week before Labor Day. On Monday morning, as he waded through a stack of disciplinary reports following a weekend fight in the general population yard that had sent eighteen inmates to the prison hospital for various injuries, his mind was also preoccupied with his sixteen-year-old son's second arrest for underage drinking and resisting arrest in a Mobile area mall, as well as a Thursday execution that was no ordinary execution.

Ella Mae Johnson, a forty-eight-year-old black mother of four from Selma was scheduled to take a seat in Alabama's electric chair for the double murder of her former husband and his homosexual lover. Despite a decent alibi for her whereabouts on the evening of the murders, Johnson was convicted by an all-white jury in Dallas County.

The media attention to the execution was already heating up, and Wiegert was rightfully concerned that once the protestors showed up, all hell could break loose outside the prison walls as the hours wound down to the six o'clock execution. Executions had become the norm in the state – four to six a year – since the death penalty was reinstated in 1976, but sending women to the chair wasn't. Johnson, who had spent eighteen years on death row, had endured two trials, four stays, and a bout with pneumonia that almost deprived the State the privilege of ending her life. She would be only the State's fourth woman since the 1920s to be executed, but the first in Wiegert's fourteen years at SACC. Five other women who had received the death penalty had been spared by four past governors and had their sentences commuted to life without parole.

But Governor Levens wasn't touched by her tearful request at the clemency hearing to commute her sentence. Instead, he chastised her for a life of indiscretions that included petty theft, disorderly conduct, substance abuse, battery, bail jumping, and, finally, first-degree murder.

Levens, whose own political career had been marked by two failed marriages, excessive nepotism in providing state jobs for his extended family, and questionable campaign contributions, would have been better off to deny Johnson's bid for clemency without passing judgement on her rap sheet, but that wasn't his style. Before Levens could finish his harsh judgement of the woman, Johnson bolted out of her seat and let loose with a profanity-laced tirade, first questioning the Governor's manhood, then assailing his personal and political missteps. She concluded her outburst by calling him a "14-karat asshole."

Clemency hearings are usually overlooked by the media, because the outcome is predictable and doesn't warrant page one news. But Michael's former employer gambled that this hearing would be anything but routine. They weren't disappointed. The fiery exchange between Levens and Johnson led off the six o'clock news and made page one in the *Montgomery Reporter*. The bold headline read: "The Gov's a 14-Karat A-Hole."

Wiegert and his first assistant, Nathan Crosby,

interviewed thirty inmates about the weekend brawl, but, as usual, the questioning offered no clear reasons for the fight. It was the classic "he said, he said" standoff for which no blame could be determined.

"We got much bigger fish to fry," Wiegert said over lunch with his staff, the majority of whom were opposed to the death penalty. Crosby, who routinely challenged his boss on his grammatical *faux-pas*, said, "It was an inappropriate pun, considering the upcoming execution, Warden." Wiegert acknowledged the reprimand then invited his youthful assistant to accompany him for a quick tour of the yard, where the protestors were already gathering. And it was only Monday.

In the past, protestors had set up their vigils outside the entrance to death row. A recent execution in July had attracted only a handful of onlookers who showed up just a few hours before the execution. Today, they observed a hundred or more people, some with tents and grills, coolers filled with beer and soda, and boom boxes resonating rap and country music. It wasn't difficult to distinguish the cultural differences between the protestors.

Wiegert spoke with an elderly black man who appeared to be the spokesperson for those opposed to the execution. "It's unconscionable to subject women to that kind of punishment," the man said, as if he were an attorney addressing a jury. Wiegert offered the usual response that he was simply carrying out the laws of the State of Alabama as the Chief Administrator of SACC.

The vast majority of protestors who supported the State's death penalty were usually area rednecks who viewed executions as an opportunity to drink and parade around the grounds with crude signs that offered their opinions on the unfortunate soul about to die. The misspelled words were proof that their education had taken a sharp u-turn after elementary school, or perhaps even earlier.

"How many people are you expecting?" Crosby asked one supporter of the death penalty. "Three hundred, maybe more," mumbled an obese man in his early thirties sipping on an Old Milwaukee through stained teeth. Wiegert and Crosby would be sleeping over in the prison suites until the execution was over.

CHAPTER 65

Sam Wiegert returned to his office, hoping to find a sanctuary from the heavy atmosphere during the week of an execution. The staff is edgy, as the meticulous plan to take a human being's life is carried out with as much dignity as possible

He instructed his secretary, Jamie Nix, to hold all calls, as he attempted to take one of his afternoon power naps on a sleeper sofa the prison had provided his predecessor. He was only five minutes into his siesta, when Nix said he had a call he might want to take.

"Dammit, Jamie, I said no phone calls!" Wiegert hollered into the intercom.

"Oh, no, I think you better take this call. The caller is extremely agitated," Jamie argued. "He said your future as the warden here could be on the line, whatever that means."

"Okay, punch him through."

"This better be Goddamn important!" Wiegert shouted into the receiver before even asking the caller to identify himself. "I've got headaches this week that a bottle of Tylenol can't fix, so make it brief and to the point."

"Mr. Wiegert, who I am isn't important, but what I have to say is. I suggest you listen closely, dial down the attitude a bit, and hear me out. Are we clear on that?"

"Yeah, yeah, but remember we have a secure line here and we'll track your whereabouts in a matter of minutes."

"Won't happen, Warden. Our technology is better than yours. Now shut up and listen."

"You got two minutes, whoever you are."

"Good, and now that I have your attention, hear me out. I have a client, a Miss Andrea Merryfield, who is in dire need of your help, Warden. It seems that Miss Merryfield is three months pregnant as the result of a sexual liaison you've carried on with the former Miss Mobile over the last six months. Because of her single status, her health insurer will not cover the cost of bearing this child. Whatever precautions you might have taken during your monthly visit to that cheap motel down the road didn't work. You understand her dilemma, don't you, Warden?"

In the moment it took to take a breath, Sam Wiegert was no longer the tough-talking disciplinarian who had rescued the prison from institutional chaos the year before Michael Tyler had arrived on death row. He felt his heart racing dangerously, and he was sweating profusely with the same kind of sweat he'd observed as terrified men took their seats in the electric chair. The silence was thick. All he could offer was a barely audible, "How can I help, sir?"

"Tomorrow at five, the west concession stand at Ladd Stadium in Mobile. No weapons, no backup, no wires, and don't be late. Understood?"

"Yes, sir."

CHAPTER 66

Sam Wiegert had inherited the job at SACC, because no sane person in the corrections field was interested in the position. Wiegert, a highly-decorated Marine with twenty years of military service, had spent four years as the number-two man under Spencer Hannaway, who, Wiegert was fond of saying "couldn't find his ass with both hands tied behind him."

Hannaway's policy of coddling the inmates had, predictably, backfired. Drugs, money, booze, cell phones, and anything else not allowed on the grounds were being smuggled in by visitors and staff. In Wiegert's first three months on the job, twelve guards had been dismissed and seventy-five people had their visitation rights revoked for one year. The inmates, including twenty on death row, who were the recipients of the contraband items had their yard and phone privileges curtailed for six months. Random drug testing was instituted, and in less than a year, all 1,000 inmates had been tested, some more than once. Repeat offenders received the equivalent of life on death row: six months in ad seg, spending twenty-three hours a day locked up.

But he didn't stop there. He segregated the general population prisoners into three groups: blacks, whites, and whatever minority groups that remained; mostly Latinos and Asians. They dined, slept, and exercised by race, a change that caused logistical nightmares for the staff during the first ninety days the new plan was in place. Wiegert then closed down the prison's tattoo parlors and sent the recreation yard's weight-lifting equipment off to area high schools and junior colleges. Various prison gangs were splintered, siphoning off members to other maximum-security prisons in the state.

But it was his final act of retribution that sent shock waves through the country's major correctional institutions. After three guards had been severely burned when an inmate tossed a lit cigarette into a dryer in the prison's laundry unit, he banned all tobacco products from the prison. The result was a slew of inmate lawsuits that went nowhere, as the ACS filed countersuits claiming prison safety trumped tobacco use. Sam Wiegert was easily the most despised man at SACC, and he couldn't have cared less.

As hard-nosed as he was, Wiegert would have done anything to postpone Tuesday, but it arrived as advertised, a humid September morning. Darkness had given way to a beautiful sunrise that colored the eastern sky.

Despite the warden's morning routine of Pepsi, occasional doughnuts, and other cholesterol filled snacks during the day, Wiegert presented a forty-inch chest and a thirty-two inch waist that supported a fit 175 pounds. The weight-lifting equipment may have been banned from the complex, but anyone employed at SACC had access to a fitness room and spa for their personal use. Wiegert constantly needled his officers about their conditioning program, particularly those who were in daily contact with the inmates.

The Warden took note of the growing crowd of protestors outside the death row unit. Two major news networks, MSNBC and CNN, had requested interviews on the Johnson execution, but he had declined both. Contrary to his predecessor, who never saw a camera he didn't like, Wiegert had an adversarial relationship with the media, which had been spawned by an ACS investigation over alleged inmate brutality in his first year on the job. Tiny cameras had been smuggled into the prison by six disgruntled guards, who had been disciplined for running a football betting pool. Some disturbing footage of the warden's "special forces" team physically and verbally abusing inmates had been leaked to the media. But Wiegert, who was the ACS's golden boy, had maintained "discipline in whatever form is necessary to preserve institutional control." Other than some formal letters of reprimand to the team – which were later destroyed – the investigation went nowhere.

After a noon lunch, Wiegert, Crosby, and a large entourage of armed officers waded through the throng of protestors, which now numbered close to three hundred. "Port-A-Potties," the latest in outdoor bathroom technology, had been provided by the prison, but it didn't stop some people from using other methods to relieve themselves.

Wiegert was a nervous clock-watcher for the rest of the afternoon as his date with Monday's phone caller approached. He left the grounds in his prison-issued Crown Victoria, then stopped by a convenience store off a service road that offered bootlegged Jack Daniels miniatures. Twenty bucks got him two drinks, a cup of ice and a Pepsi to go, the fuel he needed to meet the mystery man on the phone.

Wiegert was ten minutes early, and took a seat at a picnic bench near the stadium concession stand.

He finished the second miniature, washed it down with a Pepsi, and lit a Winston Light, another vice he'd been grappling with for over two decades. A group of grade school boys were engaged in a spirited game of flag football nearby, as the sun slowly dipped below the horizon to the west.

He didn't notice the two men in business attire approaching from behind until one of them tapped him on the shoulder and said, "Thanks for coming, Warden. We'll make this as short as possible. Looks like you got a big headache brewing outside the prison wall down the road."

"Yeah, this isn't the part of the job I enjoy. Now let's make this meeting quick. I don't have a lot of time for you guys."

CHAPTER 67

The taller of two visitors did all the talking. "For starters, please allow us to check you for weapons or wires. I'll also ask you to give us your cell phone or Blackberry with the promise you'll have it back one hour after we leave. As for introductions, you can call me Will, and my associate who is leaving to check out the area, is Bill. You're smart enough to know that's not our real names, but that will have to do for now. Other than the stylish sunglasses, we're not trying to disguise our appearances. You'll never see us again, and whatever help you might give a sketch artist will lead you nowhere. We're pretty average-looking guys, wouldn't you agree?"

"If you say so," Wiegert mumbled.

"Warden, we know about your little affair with Miss Merryfield, and we're going to do our best to keep that a secret between the three of us – well, maybe a few more than that. Our cameraman, however, really enjoyed the assignment. Now, if you choose to co-operate with us, these graphic photos and the little video of your latest romp in the sack will be destroyed. If not, they could land in the wrong hands and turn your life upside down. How we doing so far? You get the picture, Warden?"

Trying to ignore the photos that were displayed on the table, Wiegert offered a weak, "What is it that you want from me?"

"We want a certain high-profile prisoner released during the next ninety days."

Pushing the photos aside, Wiegert asked, "How high-profile?"

"A death row prisoner wrongfully convicted of first-degree murder is out of appeals, and his clemency hearing was rejected a few weeks ago. His days are numbered; he could be executed in mid-January."

A little more composed than he had been when viewing the pictures of his sordid affair with a woman some thirty years his junior, Wiegert's attitude changed dramatically. "You expect me to arrange for a convicted killer to walk out of death row like he's going for a Sunday walk in the park? You're fucking crazy and so is Bill, or whoever the hell he his."

"Yeah, part of us would agree with that, but the other part says you're going to make it happen."

"Well, gentlemen, that isn't going to happen. I assume you're talking about ...."

"Michael Tyler, inmate 234765A, cell 24 on tier two of The Row. That's who, Warden."

"Michael Tyler, the guy who killed a Montgomery television news reporter?'

"That's him, Warden. Hey, we're not asking you to empty out death row. Lots of guys in there who deserve to die for their crimes, or at least the State of Alabama says so. We just want Tyler out so he can live the life he planned before he was framed for a murder he didn't commit. And you testified on his behalf at his clemency hearing. Right?"

"While I might agree with you on his assertion of innocence, all the appellate courts have rejected every one of his claims."

"The appellate system isn't perfect, Warden. You

are aware that over twenty death penalty convictions have been overturned across the country in the last five years, including three in Alabama. Trust me, Warden, Tyler will be the fourth if given the proper opportunity.

"Now, you can take your bravado ass back to the prison, execute some poor black woman on Thursday, and act like this meeting never happened. But my associates won't like that, and we'll be instructed to distribute these photos and video, starting with your wife and father-in-law. He's the pastor of a prominent Baptist church in Mobile – Central Avenue Baptist, I believe. Then the media and internet will feast on you like fresh road kill, and, Warden, I don't think that's a path you want to walk down. Agreed?"

Resigned to the situation, Wiegert said, "All right, let's talk."

Taking a small envelope and putting it in the warden's hand, Will said, "We'll be in touch with you within a week or two. In the meantime, here's a little advance to show our good faith. You might want to help Miss Merryfield with her expenses. Now wait here for thirty minutes after we leave."

One hour later, Bill and Will were on a private jet headed to Dallas, while Wiegert was fingering through a wad of fresh fifty-dollar bills that added up to ten thousand dollars.

"Christ, these guys are serious," Wiegert thought to himself. On the way back to the prison, he made a second stop at his favorite convenience store.

CHAPTER 68

By late Tuesday, Ella Mae Johnson was already on the prison grounds awaiting her date with the electric chair. SACC was the only facility in the state that carried out executions, so Johnson was escorted south from the state's women's prison near Montgomery by the usual convoy of armed guards in three State patrol cars.

The eerie but deliberate process to carry out the execution was already in motion when Wiegert returned to his office. There were phone calls and e-mails requesting interviews, and messages from his staff that Johnson was being an "uncooperative bitch" after she had arrived. Most interesting, though, was one email on his most private account, to which only he had access.

One hour after the warden had met with Bill and Will, there was a photo of the meeting on his computer with the message, "Nice to meet you. Look forward to working with you on our little project." *These guys are good, really good.*

Nathan Crosby burst unannounced into Sam Wiegert's office with a host of problems on The Row. "You're not gonna believe the damn mess down there, Warden. Guys are tossing their dinners through the bars on to the concourse, some are pissing on the run-ways, and the noise is deafening. It's .... maddening down there."

"Calm down, Crosby. If they want to act like animals, we'll treat them like animals. Tell the guards to lock it down, turn off the electricity and water. Then announce over The Row intercom that the doors to sixteen random cells will be opened. These fortunate inmates will have the opportunity to clean up the mess, for which they will receive special food and beverage privileges, complimentary long distance phone service, and a pass or two for a conjugal visit with whatever gender they desire. What you think, Crosby? Can you sell it?"

"Me, boss?"

"Yes, you, Crosby."

"Boss, the prison doesn't have a conjugal visit program."

"Yeah, I made that part up, Crosby."

By early Wednesday morning, The Row was cleaned, order was restored, and Nathan Crosby was the recipient of ten crispy fifty dollar bills – courtesy of Bill and Will.

Michael Tyler had endured fifty-two executions over the last ten years, including four of his original rec yard friends. Only Michael and Bobby Rae Quinton remained from the hoops team that was formed in 1996, but they could always recruit a few stiffs to make five and win The Row championship each year. There were complaints from some of the teams that it was unfair to let them stay together, but Michael had an ally in one of The Row guards. Michael had provided some *pro bono* legal work for Tracy Jackson, who organized the tournament and made up the teams. The Aces led by Quinton and Tyler, would remain intact.

Michael's first two side-by-side cell friends were

long gone; Frederick Giles had been executed only a year after Michael arrived on The Row, and Walter Conway died of kidney failure a week after celebrating his 30th anniversary at SACC. Michael had since learned that the State never intended to execute Conway, and once he had reached his 70th birthday, Levens, the sanctimonious prick of a governor, had finally commuted his sentence to life without parole. In anticipation of his move to general population, the guards had chipped in for pizza, cake, and ice cream for a going away party. But Conway had said no to the move, saying he didn't want to leave his good friends behind.

Twenty-four hours before and after an execution is carried out, the entire complex is in lock down. Tuesday's eruption on The Row was a first for Michael, and it remained a mystery as to who had initiated the disturbance.

An hour before Ella Mae Johnson would come face-to-face with the State's Yellow Mama, the temperment on The Row was now surreal. There was little conversation through the bars as the time neared when the death chamber would welcome its first female in almost five decades.

Johnson's attorney had filed the last of their hopeless appeals, but the system, however motionless and unforgiving at times, would finally prevail. After her final meal of steak and lobster, two smuggled Canadian Club miniatures, and four Valium, Ella Mae Johnson calmly walked to the chamber and gave her life to the State of Alabama; number 210 since the first execution in 1920. Her final words were: "I'm ready, gentlemen. Let's light this freaking candle."

Myth would have you believe that the surge of

electricity through the chair dims the lights throughout the complex, but it's only myth. The Row is just a short walk from the chamber, and Michael watched the six o'clock version of *Jeopardy!* without any interruption of service.

CHAPTER 69

One week after the Johnson execution, Sam Wiegert received the call he knew was coming. It wasn't Bill or Will, but a different associate of the Tyler rescue mission.

"Good morning, Warden Wiegert," the caller said. "I'll only take a minute of your time to remind you of some of the particulars that were discussed with you last week. Please check your email, as you will receive a set of instructions within the minute that will detail our objectives and what is expected from you. Oh, and lest I forget, have a nice day."

Wiegert typed in his password and downloaded a message that had come in while he was on the phone. It also included a family photo taken a year ago at Disney World. *How in the hell did they get a copy of that?*

A week before Thanksgiving, Michael received an email from the Warden that he would be doing some computer maintenance work for a few days in the administration building. Michael worked with stricter guard supervision as he checked out computers in the various offices. However, nobody felt threatened by the presence of a death row inmate, because he had gained their absolute trust over the last eight years. Michael Tyler, a killer? No way.

Michael's new schedule called for him to work approximately three to five hours a day Monday through Wednesday. His discretionary bank account had grown to five thousand dollars on his minimum wage salary the warden had provided him since 1998, and if there was a wealthy inmate on The Row, it was Michael. When working in the prison administration building, he was welcome to eat lunch in the officers' dining room. It didn't rival his mother's home-style offerings, but it was a definite improvement from the swill on The Row.

After dinner on Tuesday evening which featured a morbid version of sloppy joes, Michael received a call on his cell phone from the usual anonymous caller. "Be ready, freedom is at hand," was all the caller had to say. He slept little that night after watching the movie *Rudy* that was shown *ad nauseam* on the prison movie channel during the football season.

The early breakfast tray included a note that a guard would pick him up at eleven o'clock and return him to The Row around five. He was looking forward to the annual pre-Thanksgiving dinner, which included a turkey sandwich with gravy, green beans, baked potatoes, and rhubarb pie, a Row favorite. Maybe it was just a ploy by the prison to improve the spirits on The Row, but the menus in November and December were always a welcome change. Michael, though, wondered whether he would enjoy that meal or any other at SACC.

Michael arrived at the administration building shortly after eleven, and was told the Warden wanted to meet with him before he made his rounds.

"Good morning, Michael. Please take a seat. Could I get you a cup of cappuccino?"

"Thank you, Warden, that would be nice. Been a long time – so long I can't remember."

Michael suspected the Warden had something special to say, because it was rare to meet with Wiegert in his office. He seemed uncomfortable, shifting in his chair and searching for words.

'Oh .... it's really nothing, Michael. I told your guard that I'll personally take you back to The Row around five-thirty. I've got a monthly report to get out for Montgomery, so I hope you don't mind a few extra hours."

That, too, was quite unusual. Michael had spent hundreds of days over the last eight years in the administration building, and never once had the Warden offered him a ride back to The Row. However, the only thing on Michael's mind now was the pre-Thanksgiving dinner he would miss – or would he?

"Hate to miss that nice dinner they have each year, Warden."

"Don't worry, Michael, I'll call the kitchen and have them save a plate for you. Okay?"

"That would be great, Warden. Guess I'd better get to work. I'll see you later, sir, and thanks for the cappuccino."

Michael's day consisted of cleaning up viruses by staff members who downloaded suspicious web sites, installing new software designed to create new profiles on inmates, and working with the creator of the prison web site, which was undergoing a major overhaul.

Wiegert's day was one of uncertainty and apprehension. He wasn't looking forward to Sunday's dinner with his pious father-in-law, since it guaranteed listening to another dreadful litany on the immorality of the death penalty. He could hear the rant already: "The State murdered a woman, a mother of four and grandmother of twelve, whose lasting memory is her savage death. Then the State further desecrates her body with an autopsy to determine the source of death. God and everybody else knows how she died, Sam. She was burned to death. If there's any logic to that, please explain it to me."

Around three-thirty, he received a call he wasn't expecting.

"Warden, Josh, from the Tyler rescue mission calling. Only a few hours to lift-off. I trust you're still on board."

"Yeah, yeah, Josh, or whoever the hell you are. No problem on this end."

"Warden ..... there's been a slight change in the plan. Consider it an insurance policy we had to take out to be sure you wouldn't back out. Our client is very special to us."

"Look, Josh, you have my word."

"Yes, and you're about to get a nice bonus from us, which wasn't part of the original deal."

Wiegert, who had sold his soul once he had accepted the first ten thousand dollars from Bill and Will was nevertheless offended by the group's arrogant attitude since the initial contact with him, and their dismissive characterization of him as a corrupt state official who could be bought. "Okay, dammit, what are the changes at this late hour?"

"We have someone on the line who wishes to speak with you."

"Dad, this is Aaron. Some guys grabbed me right off the street next to school and said you better do what they want or I'm toast. What the hell is going on?"

"Aaron, stay cool, put Josh back on the line."

"Goddammit, Josh, this wasn't part of the deal. You hurt my kid, and you'll end up doing the worst time you can imagine. You and your partners will never see the light of day in my prison. If you think death row inmates got it rough, you can't imagine what I'll put you through. You got that?"

That was the last communication with Aaron or Josh.

Sam Wiegert was all too familiar with the drill. His son was now the trade bait for Michael, but it was also beneficial to the warden. Aaron was now the ideal bargaining chip he needed to prove later in the investigation – and there would be a big one – that whoever these people were, would they really harm his son? Aaron was a major screw-up at times, but he was family, and the hell with the ACS policy had in place regarding hostage swaps.

CHAPTER 70

Sam Wiegert was nervously arranging papers on his desk when Michael knocked lightly on the Warden's door shortly after five.

"Come in, Michael. I'm just finishing up a little paperwork before I take you back to The Row. Take a seat, just need to turn the computer off. How was your day?"

"Fine, Warden, fine. I cleaned up most of those viruses caused by your staff downloading those sites we talked about."

Choosing his words carefully, Wiegert asked, "Michael ..... you remember those two fellows from Mississippi that visited you earlier this year? I forgot the month."

"Believe it was early February, Warden."

"Anyway, they had written me about doing a book on The Row, wanting to feature you and the guys on your rec yard basketball team. Montgomery, in their usual conservative approach to publicity, said no originally, but I told them the authors would donate some of the book's profits to the inmates' prison bank accounts, and they finally agreed. Money talks, doesn't it? Have you been in contact with them since those two visits?"

Curious over the line of questions, Michael said, "Well, we've exchanged a few letters but nothing more. Is there a problem, Warden?"

"Oh yes, a big problem, young man. Their visits were just a ruse to lay the groundwork to bust you out of here. Any comment?"

Michael paused, then lied, "An escape plan, sir? This is all news to me. And according to a recent letter from Mr. Wilheim, the book is due to be published sometime next spring. I was hoping to be around to read it."

Sam Wiegert smiled, not convinced that Michael wasn't aware of the plan or the people behind it. "At this point, it doesn't matter what you know or don't know, but the moment has arrived. Right now, I'm your most important ally in the plan, and it's time to move on. Grab your chains and let's go. People are waiting for us, and they're overly paranoid about everyone being on time."

Michael was silent as Wiegert's car exited the main gate and turned onto Highway H, driving east toward I-65. As they passed the entrance to death row, Michael took what he hoped was his last sight of Alabama's killing chamber.

Fifteen minutes later, as they passed under the interstate overpass, Wiegert finally broke the silence. "We're headed to the old county airport to make the swap."

"What swap, Warden?

"My son, Michael. Aaron was abducted after school and is with whoever your friends are."

"Friends, Warden? Honestly, I don't know anybody involved this, or whatever you want to call it. And I'm sorry that Aaron got caught up in it."

As the Warden turned left on County Highway A toward the old airstrip that had been closed five years earlier, Wiegert said, "Why they picked that airstrip, I really don't know. You can't fly any kind of plane out of there, so I assume wherever you're going, it'll be in a car."

As Wiegert's car neared the abandoned hangar that had once been home to a crop dusting service, a blinking flashlight directed them to the back of a building. A man in a hooded sweatshirt rushed to the warden's door and shouted for him to get out.

Wiegert jumped out of the car and immediately wanted to know where his son Aaron was. "Where's my boy? I get my boy, or you don't get Tyler. That was the deal."

"Shut up," ordered the man who appeared to be in charge. "Your son is safe and sound at home."

"At home?" Wiegert screamed. "What the hell is going on? I just talked to him three hours ago, and he said somebody had grabbed him off the street at his school."

"Yeah, you talked to him. It was a voice recording, Warden. Remember when we said our technology was better than yours? Your son was very cooperative. Hell, teenagers will do anything for fifty bucks. Now, say your goodbyes to Michael, because this will be the last time you will ever see him again. And, you can cancel that January 15 execution, because he won't be there to participate in it."

Wiegert was instructed to get in the back of his car, where both hands were handcuffed to a door. Michael approached the man who had befriended him after a difficult beginning on The Row. "I don't know what to say, Warden. Maybe a simple thank you will do."

Embarrassed that he had become a pawn in this improbable escape plan, a somber and reflective Sam

Wiegert said softly, "Good luck, Michael. I've always believed in your innocence."

The hooded man had one last set of instructions for the Warden. " In exactly one hour, we will contact the Mobile County Sheriff's office and let them know where to pick you up. Your car keys, cuff keys, and cell phone are in the glove compartment. It's been a pleasure to work with you, Warden. And, have a nice Thanksgiving."

A minute later, Michael Tyler, now wearing a pair of Wrangler jeans, a blue Izod golf shirt, and an Auburn baseball cap, was in a black Honda Pilot bearing government license plates, headed due east to Dothan, Alabama.

CHAPTER 71

"War Eagle, Michael. Great to see you," said the driver, who had now removed his hood. "Introductions are in order. Meet Teddy Shanlon, my co-pilot. I'm Tommy Shanlon, his first cousin."

High-fives were exchanged as Michael did his best to comprehend the last hour of his life. For ten years he had dreamed of leaving The Row as a free man through the court system, but highjacked with the help of an accommodating warden and people he didn't know was too much to believe.

Teddy Shanlon spoke. "Michael, you probably have a million or more questions about what has just transpired. While we are recruits of the code word "Network" that orchestrated your escape, most of the people involved are cloaked in anonymity. The Einstein of the plan, we are told, resides somewhere in Texas or Oklahoma . That's as much as know. It should come as no surprise to you that we're not the Shanlon cousins, either. With the exception of one or two individuals in The Network, we're just two normal-looking guys with phony names. Any questions?"

"Only one right now, Michael asked. "When you greeted me with a "War Eagle," was it because of my ties to Auburn, or because some of the people involved in The Network are Auburn alums?"

"Not some, Michael, all of them," Teddy laughed. "Our part of the a plan is to deliver you to a "friend" in

The Network who will deliver you to a destination unknown to us. We then go back to our regular lives and, hopefully, you can start a new one. I understand you missed your pre-Thanksgiving dinner tonight, so we picked up a couple of turkey subs for you. There's also a few Mountain Dews in the cooler for you."

"How did you know that I missed dinner on The Row?" Michael asked.

"You'll hear this a lot over the next few days and months, Michael: our technology is better than the Alabama Corrections System. We like to think we know what they're planning to do before they do it. Now, I have a phone call to make to the sheriff in Mobile County. All hell is about to break loose, and I wish we there to enjoy it."

Timeliness was everything to The Network, and at 7:15, exactly one hour after Michael had climbed into the back of the Honda Pilot, Teddy made the call.

Brandon Jacobs, the Mobile County Sheriff, was at his son's high school basketball game where he was paged by his dispatcher's urgent phone call. "The Warden of SACC is handcuffed to his car at the old county airport, and a death row inmate has escaped. Please advise a course of action."

The call set in motion a plan that made anyone traveling north or south on I-65 wish they had taken another route on the eve of Thanksgiving. The timing was absolutely brilliant.

Two hours later, Michael and the Shanlons checked into the Dothan Holiday Inn. The bill for the three rooms had been prepaid by a wire transfer from an account in Norman, Oklahoma, and was closed on the following day.

CHAPTER 72

A brilliant sunshine greeted Michael the next morning when he opened the drapes of room 238 of the Holiday Inn. He had slept little, fearing a knock on the door in the middle of the night would bring an end to his short-lived freedom. He had spent the last 4,000 days under the scrutiny of guards with guns, tasers, and night sticks, who barked orders and controlled almost every minute of his daily existence. He had paid the State of Alabama with the best years of his young adult life, and the rage he felt for the failure of the legal system to right a wrong had finally reached the breaking point. He sat on his bed and, for the first time in almost eleven years, he cried.

The news of his escape was all over the early morning TV news shows, and the complimentary *USA Today* left outside his door featured Michael's photo in living color. The headline in bold 48-point type was loud and clear: "ALABAMA DEATH ROW KILLER ON THE LOOSE."

The accompanying story rehashed everything from his first high school touchdown to his last day on The Row. There was speculation on Warden Sam Wiegert's role in the brazen escape, as well on the unusual bond that had been forged between the top administrator of a maximum security prison and a prominent death row inmate. Wiegert would have a lot of questions to answer.

The TV reports covered by a helicopter showed traffic backed up five miles north and south on I-65, as all vehicles were stopped for an inspection. Over one hundred local, county, and state patrol cars were part of the highway assault over a seventy-five mile corridor of the interstate between Mobile and Montgomery. The assumption was that Michael had an hour's lead and was probably headed north towards Montgomery. Instead, he was one hundred miles to the east and soon to be in the air, destination unknown.

Teddy Shanlon knocked on Michael's door at eight o'clock indicating they were ready to leave for the airport, a private airstrip twelve miles southwest of Dothan, to meet another ghost in The Network. As they arrived, a sleek Gulfstream G200 jet was landing, using every inch of the 6,000-foot runway, leading to a small concourse which was void of any other aircraft. It taxied to the airport tower that was manned by one person and came to a stop. They waited in the car until the door to the plane had been opened, the steps lowered, and the pilot beckoned Michael to board. He thanked the Shanlons, or whoever they were, for their hospitality, and they parted with a "War Eagle."

"Good morning and welcome aboard, Michael. Captain Jon McMullen at your service."

"Thank you, Captain, but that's not your real name is it?"

"No, Michael, but I did fly for a major airline for thirty years, recently retired. Take a seat in the cabin, we'll be airborne in ten minutes. Oh, nice photo in the paper this morning."

"Thank you, but those prison mug shots aren't very flattering. Our destination is?"

"I'll get my instructions once we're airborne.

Help yourself to some coffee, milk, or soft drinks. The pastries on that tray are delicious."

Minutes later, the jet was thundering down the runway to a rendezvous with a powder-blue sky overhead. Twenty-four hours ago, Michael had been a nobody, eating an undercooked egg and burnt toast for breakfast. Now he was the toast of a mysterious network of Auburn grads who believed so strongly in his innocence that they would do almost anything for a college football jock.

He thought of his mother saying a thousand times over that prayer and patience would get him through this ordeal; that God would undo the injustice of his imprisonment. Pastor Roberts would accompany Margaret and Ralph on their monthly visits, where they spent most of the allotted three hours with hands clasped in prayer. He thought, God had finally intervened, but why did it take him ten years?"

An hour later, they were touching down at another private airport, probably owned or operated by someone with a connection to Auburn. Captain McMullen brought the plane to a stop within a few yards of a silver Cadillac Escalade, and a tall slender man in a navy blue windbreaker stepped forward and introduced himself as Myron DeBauche. "War Eagle, Michael. Welcome to Richmond, Virginia, and Happy Thanksgiving." Michael thanked Captain McMullen for his role in The Network, wondering if he'd ever see him again.

CHAPTER 73

Michael took a seat up front with DeBauche, a wealthy hedge fund manager, but before Michael could ask his standard question, it was answered for him. "Yes, my real name is Myron DeBauche, Michael. I am one of the few people in The Network whom you will get to know with no alias. The secrecy of the group is what makes it so special. The CIA would be envious of this operation.

"I'm your mentor, so to speak, for as long as it takes to resolve your legal issues with the State of Alabama. If things should deteriorate here in terms of blowing your cover, you will be moved to a new location. Consider yourself in the Witness Protection Program, and I'm the United States Marshal whose responsibility it is to keep you out of harm's way – with your cooperation, of course. Any questions?"

"Sir?"

"Call me Myron, Michael. You're not in prison anymore, where respect is expected, but never earned. Think of The Network as a group of fraternity brothers from school embarked on a mission to save not only you, but also the State of Alabama the embarrassment of executing an innocent man. You are innocent, aren't you, Michael?"

"You better believe it, Mr. DeBauche, I mean, Myron." Michael had only one question for the newest member of The Network. "Why Richmond, Myron?"

"Simple, Michael. We've done our homework. We couldn't find one single former professor or coach who was at Auburn when you were, who has a similar position at either of our two fine universities here, Virginia Commonwealth or Richmond. The number of Auburn alumni, including me, living in the area is relatively low – twenty-three since 1985. You played football only two years before your knee injury, then blended nicely into a student body of 20,000 or more. You've aged fifteen years, lost twenty-five pounds from your playing weight, and have that nasty scar under your right eye incurred while playing basketball in prison. Other than that absent pinkie on your right hand, which I'll address soon, you're a changed man."

"And the chances of me running into one of the other twenty-two alumni here is....?"

"Low, Michael. Very low. In fact, I will provide you a list of their names and professions. Good, now let's get you settled in. We can talk more later."

They drove along the James River to the north side of Richmond and pulled into an upscale townhouse development that Myron said a business friend of his owned. "Here's your new home, Michael – 123 Elmwood Drive."

The newly furnished townhouse was more than Michael had expected. From eighty square feet to twelve hundred in twenty-four hours was like a trip from hell to the Hamptons.

After a quick tour of the premises, Myron asked Michael to join him at the kitchen table. "There's food and drinks in the refrigerator, clothes in the bedroom closet, everything to make your stay here as comfortable as possible. The rent and utilities are taken care of, which means the only expenses you'll have are personal – going to the movies, dining out, etc. To pass the time, you might think of writing a book on your journey. All it needs is the perfect ending.

"Now, there are a few ground rules you must follow, because the State of Alabama, and now the FBI, will exhaust every resource they have to find you, and return to you to death row. Understood?"

"Yes, Myron."

Myron then emptied the contents of a manila folder on to the table. It included Michael's new identity, driver's license, Social Security number, and the complete background of Shane Couples, formerly of Terre Haute, Indiana, who existed on paper only. "Study it, devour it, memorize it. In the course of a conversation with a stranger, and you being new to the city, they'll want to know more about you than you about them. This is crucial, Michael. If I sound a little too harsh, please excuse the tone. The Network has invested time and money, risked their professional careers and families to spring you out of that shit-hole they call a prison in Alabama, and we can't chance having our secrecy compromised."

Myron then took a cell phone from his jacket pocket. "This is one of those burn phones that has 250 minutes of call time. Any calls you make are not traceable, but I would strongly suggest that you resist the temptation to call your family or friends in Alabama, because their lines will be tapped for as long as you're on the loose. You don't need to contact me unless you're standing in two feet of water or the apartment is on fire. I'll call you at least once a week on the land line. And under no circumstances are you ever to invite anyone to your apartment. An apartment with no family photos or other personal items makes people suspicious as hell. And finally. Remember those two journalists from Mississippi who visited you back in February

"Yes, they wanted to do a story on me and other friends about our life on The Row."

"Well, when they left, they retrieved a paper cup you had used for a soda. Its purpose was to save your DNA. A forensics lab in Europe replicated a prosthetic finger with your same skin tone for you to slip over the nub of your pinkie which was severed in a ....?"

"Repairing one of my dad's lawnmowers. Yeah, it was dumb."

From his jacket pocket, Myron retrieved a small jewel box. "Well, here's your new pinkie, Michael. Go ahead, try it on."

Michael slipped the prosthetic finger over the stub of his partial finger.

"Fits perfectly, Myron."

"A few words of caution, Michael. If you must shake hands with someone, don't grip the person's hand too tightly. You don't want it coming loose or falling to the ground and sending them into cardiac arrest."

Checking his watch, Myron said, "Now, unless I return home for Thanksgiving dinner with my family and in-laws, I will incur the wrath of angry Virginians, which is unlike any other on earth."

After Myron departed, Michael opened a small envelope that said "miscellaneous living expenses." Inside were fifty twenty-dollar bills. He would be going out to dinner tonight, and maybe shopping over the weekend.

CHAPTER 74

Late Friday evening, Bruno Romano was alone in his office, which also served as his new home. Recently divorced because of his devotion to the Defense Project, and not his family, he now poured more time and research into his work. He had just finished his third novel, *Wrongful Conviction*, which like the first two, had made the trip to the top of *New York Times* Best Seller's list. It was a blissful February evening, as Mother Nature had uncharacteristically blessed Montgomery with five inches of fluffy white snow. He drained the last of an Amaretto on the rocks, as he savored his newfound wealth and independence. The combination of the liquor and the dancing flames of the gas fireplace had him dozing off in his recliner, when the ringing of the phone jolted him out of his stupor. Who the hell could be calling at what time – midnight?

Grabbing the phone, Romano grumbled into the receiver, "Before I even ask who is calling, do you know what time of the night – or morning – it is?"

"Mr. Romano, sorry about the hour, but we just discovered something new in the Michael Tyler case that might help him. You are still handling his appeals, right?"

"Yes, but who am I talking to?"

"Jordan Henry, second-year student at the Law Center."

"Well, Jordan Henry, didn't the Center teach you anything about calling people in the middle of the night?"

Attempting to humor Romano a little, Jordan replied, slightly slurred, "Ah, we take that course next semester, sir."

"Funny, Jordan, so very funny. Now that I'm at least partially awake, tell me what you have that can help Michael Tyler."

"A video, Mr. Romano. It explains it all. We can be at your office in ten minutes."

"Now?" Romano protested. "Jordan, it's past midnight. Oh, what the hell, come on down."

"Do you have anything to drink, Mr. Romano?"

"Drink? You sound like you might have had enough already. Yeah, I got some cold beer. Hurry up, back door."

Ten minutes later, Jordan Henry and fellow law student Kevin McKenzie were seated in Bruno's office, anxious to tell their story, and clutching their video as if it were a winning lottery ticket.

"All right boys, what you got?" asked Romano.

Henry was the spokesperson. "We have the video of the last day of the trial. You know, the one the Law Center taped."

But before Henry could proceed any further, Romano interrupted the conversation. "Look, I've seen that same video a hundred times or more. What's so special about your copy?"

"The ending, Mr. Romano. The real ending."

"Well, the ending I viewed was the jury finding Michael Tyler guilty of first-degree murder, and Judge Brian Brendle then overriding the jury's sentence of life without the possibility of parole. That's all I remember, boys."

But Jordan Henry persisted. "Then you missed the real ending, sir."

Romano suspected the two students were onto something he might have missed. "First of all, what is your interest in a ten-year-old video?"

Kevin McKenzie finally spoke. "Well, it's the Tyler case, and we've never seen the video of the trial, and now he's escaped."

"What about those beers you promised?" Jordan asked.

Grabbing two Coors Lights from the refrigerator, Romano said. "Okay, it's your show, boys. Let's see what you got that woke me up past midnight."

Henry assumed control of the conversation, explaining to Romano that they had checked the video out of the Law Center case files earlier in the day as part of a school assignment. "We were planning on watching it Saturday, but with the snow, we decided to watch it tonight. It's about two hours long, but we've cued it to the ending where the jury's sentence is announced."

Inserting the tape into Romano's VHS player, there was Brendle just as he was ten years ago, overriding the jury's Life Without Parole recommendation and sentencing Michael to death.

"Now, here's the real ending, Mr. Romano. You won't believe it. The camera is still running, the sound is on, and now there's just a still shot of the defense table for exactly seven minutes and twenty-three seconds. Watch closely. The filming resumes, and the picture is that of Anthony Romano sitting at the defense table putting some papers in his briefcase. We can only assume that everybody, including yourself, who has seen the video, had turned it off after the sentence override. Well, it's not over. Look what we have here."

Bruno Romano moved closer to the TV, where the late Monsignor Patrick Reilly was approaching Anthony Romano from behind. "Now watch and listen carefully," Jordan said.

Bruno watched as the Monsignor spoke in harsh language, calling his first cousin a twenty-first century Judas Iscariot. "Did he really call him a sorry son of a bitch, too? Why the offensive language?"

The Monsignor's voice was slightly muffled, but clear enough to hear him say he recalled a confession Anthony had made to him shortly before the trial, that he had played a role in the death of Maureen O'Brien. There was also the question of confessee/confessor confidentiality, and the Monsignor said he would honor it unless "he had a bad hair day one morning." A bad hair day?

Bruno took a seat behind the desk before his legs failed him, desperately trying to comprehend the unbelievable scene that had just played out before him. He tried to rationalize the startling development but he couldn't. Anthony? Involved in Maureen's death? No way! His cousin was in love with money; women came in a distant second.

Grasping for some answers, Bruno asked, "Any theories, boys?"

Jordan Henry spoke. "Our theory, Mr. Romano, is that the Law Center student doing the taping must have left the courtroom, maybe to use the bathroom, and left the camera running. When he returned, Monsignor Reilly and your cousin had already left the defense table. He then turned off the camera, unaware that in his absence the camera had recorded the most baffling five minutes of courtroom history. The old Perry Mason shows can't match this shit. Excuse me, sir."

"That's okay, Jordan, I was thinking the same thing. Gentlemen, the hour is late. Let's all get some sleep and talk about it some more in the morning. Maybe ten?"

"Well, Mr. Romano, Kevin and I were planning on going home to Huntsville for the weekend," Jordan explained.

"Guys, I don't care if you live in Houston. Be here at ten. I'll make it well worth your time."

Thinking it might mean money, Jordan replied, "At ten, Mr. Romano."

CHAPTER 75

Bruno Romano got little sleep that night, his mind swirling in a hundred different directions over the early-morning revelation and what the future held for Michael. He wasn't part of the mysterious Network, and had no idea where Michael was hiding out. The police and FBI had interviewed him on two occasions, but he had prevailed against wire-tapping, because of the lawyer-client privilege.

He wasn't questioning the validity of the video, but in the event of a hearing to admit new evidence, the State would argue whether the confession had actually taken place. But if Anthony was intent on receiving absolution, why would he have confessed to the Monsignor, who would have easily recognized his gravelly voice? He could have visited any of the other three Catholic churches in town to repent his sins. Was there a history between the two, and was the Monsignor settling an old score? Anthony was part of the group that played bridge once a month at Monsignor Reilly's place, but that was their only social connection. What could have transpired to trigger his accusation? Bruno came to the conclusion that he had attended the trial for a reason.

Bruno was also concerned that requesting a hearing to admit new evidence would land him back in Circuit Court before Winston Kennedy, the former prosecutor in Michael's trial. Kennedy had personally prosecuted over twenty cases in his seven years as the State's Attorney General, and never had one reversed on appeal.

Jordan Henry and Kevin McKenzie arrived at ten, hoping this second meeting would be short but financially rewarding.

"Good morning, gentlemen," Bruno said. "Let's retreat to my office. I promise not to keep you for long. Coffee and pastries for anyone? Get what you need in the kitchen."

Both students returned, armed with a plate full of sweets for their trip north. Romano told them he wanted to treat them as clients, insisting that what was discussed among the three would not leave the room. He asked if he could record their conversation, and they agreed. But first, he wanted to know something about them.

Jordan, the pitchman for the two, said his father was a CPA in Huntsville, while Kevin's family was in the real estate business. They had grown up a few houses apart from each other, attended the same schools, and both had decided on law school. Long-time buddies.

A little satisfied, but still fearful that this latest development could go public, Bruno said, "Sounds good. For openers, though, I'm keeping your copy of the video. My trust in the legal system is in the red numbers right now, and only Michael's acquittal will change that. Not only are you clients, but you're also employees of the Alabama Defense Project. Reaching into a desk drawer, he took out $250.00 in cash for each new employee. And your lips are sealed about your discovery. Right?"

There was no answer as the two law students

paused to let this sink in. "I'll take that as a yes, boys," Bruno said. "Have a great weekend and check with me after classes on Monday. How about dinner that night? Ribs at one of my uncle's restaurants?"

"Yes, Mr. Romano," they said in unison. "See you Monday."

Bruno replayed the video over and over that afternoon, hoping to dispel the nagging thought that his cousin was somehow involved in Maureen's death. Should he confront Anthony or go straight to the Attorney General to pursue Michael's possible ticket to freedom? He enhanced the images on his TV screen and it was the Monsignor's use of the word 'role' in recalling the confession that caught his attention. He had played a role in the murder, but was he the lone perpetrator? Bruno would need more. He needed to meet with Anthony, covertly obtain a DNA sample and fingerprints, and proceed from there. He remembered Captain Rabas' testimony that listed no less than twenty smudged and partial fingerprints in the O'Brien residence. Could one of them belong to Anthony? The Defense Project had all the fancy toys the forensics labs had, including the FBI database system for matching fingerprints. All the prints taken from the party had been entered into the system, but no matches had been found. With a fresh set of Anthony's, they just might find a match.

The two cousins had not been particularly close since they went their separate ways ten years ago, the same year Anthony took on the Tyler case *pro bono*. Their relationship had widened two years later, when Anthony had dropped Michael, and Bruno had taken over the case through the appeals system. He would make the call next week.

CHAPTER 76

Three months had passed, and Michael Tyler was still the most anonymous Auburn alumnus in Richmond. Other than Myron Debauche, none of the other grads living in the area had crossed paths with Michael, who was now number one on the FBI's "Top Ten Most Wanted" list. He had checked out his mug shot on one of the posters in a nearby post office, and was relieved to see that the photo taken when he arrived on The Row was a bad resemblance to him ten years later. There were at least ten brothers in the Montgomery projects who looked like Michael Tyler in 1996 when he arrived on death row.

Michael had followed Myron's suggestion that he start writing a book on his saga, and he was now up to two hundred pages. He hoped his mother, the English major, would edit his copy someday soon.

One morning Michael returned home after his daily three-mile run through a local park near his townhouse, to see the red light blinking on his phone. It was a message from Myron, whom he hadn't heard from in over two weeks. "Urgent, Michael. Call me on my cell."

Michael reached Myron in a meeting, but heard him asking people to wait while he took this important call. "Okay, Michael, I'm here. I don't want to use the phone, so I'll stop by the apartment around noon. Got some interesting developments in your case. I'll bring some food over from the cafeteria."

Before Michael could probe a little more about Myron's call, the line went dead. He could be a man of few words.

At noon, Myron was sitting in Michael's kitchen, munching on some pasta concoction that was sadly reminiscent of a similar dish on The Row. He finally took a break and went into the details about the latest development in the case. Myron told him about the existence of the video, then continued.

"Last night The Network intercepted an email from your attorney in Montgomery to a retired Alabama Supreme Court judge, asking for his advice on the admittance of a trial video as the basis for an evidentiary hearing."

"Who was the judge?" Michael asked.

"A Lorenzo Consentino, Michael. Does the name ring a bell?"

"It's definitely Italian. Could be some relative to Bruno Romano. Wait, I remember him saying something about an appellate judge who had ties to the family, Maybe that's the connection, Myron. What was the message?"

"I'm paraphrasing now, as I don't have an exact copy of it, but apparently a video exists that suggests your initial attorney made a confession to a priest prior to your trial that he had played a role in the death of the lady you were convicted of killing."

There was a long pause and Myron continued. "Did you hear what I just said, Michael? Are you alright?"

Michael was glad he was sitting, because his feet didn't seem to be touching the floor. "Did I hear you correctly? There's a video of Anthony Romano being accused of killing Maureen."

"No, the email said he might have had a 'role' in the murder. 'Role', that's the key word. My question is, what were the circumstances that someone videotaped him and the priest at the trial? Any ideas, Michael?"

"None, Myron. But it's the best news I've had in the last eleven years. Where do we go from here? Do we call my attorney?"

"No, Michael, we don't right now. The Network will analyze the situation and determine a course of action. I'll keep you informed as best I can. For once, time is on your side. Take a nap, you deserve it."

Michael would take Myron's advice and take an afternoon nap. An hour later, the phone interrupted Michael's dream of going home to Montgomery a free man. The caller was Bruno Romano.

CHAPTER 77

"Michael, my friend, how are you?"

"I'm doing just fine, Bruno, but how did you find out where I am? I'm just a little confused, because the people behind my current situation are so secretive."

"You mean The Network, Michael?"

"You're part of it now, too?"

"Took the oath two hours ago," Bruno joked. "Was told I'm only the fourth person in The Network you know who isn't using an alias. I wanted so badly to be a Billy Bob or a Joe Willie, for maybe a month or two."

Laughing, Michael remarked, "I hear you have some good news to share with me, Bruno. My friend here said an email you sent to a former judge in Alabama had been intercepted. Is that right?"

"Yeah, your friends are good," Bruno admitted. "Yes, Judge Lorenzo Consentino, a former appellate judge, is a second cousin to Anthony's dad. He's been retired since 1990, and has written several books on the flaws in the appeals system, and how they have an adverse effect on defendants. The judge isn't too well liked by his peers, because he's been an extremely vocal critic of how haphazardly they dismiss death penalty appeals. On some fifty appeals over his twelve years on the court, he almost always voted for the defendant."

"So, Judge Consentino was a maverick on the

death penalty. Did he respond to your email?"

"He said he would in the form of a letter. Wanted no electronic trail left behind that could lead to you."

Bruno went on to explain how the events of the last twenty-four hours had led to the email. "Late Friday evening, two second-year law students from the Law Center came to me with a videotape of your trial. You'll remember that the Center taped the entire trial. Apparently, the student doing the taping, whom we've identified as Paul Brandies, a real estate and corporate lawyer from Mobile, left the courtroom right before Judge Brendle overrode the jury's sentence, but forgot to turn off the camera. I talked with him this morning, and he remembers suffering from a bad case of the runs, which led to his third or fourth bathroom break of the morning. When he returned, he realized the camera was still running, but he said it was no big deal. He just turned it off, packed up the equipment and headed back to the Center.

"He said the standard procedure was to edit the taping to about two hours' worth. However, because of the trial's significance, he was instructed to make a dozen copies of the final product. Brandies said he watched the video four or five times, but never saw the final ending the two students had, because he always rewound it from the point the court was adjourned. It was then, after about a seven-minute delay in the taping, that Monsignor Patrick Reilly confronted Tony Romano at the defense table about a confession he had made to him that he had a role in Maureen's death.

"It's inconceivable to think of the hundreds of times this video has been viewed by students and professors over the last ten years, that two students with a light buzz from a twelve-pack of beer were distracted long enough to let the real truth come forward. Michael, you may owe your life to them when this sorry saga is finally over, and you can tell the State of Alabama to write you a fat check for five hundred and fifty thousand dollars. That's fifty thousand a year for the insult of labeling you a killer. Add to that the million or more the State has already invested in your case, and maybe people will sit back and wonder if they're really getting their money's worth in this death penalty charade."

Michael was excited, pacing back and forth with his cell phone. "Where do we go from here, Bruno?"

"A word of caution, Michael. I'm sure I'll hear from somebody in The Network soon. We'd like to be able to determine the validity of the confession, but unfortunately the good Monsignor is deceased, and Anthony could deny he ever made the confession. The Monsignor had occasional flashes of senility, and this might have been one of those moments. We've got another avenue to approach here, and that's matching Tony's prints with those that couldn't be identified in Maureen's home. Hopefully, we'll get lucky. For the time being, keep the faith. Remember, there can be no further communication between us. Even with those high-tech throwaway phones The Network is using, there is a risk involved. Anything else, Michael?"

"My parents, Bruno. Any contact with them?

"I went to see them after your escape. They've been hounded by the FBI, who think they were part of the plot to hide you. Your old man came close to decking one of them a few weeks ago when they pushed a little too hard for information. I got a restraining order against the Feds and State from talking with them unless an attorney is present. A former classmate of mine, Peter Gorgas, a nasty litigator from Mobile, is representing them. He and the FBI have an adversarial history, and he relishes any opportunity to go to war with them. I'll have Peter contact them to let you know you're doing fine."

"Thanks, Bruno. This is great news."

CHAPTER 78

Good morning, cuz," Bruno Romano said into the speaker phone after Tony's secretary had put him on hold for five minutes. "Didn't she tell you that one of your rich and famous cousins was on the line?"

"Which one?" Tony asked. "There are several in the family, and those that aren't are always bugging me for money. What can I do for you today? I know it can't be about money."

"No, it's not, Tony. It's about Michael Tyler."

"Oh, our Michael. The same Michael Tyler, who by all accounts masterminded his miraculous escape from Alabama's death row with the alleged help of an unscrupulous warden, and who has avoided the blood hounds for what – three months now?"

"I'm looking ahead, Tony. If he's apprehended, he'll be back on death row and executed in a matter of months. Just want to go over key parts of the trial transcript one more time and see if there's anything we missed."

"The only thing we missed, Counselor, was a credible judge, who disagreed with the jury's sentence. Then you actually draft some lame appeal three years later questioning my work in the trial, and now you expect me to help you save his ass. Did you ever think he might have done it, Bruno?"

"A few times, Tony, but no, he didn't do it. Give me a few hours some morning this week, and that'll be the end of it. That's the least we owe the kid. I keep calling him a kid out of habit. Geez, Tony, he's thirty-four years old, has two degrees, passed the Bar while on death row, and is number one on the FBI's Ten Most Wanted list. Ironic, huh?"

"Well spoken, Bruno. Okay, you can have me for three hours on Wednesday morning. And your place, please. The coffee here sucks. See you at nine."

"Thanks, cuz."

"Quit the cuz shit."

Tony arrived at Bruno's office at nine sharp on Wednesday, hung over from his Tuesday night poker game.

"Damn, Tony, you look like death warmed over," was Bruno's greeting.

"Maybe, but I got five grand in winnings to prove the night wasn't a complete waste. Coffee and maybe one of those tasty omelettes you're famous for would help, too."

"I'm way ahead of you. Let's head to the kitchen where we can yak at the table."

"Damn, Bruno, with your cooking skills, how in the hell did that wife of yours ever run you off?"

Bruno ignored the question, then satisfied Anthony's curiosity about the meeting. "No, we're not going to try and decipher the entire transcript page by page. And beating up on Judge Brendle's perceived racism won't get it, either."

"*Perceived* racism?" Tony asked. "Instead of the traditional judge's black robe, he should have been wearing a freaking Klan outfit!"

"The one other problem I have is that any new evidence would land us back in Circuit court before

Winston Kennedy, who isn't likely to touch anything that could lead to an acquittal."

Tony agreed with his cousin. "And you're on some kind of a high thinking the s.o.b. would allow a new evidentiary hearing to overturn a conviction that he used to get elected to his judgeship. Unless you got a video of the guy doing Maureen, you got nothing. Michael's only hope is to stay clear of the law. I repeat, he has to stay clear of the law."

"Well, we might have something close to that, Tony. We'll see how it plays out." The two cousins spent the next three hours reviewing key parts of the trial transcript Bruno had highlighted, but, as they expected, nothing new presented itself.

Bruno sat back with a heavy sigh and thanked his cousin for meeting with him. "I hope it wasn't just for the coffee and omelettes."

"No, Bruno, was great to see you. We should get together more often."

"I agree, Tony."

Bruno got up to shake his former law partner's hand and finally asked the question he had repressed over the last ten years. "Anthony, were you ..... seeing Maureen?"

Without any hesitation, Tony said, "You probably heard that from some of the Mayor's cronies, who all seemed to have a book on her social life, which there was very little of. She was a very private lady, but to answer your question, no. We had lunch a few times, and she subbed in our bridge club at the Monsignor's place. And, I'm a happily married man, Bruno. That's it. Nothing that will ever make good fodder for your next novel. You take care."

Bruno doubted Tony's denial, but his mission

was accomplished. Tony's DNA and prints were on the coffee mug and utensils, and in a few hours he would match them to the lab results taken from the O'Brien home.

CHAPTER 79

If Anthony Romano was having an affair with Maureen O'Brien, the initial sweep for prints by forensics found nothing that could cast suspicion on his possible involvement in her murder. Romano was vacationing with his family in Mississippi at the time of Maureen's party for Monsignor Reilly's bridge club, and none of the guests were compelled to offer their prints as all had solid alibis for their whereabouts on the night of the murder. But the headboard print found by forensics was a definite match to the one Anthony left on the coffee mug on his visit to Bruno.

Bruno, the only non-Auburn alumnus in The Network, was now left to decide whether to pursue an evidentiary hearing on the contents of the video the two Law Center students had discovered. He faxed a request to Judge Kennedy late Wednesday evening, requesting a Friday meeting with the judge to consider his motion. On Thursday morning, Kennedy's clerk left a message on Romano's voice mail that he would meet with him Friday morning at eleven o'clock. "PS: Bring the evidence."

Bruno knew the tenor of the meeting would focus on Michael's escape more than his request for a new hearing. The pleasantries had hardly been exchanged when Kennedy jumped on Bruno, wanting to know where Tyler was hiding out. "Now let's cut to the chase here, Counselor. Where is your client, Michael

Tyler?"

"Judge, I haven't been in contact with Michael since his escape from death row. I have no earthly idea where he is calling home now. This meeting has to do with new evidence that is pertinent to his claim of innocence, and that's all."

Randall Simmons, who had succeeded Kennedy as the Attorney General, objected. "The State requires the defendant to be present for an evidentiary hearing, unless he is incapacitated in such a manner that he cannot attend."

"Well, you just answered your own argument, Mr. Simmons," Romano responded. "Michael Tyler is, in your own words, incapacitated. There's case law to support my argument, a U.S. Supreme Court ruling in a West Virginia case back in the late 1970s, I think. Give one of your twenty assistants something to do tomorrow, and look it up."

Kennedy intervened, "All right, what is the new evidence, Mr. Romano?"

"The new evidence is in the form of a video that supports our claim. And no, I don't have it with me, but I promise to make it available at the hearing."

"Oh, you'll have it available for the hearing, Counselor?"

"Yes, you heard me correctly, Your Honor."

"Well, what if I don't grant this hearing?"

"Let's make this easy on everybody, Romano persisted. "If this hearing is not granted, the video will be in the hands of every major media outlet within the next forty-eight hours. The State of Alabama will have its repulsive racist past revisited, something you, Your Honor, and Mr. Simmons, could have prevented. If that isn't reason to grant me a hearing, then there's the issue of Maria Collins, Your Honor. I look forward to hearing from your clerk before five today. Thank you, gentlemen."

Bruno received a call at three-thirty in the afternoon; the hearing was scheduled for the following Tuesday morning in Circuit Court.

CHAPTER 80

Bruno's next call was to Myron DeBauche in Richmond.

"Stay put, Bruno. I'll call you back in a few hours. Great work. The Network will be pleased at the news about the hearing."

Bruno decided a short nap was in order; he had a hunch he was headed to Richmond. An hour later, the phone interrupted his sleep. It was Myron. "Grab an overnight bag, Bruno, you're due in Richmond tonight."

The plan was for Bruno to drive to Selma, where The Network jet would meet him at the old Craig Air Force base airstrip. Myron insisted that a trusted friend or two act as an escort. "After that meeting today, the law might have a tail on you."

Bruno immediately called Jordan Henry and Kevin McKenzie. "Gas up the old Chevy, boys. Road trip upcoming. I'll meet you at five sharp at the Montgomery Mall fountain. I'll have a slight disguise: sunglasses, faded jeans, dirty sneakers, and an Atlanta Braves cap that has seen better days." His new employees had a slew of questions for their boss, none of which he would answer. Bruno slipped them each a fifty and told them to keep their mouths shut and their cell phones on.

As planned, The Network jet was rolling to a stop as they approached the hangar. Bruno got out of the car and Jordan and Kevin headed back to Montgomery. Captain McMullen greeted Bruno, and within three minutes the jet was breaking through a small cloud cover headed east for Richmond.

"Sorry for the short notice, Mr. Romano, or I would have some snacks and drinks for you. Our flying time is fifty-five minutes. If you'd like, you can sit up front with me and be my co-pilot."

Bruno was overly curious about The Network's connections to fly into a government-controlled airstrip on such short notice. "The Network must have some special friends in high places."

"You really don't need to know, Mr. Romano."

"Make it Bruno, captain."

"Yes, sir."

Fifteen minutes into the flight, Captain McMullen took his hands off the stick and said, "You take over the controls while I hit the head. Be back in five."

Bruno thought he had suffered his first heart attack, but the Captain pointed out the horizon indicator, and showed him how to maintain a level altitude. At seven-thirty they landed in Richmond, where Myron was waiting at a private gate. "Welcome to Richmond, Bruno. I trust you approve of our travel accommodations. Did the good Captain let you fly the plane?"

"All of a few minutes, Myron, but hardly long enough to earn my wings."

As Myron's Cadillac was exiting the airport, Bruno's curiosity was getting the best of him. "Myron, may I ask you a few questions about you and the other people behind Michael's escape?"

"You may, Bruno, but I don't have a lot of the answers that would satisfy your inquisitiveness. I'm told there are maybe fifteen to twenty influential Auburn alumni around the country – most for their financial support – who are involved in the plan. I know only one or two by their real name; the rest are enjoying being someone else for the time being. That's all I can tell you. Now, bring me up to date on the evidentiary hearing."

"I brought the video with me, if you think we should show it to Michael. The quality is good, but I don't want to get his hopes too high, because there's no definitive denial from Anthony that he ever made the confession to Monsignor Reilly. The Monsignor is doing all the talking, calling him some unpriestly-like names along the way. And then there's the word 'role' that Anthony supposedly used in his confession to the Monsignor. Unfortunately, the Monsignor isn't here to verify that the confession took place."

"Didn't he die only a week after the trial?" Myron wanted to know. "Didn't some kid run over him with his car?"

"Yes, according to the local police report, the Monsignor stepped off the curb outside his church and was struck by a teenager who was driving with an expired license, and under the influence of alcohol as well. The kid got six months in juvenile detention and had his driver's license suspended for eighteen months. Killing a member of the clergy carried no more weight than running down a stray animal on the interstate. I hate to admit this, but I think the Monsignor's death could have been planned by Anthony. He couldn't risk the confession going public, and I honestly believe the Monsignor, had he lived, would eventually have broken the vow of silence if it came right down to Michael being executed."

But Myron wasn't buying into Bruno's theory. "Bruno, didn't the kid explain later on that there was no conspiracy, that he didn't know anyone in the Romano family?"

"Yes, and he also apologized to the parish and in person to Bishop Schmitt in Mobile; said he couldn't imagine intentionally killing a man of the cloth."

Bruno suggested that Myron take the video with him and view it before they met with Michael. "I've got it cued to the end where the sentence is announced; then there's the seven-minute, twenty-three second delay before the Monsignor and Anthony get together at the defense table. I'd rather you watch it alone, because I don't want to influence your opinion. It's pretty powerful stuff."

That's fine with me. I'll look at it tonight."

"I have a room for you at the downtown Hilton. Michael's not aware you're in Richmond, and I think it's best he doesn't know for now. He's got some serious anxiety issues right now, which is not unusual, given the latest developments. There's a great steak house across the street if you're looking for a good meal. I'll call you early tomorrow morning, then we'll head over to Michael's apartment and decide where to go from there."

CHAPTER 81

It had been six months since Bruno last saw Michael at his clemency hearing, and he marveled over his physical appearance. "Obviously, your gracious host has had a profound effect on your rehab, young man," Bruno told him after a lengthy embrace.

"I wasn't expecting you, Bruno, but I hope you're the bearer of good news. I'm ready to put these last eleven years behind me and move on with my life."

Myron nodded his approval. "Bruno has good news, Michael, so I'll let him do the honors."

"On Thursday, our motion for an evidentiary hearing was granted by none other than Judge Winston Kennedy, to consider our new evidence that wasn't available at your trial. It involved a video tape the Law Center shot the day your sentence was overridden by Judge Brendle."

Michael acknowledged the video program. "I'm aware of those trials the Center taped. I was involved in a few of them myself, including my own trial."

"Good. I plan to show the video at the hearing, at which time Kennedy will have several options. The least desirable of them we won't dwell on right now."

"I know that one, Bruno. Deny the new evidence and then send me back to death row to complete my sentence."

"Michael, let's not get ahead of ourselves," Bruno cautioned. "First of all, you won't be in court to hear it, because you're what the system says is incapacitated, and there's case law to support it."

"Yes, Bruno, a 1978 case in West Virginia. Some inmate claimed a bad back prohibited him from traveling to the hearing. And, he also said what was the purpose of showing up in a faded 10-year-old jumpsuit and chains when he wouldn't be allowed to speak."

"You know your law, Michael, but then I'm not surprised. And, as I pointed out to Myron, the good Monsignor is deceased, which leaves Anthony as the only party left to explain the confession. He might confirm he regularly went to Monsignor Reilly for confession, but deny that he ever spoke to him about being involved in Maureen's death."

Michael was silent, pondering the possibility of yet another setback by a system that had failed him, first as a defendant and now as an attorney at law.

Bruno spoke. "Let's address all the legal options Judge Kennedy will have at the hearing, beginning with the worst. One: if the video is tossed, then the search for you continues, and you're still under a death sentence. Two: if the video is allowed, and a second trial is ordered, you would have to return to Montgomery and turn yourself in. Kennedy wouldn't touch a trial *in absentia.* A second trial would drag on for a year, the State's way of punishing you for your escape. Three: the best-case scenario is that Kennedy admits the tape and the State, convinced that the conversation is legitimate and implicates my cousin, calls for a direct acquittal."

"And what are the chances of that playing out, Bruno?"

"Not bad. A second trial is more realistic, but we hold all the aces this time around. The tape is good which we will show you shortly, but Anthony would have a difficult time explaining his bloody thumbprint on Maureen's headboard in her bedroom. The State's forensics team didn't miss it when they swept the house for prints, but they couldn't find a match in the Federal database. But now we have Anthony's prints from a coffee mug, and they're a perfect match."

"The video?" Michael asked.

"Yes, Michael," Bruno replied. "I believe Myron has something to say about that."

"But here's the game-changer. After viewing it last night, I emailed it to our retired judge who has been advising us on our legal strategies. He believes the video will cast suspicion on Anthony and add a little drama to the hearing, but even if that's rejected, his fingerprint on the back of Maureen's headboard will doom him. He calls it a win-win situation."

Bruno wanted to know if The Network had a contingency plan in place, should the hearing not go well.

"Yes, we would return to Richmond. We have a second location in mind, but that scenario was based on Michael's identity being comprised here," Myron explained.

"How long are we talking about?" Michael asked.

"Indefinitely, Michael. We're in this for the long haul. Money is no object here. If we have to send you out of the country where there's no extradition agreement with the United States, then that's what we will do. How does Morocco sound?"

"This is all too much to believe, Myron."

"Yeah, only Hollywood can make this stuff up. If you're ready, Michael, let's watch the video."

With almost no expression, Michael watched as

Monsignor Reilly confronted Anthony at the defense table. For five minutes the clergyman verbally attacked him, questioning the oath he took when admitted to the bar to pursue his client's cases with truth and honor, and now his willingness to send an innocent man to his death. The question Michael had asked himself when he first met Anthony – why would Romano be interested in his defense and provide his services for free and then insist that Michael not testify -- was finally answered: Anthony Romano had killed Maureen O'Brien!

"What do you think, Michael?" Bruno asked.

With only minimal expression, Michael said,"I believe we should go back to Montgomery."

"Good," Myron replied. "Let's give this a day or two to sort things out. Bruno can spend the weekend here, and that will give you both time to think this through. I can have The Network's jet ready in a few hours' notice if Montgomery is the next destination. Michael, you know where the best nightclubs and restaurants are, so treat your attorney to a night or two out on the town."

CHAPTER 82

Late Sunday afternoon, Bruno and Michael were headed to Selma aboard The Network jet, hopefully leaving behind the secret hideaway Myron DeBauche had provided since the most efficiently-coordinated death row escape in the twenty-first century.

Bruno was on the phone, first to Jordan Henry and Kevin McKenzie, to have them meet the plane in Selma at two o'clock, then to his staff in Montgomery, to give them a three-day paid holiday starting Monday. Michael would be spending the next three days in Bruno's living quarters above his law office, only a short block from the courthouse.

Michael had insisted on rolling the dice on a direct acquittal, believing that the video alone would vindicate him. He had convinced himself that the State of Alabama was embarrassed over his trial and the polls that said an innocent man was sitting on death row waiting to be executed. Michael was the poster boy for everything wrong with the death penalty in Alabama, beginning with judicial overrides of juries.

They spent the majority of Monday going over the hearing procedures and whom to call first to the stand: the Law Center students who had discovered the seven-minute gap in the action of the tape, or Paul Brandies, who did the actual taping of the trial ten years ago. They decided on Brandies, whose testimony would set the stage for the students to tell their extraordinary story. Brandies was now a junior partner in his uncle's firm which specialized in corporate and real estate law. He had a passion for criminal law, but family ties in the forty-five year-old firm that bore his surname offered him a satisfying career in fields that didn't involve dealing with the dregs of society.

The day of reckoning had finally arrived. Michael and Kevin McKenzie would wait in Bruno's office with an audio device that would allow them to track the hearing word for word. They listened closely as Judge Winston Kennedy addressed the courtroom, which included Michael's family and friends and out-lined what the hearing options were.

"We are here today to determine the validity of evidence that was not available in the 1995 trial of the State of Alabama versus Michael Tyler. If I determine the evidence is creditable, I will consider ordering a new trial. If the evidence presented does not meet the court's legal standards, Mr. Tyler is still regarded as a fugitive from justice and remains under the court's death sentence. This hearing is different from most, because of the defendant's absence, but that will have no bearing on my decision. He is within his rights not to appear. Mr. Romano, you may begin. Please call your first witness."

Bruno thanked Paul Brandies for making the trip north to testify.

"Glad to be here, Counselor."

Bruno asked if Brandies would explain the Law Center's role in the Tyler case.

"A major part of the Center's curriculum was videotaping various trials around the state for class-room analysis. We taped both civil and criminal trials, probably four or five a year. I believe the Center has over one hundred such trials on file." Brandies went on for a few more minutes about the Center's program, and Randall Simmons, Judge Kennedy's successor, anxious to be heard, objected. "Is there a question somewhere in this testimony?"

Romano, loathed interruptions on his direct examinations, and before Kennedy could rule, told Simmons he could ask all the questions he wanted on cross. It brought a pained look toward Romano from Kennedy, who said, "That's my role in this hearing, Counselor. You may continue."

But Simmons wouldn't let the issue die."There's an objection before the bench, Your Honor."

"All right, Counselor. Mr. Romano, a question or two might move the testimony along and appease our Attorney General. Does that suffice, Mr. Simmons?"

"Thank you, Your Honor."

Ignoring Kennedy's ruling, Romano asked Paul Brandies to continue. "In my final year at the Center, I was one of seven or eight students who routinely taped different trials."

Turning toward Simmons with a martyred look, Romano asked Brandies, "Did you tape the majority of the Tyler trial?"

"Yes, I did the majority of it, Mr. Romano. We were short a few students because of semester exams, so I missed only one day."

"Now, if it doesn't bother the State too much, Mr. Brandies, would you please explain the procedure that follows when you've completed the taping."

Simmons was on his feet to object to Romano's remark, but Kennedy shut him down before he could speak. "Mr. Brandies, you may answer Mr. Romano's question."

"Thank you, Your Honor. After the trial is over, we edit the tape down to about three hours of actual court time."

"How much footage of court time was taped in the Tyler trial?

"Can't be specific, but usually a trial that takes seven to ten days, will yield maybe thirty to forty hours' worth."

Romano was now on the doorstep to exposing the flaw in the tape that would be the defining moment in the hearing. "Have you viewed the finished product recently, Mr. Brandies?"

"Yes, in your office yesterday."

"Mr. Brandies, did the video you viewed yesterday differ from the original you prepared ten years ago?"

"Nothing that I could determine, sir."

"How many times did you view the video while a student at the Center?"

"I'm guessing maybe three or four times before I graduated."

Romano plodded on. "Let's go back to the day the sentence was pronounced. Anything unusual about the day while you were taping?"

Brandies forced a sheepish grin. "Yes, I had a major dysentery problem that day."

"You had the ...."

"The runs, Mr. Romano."

Romano tried to make light of the situation. "Bad pizza, maybe?"

"Bean soup," Brandies said.

Romano seemed amused at the dialogue, but Kennedy wasn't. "Can we get to the heart of the issue here? The Court isn't the least interested with what

Mr. Brandies had to eat the day before."

Romano resumed his questioning. "Were there a few times you had to leave the courtroom to use the bathroom?"

"Yes, maybe three or four times."

"When was the last time?"

"Just before the sentence was read."

"And how long were you gone?"

"I can't give you an exact time, sir. Maybe ten to fifteen minutes. I ran into a few friends from the Center in the lobby. They said the judge had overridden the sentence."

"Did you leave the camera running while you were gone?"

"Apparently, yes."

"When you finally returned to the courtroom, Mr. Brandies, what did you do next?"

"I turned off the camera, packed up the equipment, and went back to the Center."

"When did you start editing the tape?"

"It was a Friday, so I decided to put it off until Monday."

"And when did you complete the editing?"

"In about two weeks."

"Thank you, Mr. Brandies. I have no additional questions."

Without leaving his chair, Randall Simmons asked the Mobile attorney. "Mr. Brandies, could the video tape have been altered over the last ten years to produce a desired effect?"

Brandies, who had shown little emotion on the stand, rose to challenge the Alabama Attorney General. "Excuse me, sir, a desired effect?"

"Withdrawn. I'm through with this witness."

“You’re damn right you are,” muttered Brandies.

“I’ve heard enough Counselors,” and Kennedy banged his gavel, calling for a short break.

CHAPTER 83

During the break, Bruno huddled with Jordan Henry, who would yield the second dagger against the State's case. "This is your big day, Jordan. An hour from now, your testimony, along with the video, will lift a decade of injustice, and you and Kevin will be the new darlings of the media. We've rehearsed your testimony regarding the night you watched the video, and to the point where you left to take a phone call, and Kevin stepped outside to check on the snowfall. Pretty basic stuff. Don't let Simmons try to rattle you on cross, because there's nothing he can challenge. The video will speak for itself."

Jordan, who had played high school football and was a state champion wrestler, was an impressive twenty-three-year-old law student. His blond locks, engaging smile and lively blue eyes were testimony to his selection as his high school's most handsome male.

Romano slowly approached the witness box and thanked Jordan for coming to testify. "Jordan, how did you become involved in this case, which led to this evidentiary hearing?"

"It goes back to the night of February 14, when my roommate, Kevin McKenzie, and I were watching the video-tape of the Michael Tyler murder trial at our apartment."

"And why were you watching this particular video?"

"Our class had been assigned a review of the trial for a course in felony murder. We had checked out the video that morning and planned to watch it over the weekend. It was a popular video; I think the library had a dozen of so copies of it."

"At approximately what time did you start watching the video?"

"It was around seven-thirty that evening."

"Did you watch it from start to finish or did you take a break or two in between?

"Maybe two or three breaks. We were cooking a frozen pizza in the kitchen, and Kevin left a few times to check on that."

"Can you recall what time you thought the video had reached its ending?"

"Right around the ten o'clock news. We watched the sports report, then went back to the video. We saw the jury's sentence announced, and then the judge's override."

"Now, this is extremely important, Jordan. What happened right after Judge Brendle's override of the sentence?"

"Actually, two things. The phone rang, which I took in my bedroom, and Kevin went outside to check on the snowfall."

"And how long were you both gone before you returned to the TV?"

"Maybe five to ten minutes."

"Was the video still playing when you returned?"

"Oh, yes, it was, and I believe that's why we're here today."

Okay, Jordan, tell the court what you witnessed on the TV."

"Mr. Anthony Romano, the defense attorney, was

engaged in a rather heated discussion with a minister or priest."

"That would be the late Monsignor Reilly."

"Yes, Monsignor Reilly, Mr. Romano."

"How long did the conversation go on, Jordan?"

"Well, it appears we caught the tail end of it, so we rewound the video to the judge's override."

"After the judge's override, what appears on the screen?"

"People are filing out of the courtroom, and the camera is focused on the defense table. We assume the taping is over, but we're wondering about the Monsignor and his conversation with Mr. Romano. We thought we might have missed the entire segment."

"And did you?"

"Initially, yes, but after a seven-minute delay or so, Mr. Romano returns to the defense table to retrieve some papers, and Monsignor Reilly approached him from behind. He was quite upset."

"So noted, Jordan. Now, can you be a little more specific on the time lapse after the courtroom empties and the screen is just a still shot of the defense table to when Anthony Romano and Monsignor Reilly appear together at the table?"

Simmons was in his feet objecting. "Asked and answered, Your Honor."

"Overruled," Kennedy snarled. "Mr. Henry, you may answer the question."

"It was exactly seven minutes and twenty-three seconds. Their conversation was five minutes long. We timed it several times."

"When did you get in touch with me about your discovery?"

"It was later that night, or early in the morning.

I remember you being upset when we called so late."

"Yes, I recall, Jordan. Your Honor, unless Mr. Simmons has any questions for this witness, I would request that we set up the video equipment to show this dramatic ending, which will clearly absolve Mr. Tyler."

Kennedy looked in the direction of the Attorney General, who appeared frozen in his chair. "Mr. Simmons, do you have any questions for Mr. Henry?"

"Just two, Your Honor. Mr. Henry, were you reimbursed by Mr. Romano to appear here today?"

Peeved by the Attorney General's constant needling, Romano objected angrily, "What's the relevance?"

"Sustained, Counselor. Mr. Henry is not here appearing as an expert witness for which he is entitled a fee. He's here to recount the events of February 14, and really nothing else that I can determine from his testimony. If Mr. Romano comped a meal at one of the family restaurants for Mr. Henry, that would suffice. Anything else, Counselor?"

"Yes, nice looking sport coat, Mr. Henry. Was that comped, too?" Kennedy shook his head in disgust. "That's it Counselors, I'll see both of you in chambers. And Mr. Simmons, bring your checkbook with you."

CHAPTER 84

"This won't be long, gentlemen. For openers, Mr. Simmons, you can write a check for one thousand dollars to my favorite charity, the Boys and Girls Clubs of Alabama."

"One thousand?"

"Yes, I can make it twice that if you'd like, Mr. Simmons."

"And why are you smiling, Mr. Romano?"

"I like your style, Your Honor."

Kennedy then instructed the two attorneys on how the rest of the hearing would proceed. "We're going back to the courtroom to view the video, then I will retire to my chambers and render a decision. Mr. Simmons, to ensure that we preserve the noble and legal interests of the State of Alabama, you will object, for some lame reason, why the video is of poor quality and doesn't present a clear and convincing reason to be admitted in a new trial. I will probably overrule your objection and, hopefully, one way or the other, we can all put this eleven-year fiasco to rest. Think about it, gentlemen. All because a twenty-three-year-old law student had to take a piss."

"No, Your Honor, to answer the phone."

"Whatever."

A large screen had been set up in the courtroom, and the moment of truth had finally arrived for Michael Tyler and his family. Judge Kennedy asked that Mr. Romano explain briefly for the courtroom what part of the video they would be viewing first.

"Your Honor, we will begin with the sentence override and the events that followed. There will be a seven-minute, twenty-three second delay in the video that is nothing but a still picture of the defense table before Monsignor Reilly and Anthony Romano return to it. I trust it won't be too ...."

Kennedy offered, "If you're wondering if we can all survive seven minutes and twenty-three seconds of unadulterated silence, we can. Please begin."

There was an eerie silence in the room as Bruno Romano depressed the play button to the video. Over one hundred eyes were glued to the screen as Anthony Romano's ultimate betrayal to his profession was played out.

Bruno was ashamed to be a Romano, knowing the undeniable guilt that would be attached to future generations of the family. The pause in the video gave him time to reflect how closely their lives had paralleled each other, from their early days at St. Boniface to washing dishes and bussing tables at the two family restaurants. Two years younger and a smaller version of Tony, Bruno had watched with pride as Tony became a football icon at Sidney Lanier High School, then eventually earned a scholarship to play at Duke. Bruno had chosen Vanderbilt, because a love interest from high school had enrolled there at the same time. He had lost his virginity to Loraine Dugan, and despite several breakups over the next three years they had married in his final year of law school.

The stars were telling them something different, but they ignored the warnings and further complicated the tenuous relationship by bringing three children into the world. By the time Mark, the oldest, was ten, Bruno had moved out of the house and into his office. And every month afterwards, he had written a check to Loraine for five thousand dollars.

There were voices and images on the screen now, as the Monsignor ambled up the aisle and leaned over the chair next to Anthony. There were no pleasant exchanges as the Monsignor launched into a heated verbal attack of Bruno's cousin. Anthony looked up at the old priest only briefly, barely acknowledging his presence. The beads of perspiration from his forehead seemed to drip off the big screen; the same experience Bruno had when he'd made his first confession as a second-grader: "Bless me, father for I have sinned."

Since the students' discovery of the shocking climax to the video, Bruno had viewed the ending over and over and had it memorized. He mouthed the words as if he were watching a silent movie, giving actual voices to the two actors. Monsignor Reilly was passionate, grasping Anthony's arm like a father disciplining his son for some major transgression. Anthony never responded, instead, burying his head in his huge hands, weeping uncontrollably, not wanting to face the wrath of his confessor. Then it was over, and there was a collective sigh in the courtroom after Bruno punched the button to stop the video. Randall Simmons made an attempt to object, but Kennedy dismissed him before he could get to it. *Shades of Harold Christian,* Bruno thought. Kennedy called for a short recess and then retreated to Christian's old chambers, where he would consider the defense's motion to admit the video as evidence in a second trial.

Kennedy took his seat in Christian's favorite chair, one of the few remaining symbols of Christian's thirty-year reign as a judge. Only one other item was missing – a bottle of Southern Comfort which had always been present when attorneys scrimmaged over motions and arguments before him. He wondered how Christian would have handled this legal mess. Hell, he knew. It never would have reached this point.

He made his decision quickly, then returned and addressed the packed courtroom, reiterating his comments on the options he had made in his opening remarks."This hearing is not about guilt or innocence, although any decision I make may determine the course this case will take. Therefore, I am ordering that the video the defense has presented is sufficient to order a new trial. I am ...."

Randall Simmons rose and asked to be heard. "I'm sorry to interrupt you, Your Honor, but the video speaks for itself. Yes, Anthony Romano could deny he ever made the confession prior to the start of the trial; however, his actions and demeanor in the video speak volumes about his sense of guilt and remorse. I would take the word of Monsignor Reilly in this case. And now I have been handed other incriminating evidence by Mr. Tyler's attorney that clearly implicates Anthony Romano in Maureen O'Brien's death. Therefore, I am asking the court to issue a direct acquittal in this case. On behalf of the State of Alabama, I offer my most sincere apologies to Mr. Tyler, his family and friends who have endured this agonizing process over the last eleven years."

Pastor Roberts, who had been at the Tyler's side throughout the trial, raised his hands to the heavens and shouted, "Praise the Lord! Yes, there is justice in Alabama!" The courtroom erupted into a thunderous roar and Winston Kennedy did nothing to stop it. In fact, he appeared to endorse the celebration, even though it was at his expense. After the decibel level had subsided, he spoke to the court.

"The Court concurs, Mr. Simmons. But before we adjourn, I would be remiss if I, who prosecuted Mr. Tyler, didn't also offer my apologies to the defendant. It would be more appropriate if Mr. Tyler were present to hear it, but, given the bizarre circumstances of his escape and subsequent flights to parts unknown, that will have to wait."

Almost on a signal, the doors to the courtroom opened, and there was Michael being escorted to Kennedy's bench by two smiling bailiffs and Jordan Henry and Kevin McKenzie.

Michael was apologetic, then told a harmless lie. "Sorry I missed this hearing, Your Honor. My flight was delayed two hours in Atlanta. Some things never seem to change."

CHAPTER 85

Judge Kennedy stepped down from the bench and extended his hand to the man whose prosecution had sent him off to death row by a racist judge. He thought Brian Brendle should be here offering the state's *mea culpa* to Michael and the others he had screwed over with his jury overrides.

"Michael, please join me for a moment, or for as long as it takes to offer this Court's apologies. Ten years ago, I participated in a travesty of justice. I questioned my own work at the time and how it played into a guilty verdict. We had a contaminated crime scene, confusing testimony, perjured testimony, and more than enough reasonable doubt to warrant a not guilty verdict. But the jury thought otherwise, and that's their prerogative.

"It was then that Judge Brendle should have overturned the jury's verdict, but given his history in trials with black defendants, that wasn't going to happen. Then he confirms his true racists colors by overriding the sentence of life without parole for death.

"Tomorrow, I am asking the Governor to place a moratorium on all death penalty sentences involving jury overrides until a thorough analysis of each case is made to ensure that the verdict and sentence meets the guidelines established by the Attorney General's office. I may be committing political suicide in a state that relishes the death penalty with the same fervor as they do their football, but this is the fourth conviction to be overturned in the last five years. Eight years ago, the State executed the wrong man, because DNA evidence was denied, then the real killer steps forward a month later claiming he needed to "cleanse his soiled soul." How many people have taken a seat in that chair whose claims of innocence have fallen on deaf ears? The judicial overrides in death penalty cases must stop.

"We spend more money per capita executing people than most other states in the country that have the death penalty. Instead of improving the well-being of our children living below the poverty rate, which is also one of the nation's highest, we execute people at a tremendous cost to the taxpayers of this great state. And the overwhelming majority of those condemned to die represent that group.

"Michael, you are an exception to all the men and women waiting to die on death row, and to deny you the career that you had so diligently planned when you entered Auburn University fifteen years ago would be inexcusable. Please accept my personal apologies and best wishes to you as a member of the bar. You will do well. This court is adjourned."

Michael was engulfed by his parents, Pastor Roberts, and other well-wishers who dominated the gallery. He was besieged by the media for his reaction to the acquittal and where he had been hiding out after his escape, but all he would say was, "I'm relieved. I'll talk later."

When the courtroom had almost emptied, Judge Kennedy called Bruno aside and asked, "Counselor, who in the hell is Maria Collins, and what role did she have in this case?"

"I have no idea what you're talking about, Your

Honor."

Kennedy smiled. "That's what I thought."

Bruno suggested they have a victory lunch, but Michael declined, wishing to return to Greenville to start the healing process. He asked his dad if Hercules would still remember him.

"I think so, son. He's missed you as much as we have."

An hour later, they were turning into the driveway of their home on Maple Street, and there, snoozing on the front lawn, was Hercules. Michael ran to him and picked up the old warrior, letting him rest his chin on his shoulder. Hercules licked his face affectionately, something he reserved for Michael only.

Later that evening, when Michael was relaxing on the back porch, Hercules, now 140 years old in dog years, limped to his dad's tool shed and returned with the frayed football he and Michael had played with in another lifetime when they would go to the high school field, and Michael would throw the ball as far as he could. There were times when it seemed Hercules would beat the ball to its landing spot, then return it to his master for another throw. Michael's arm would tire long before Hercules' legs did.

Despite a near crippling stage of arthritis today, Hercules nuzzled Michael's leg, indicating that he was ready for their favorite game of fetch. Michael tossed the ball about fifty yards to the edge of the property, and Hercules hobbled at half-speed to retrieve the ball. He returned it to Michael, setting the ball at his feet. Michael threw it one more time, but old Hercules was panting heavily, and he laid down beside Michael and rested. Tomorrow was another day for play.

EPILOGUE

Michael finished his book, *Michael: My Ten Years in Hell,* which became an immediate best seller. Two months after his acquittal, he received a check for five hundred and fifty thousand dollars from the State of Alabama for his eleven years of wrongful imprisonment, and he donated half to Pastor Roberts toward the construction of a new church. He also received the full proceeds of Maureen's life insurance policy, which had been held in escrow pending his execution. That he gave to the Greenville school district.

Jordan Henry and Kevin McKenzie, who discovered the crucial lapse in the video, also benefitted from Michael's riches. Their tuition, and room and board while attending the Law Center were covered, in addition to a fifty thousand-dollar bonus for each.

After a national book signing tour, Michael went to work for Bruno Romano's Defense Project. His first case was lifting the death sentence for his old friend, Bobby Rae Quinton. The sentence was reduced to life in prison by a new circuit court judge in northeast Alabama, and shortly afterward Bobby Rae was paroled. With the help of a speech therapist, Bobby Rae finally corrected his stuttering and then hit the lecture circuit, earning six figures per speech on his opposition to the death penalty. And with authors like Bruno and Michael in the picture, a book on his life was likely in the works.

Anthony Romano negotiated a plea bargain to avoid the death penalty, and was sentenced to twenty-five years to life. The SACC finally had a genuine rich man and another lawyer. It was later learned from Tony's wife, Charlene, that her husband had carried on a secret, but stormy, six-month affair with Maureen, and he was incensed when Maureen wanted to end the relationship. He admitted that the confession he made to Monsignor Reilly was at a different church, and he was unaware the Monsignor was filling in for a priest who was on medical leave. However, he never offered any reasonable explanation why he chose to kill Maureen in the manner that he did.

Sam Wiegert was suspended without pay for two months for his role in Michael's escape but the extra fifty thousand-dollar payment he received from The Network more than compensated for the fourteen thousand dollars in salary he lost. His secret affair with the Mobile beauty queen remained a secret.

Judge Brendle lost his bid for a fourth term, but even in defeat he never apologized to Michael for his ten years on The Row. His other sentencing overrides were being investigated by the Attorney General's office. The Mississippi authors did as promised; donating fifty thousand to The Row's inmates that averaged out to nearly five hundred dollars per man.

Michael never again heard from anyone in The Network, but he knew that somewhere they were all smiling, knowing their mission had reached a successful conclusion.

"WAR EAGLE!"

AUTHOR'S NOTES

Although this book is a work of fiction, it should be noted that the majority of cities and schools mentioned in the book are real. The others I just made up. None of the activities mentioned in the story are meant to impugn any town's reputation or history. I created those, too. I lived the better part of two decades in Montgomery, Alabama, where I became interested in the death penalty and its application.

My legal "training" comes from tv shows, books, and conversations with practicing attorneys. I may have stretched the interpretation of the law at times, but it was done only to enhance the story.

I must critique my own work, though, in suggesting that Alabama has passed a lottery or has a statewide Office of Public Defenders in place. However, jury sentencing overrides in Alabama are indeed real, and have been in effect since the repeal of the death penalty in 1976. They remain a controversial topic, and Alabama is one of only three states that allow the practice.

Special thanks to friends and family who encouraged me to complete the book after numerous mishaps along the way almost derailed the project, then offered their editorial opinions on the first of many drafts. Thank you all.

www.ingramcontent.com/pod-product-compliance
Lightning Source LLC
LaVergne TN
LVHW020534100826
845148LV00010B/1462
* 9 7 8 0 9 8 2 9 4 7 0 1 2 *